THE DOG
WHO CAME FOR
CHRISTMAS

More heartwarming novels by Sue Pethick

Boomer's Bucket List

Pet Friendly

Published by Kensington Publishing Corporation

THE DOG
WHO CAME FOR
CHRISTMAS

Sue Pethick

KENSINGTON BOOKS
www.kensingtonbooks.com

KENSINGTON BOOKS are published by

Kensington Publishing Corp.
119 West 40th Street
New York, NY 10018

All Kensington titles, imprints, and distributed lines are available at special quantity discounts for bulk purchases for sales promotion, premiums, fund-raising, educational, or institutional use.

Special book excerpts or customized printings can also be created to fit specific needs. For details, write or phone the office of the Kensington Sales Manager: Kensington Publishing Corp., 119 West 40th Street, New York, NY 10018. Attn. Sales Department. Phone: 1-800-221-2647.

Kensington and the K logo Reg. U.S. Pat. & TM Off.

ISBN-13: 978-1-4967-0907-3 (ebook)
ISBN-1-4967-0907-1 (ebook)

ISBN-13: 978-1-4967-2321-5
ISBN-10: 1-4967-2321-X
First Kensington Trade Paperback Printing: October 2017

10 9 8 7 6 5

Printed in the United States of America

Give the boy a dog and you've furnished him a playmate
Always true and faithful as can be.

—Berton Braley

THE DOG
WHO CAME FOR
CHRISTMAS

CHAPTER 1

"One, two, three, four . . ."

Kieran gasped as he ran, his words coming out in a harsh whisper.

"Five, six, seven, eight . . ."

He'd already counted to a hundred four times, and Cody was still chasing him.

"Come back here, freak!"

"Thirteen, fourteen, fifteen . . ."

He stole a glance over this shoulder; Cody was getting closer. Kieran closed his eyes and forced his spindly legs to pump harder.

"Twenty-one, twenty-two . . ."

Why hadn't he run for the school bus instead of hiding in the bathroom? Even if Cody had caught him, the worst he'd have gotten would have been a wedgie or a sock on the arm. Now, with the safety of the school grounds behind them, there was no telling what Cody Daniels would do to him. All Kieran could do was keep running and hope the older boy lost interest and gave up.

There was a crack in the sidewalk up ahead. Kieran swerved to avoid it and landed badly, crying out as pain, then terror, shot through him. He'd lost count! What number was he on? His lower lip began to tremble and hot tears pricked his eyes. It felt as if the world were crashing down around him.

"It's okay, bud. Just start over again. You can do it."

Kieran swallowed hard, feeling his grandfather's words pour over him like a soothing balm. Yes, he could start over. The numbers were always there, always neat and orderly. Numbers could be relied upon when everything else—parents, home, friends—failed him. Gritting his teeth against the pain, he ran on.

"One, two, three," he muttered. "Four, five, six . . ."

"I'm gonna get you, you weirdo. You won't get away this time!"

The sidewalk ended, and Kieran plunged ahead, dodging tree roots and gopher holes, struggling to keep his balance as a car went by. What if Cody never gave up? What if he pursued Kieran forever?

"Thirty-six, thirty-seven, thirty-eight . . ."

Running blindly, driven by fear, Kieran didn't notice when they passed the last house. The neat brick homes—decked out in Christmas finery—had given way to dense tracts of hickory and pine that lined the street on both sides. The boy shuddered, remembering his mother's warning about the woods, its pathless understory a tangled mass that grabbed the ankles of wayward boys, making them easy prey for the critters who lived there.

Behind him, Cody was crashing through the dry grass like a mad bull. Kieran glanced at the forbidden territory and shuddered. No one in his right mind would plunge headlong into that maze of hidden dangers, he thought. A boy would have to be truly desperate to take that chance.

Exactly.

He pivoted, felt himself start to skid, and saw Cody's arm reach for him. As Kieran shied from the grasping fingers, he felt his sneakers regain traction and made a desperate leap into the weald. He tripped and almost fell, his skinny arms windmilling for balance, then took off again. From the safety of the roadside, Cody flung his final, breathless taunt:

"You're in trouble now, freak. No kid's ever come out of there alive!"

Deeper into the woods Kieran ran until his legs gave out and he tumbled to the ground. Muscles quivering, his hands stinging from the brambles that raked them as he'd passed, he closed his eyes and gasped for breath. His desperate plan had worked. Now all he had to do was find his way home.

Kieran stood up and looked around. In the headlong rush to escape, he hadn't noticed where he was going, and it didn't take long for him to realize that he was lost. Worse, there were strange noises in the woods; even a Cub Scout with a Webelos badge could get spooked. As he made his way deeper into the dimly lit copse, trying to find a way out, his senses were on high alert.

A crow cawed a warning and flew off as he passed. Something skittered through the leaves and disappeared into the shadows. He swallowed hard, feeling the urge to count again begin to build inside him. Kieran shook his head and pushed the compulsion away. Counting out loud was one of the things that had gotten him in trouble with Cody, something that made other kids shy away or giggle nervously. Sometimes Kieran thought it would be better if all the kids treated him like Cody did. At least that way, he'd know if they were just pretending to be his friends while whispering behind his back.

A protracted growl from his stomach reminded him that

he should have been home by now, sitting down to his after-noon snack. His mother would be home late, and Dylan and McKenna would be glad of his absence, if they noticed it at all, but Grandpa Wendell would worry if he got home and Kieran wasn't there. The boy stifled a sob. He hadn't just outfoxed Cody, he thought, he'd outfoxed himself.

Something moved in the leaves behind him. Kieran whipped around and peered into the deepening shadows, feeling his heart pound as he remembered Cody's parting words.

"No kid's ever come out of there alive!"

He'd thought Cody was just trying to scare him, but what if it was true? What if there really was something bad, like an evil force, that might keep him there forever? The thought turned his bowels to water.

He heard it again: a tentative footfall, closer this time, then a narrow shaft of sunlight revealed a pair of yellow eyes staring at him from the shadows. Kieran felt his throat tighten as he stood rooted to the spot, unable to make a sound. Memories of his family flooded his mind, and as he thought about the peo-ple who loved him and would miss him in spite of everything, Kieran began to cry. Salty tears spilled down his face, and he collapsed on the ground, regretting the foolish act that had de-livered him from Cody's simple beating into the jaws of a monster.

The sound of dried leaves being crushed underfoot grew louder as the thing in the shadows closed in. Kieran tried to count again—just to calm himself—but when the numbers failed him, the impulse to wince overcame him. Once, twice, three times he screwed up his face, an eruption of tics he was helpless to stop. Shame burned his cheeks. At least no one would know how weak he'd been at the end.

Then suddenly, Kieran felt a gust of moist, musty air on his face, and something rough and wet began scrubbing away his tears. Startled, he drew back and opened his eyes.

It was a dog, with fur that was every shade of grey. It had a long snout and a large black nose and whiskers that covered its mouth and chin like an old man's. Shaggy ears stuck out on either side of its head like bats' wings, and its close-set eyes had a look of perpetual anxiety. It looked so funny that Kieran burst out laughing.

The boy's reaction seemed to please the dog, who set a front paw gently on his arm, an unmistakable gesture of reassurance. Kieran reached out a shaky hand, giving the animal a tentative pat, and the dog lowered its head, quietly demonstrating where and how it wished to be stroked. By the time his near-hysterical laughter had stopped, so too had the boy's facial tics.

Then the long grey snout gave him a shove, urging him onto his feet. The boy stood, brushing away the fragments of leaf and vine that clung to his clothes, and looked around.

"Can you get us out of here?"

The dog cocked its head as if listening for something and turned back the way it had come, then paused and looked back as if waiting for the boy to follow. Kieran bit his lower lip. Even if the dog could only lead him to its own home, at least he'd be out of the woods, but it wasn't wearing a collar, so it might be a stray. In which case, he thought, the only direction it would lead him was farther into the wild.

Nevertheless, he'd had no luck trying to escape on his own, and staying put was no longer an option. December dusk came early in the South Carolina piedmont and temperatures fell precipitously once the sun set; Kieran's coat wasn't warm or waterproof enough to keep him safe if it dropped below freezing. Under the circumstances, he figured his best bet was to follow the dog and hope for the best.

"Okay," he said. "Guess I'll just have to trust you."

At that, the dog took off, with Kieran close behind. Noting how the animal avoided the obstacles in its path, veering around fallen logs and giving a wide berth to the red-orange poison ivy, Kieran wondered if the dog had been living in the woods. If so, he thought, maybe it'd prefer a nice, warm home— one in which a nine-year-old boy lived.

Kieran heard a car and realized they must be near a road. In his excitement, he didn't watch where he was going and stumbled into a broken branch that caught him under the arm, tearing a hole in his coat. He stopped and smoothed the frayed edges of the material, hoping his mother wouldn't notice the damage before he'd had a chance to stitch it up.

The sounds of traffic were unmistakable now, and Kieran was surprised at how busy the road ahead seemed to be. How far had he wandered? Was he still in Bolingbroke, or had he crossed into the next town? But as he stepped out of the trees, the boy saw that he was only a few dozen yards from where he'd entered the woods. For all his Boy Scout training, he'd still made a rookie mistake: walking around in circles.

He turned back and beckoned to the dog.

"Hey, boy, we're almost home. Come on."

The dog took a step back, unwilling to emerge from the cover of the woods.

"It's okay," Kieran said. "The cars won't hurt you."

But the dog refused to be coaxed. Kieran stepped forward and held out his hand, but instead of coming closer, the dog turned and went crashing away. In seconds, it was gone.

Kieran waited for several minutes, hoping the dog would return, but with time running out and his stomach now painfully empty, he reluctantly decided to go. Then something caught his eye: a tuft of grey fur that had caught on a bramble when the dog ran off. He plucked it from the branch, tucking it into his pocket, then stepped out of the woods and ran for home.

Wendell was fixing dinner when he heard the front door slam. As Kieran ran into the kitchen, he glanced at his watch. The boy was late, but he seemed cheerier than usual, and Wendell decided not to ask for an explanation. Boys Kieran's age were fond of dawdling on their way home. If his grandson had gotten distracted chasing bugs or looking for crawfish, it was no concern of his.

The boy took a seat at the table, and Wendell poured him a glass of sweet tea, setting it out with a box of Ritz crackers.

"How was school?" he said, taking a cracker for himself.

Kieran guzzled the entire glass of tea before answering.

"Fine." He stuck a cracker in his mouth and reached for another. "May I be excused?"

Wendell frowned. First the late arrival and now the hurry to run off. If it wasn't for his grandson's lighthearted mood, he'd have sworn something was wrong.

"What's the rush? No time for an old man?"

Kieran gave him an impatient look.

"I'll be right back. I need to check something in my room."

"Okay then, go on," Wendell said. "But if there's a problem, you know you can tell me about it, right?"

"Of course," Kieran said, hopping down from his chair. "Why wouldn't I?"

As the boy ran off, Wendell told himself to be patient. If something was going on, Kieran knew his grandfather would lend a sympathetic ear. He grabbed another cracker and checked on the lasagna. The sauce was bubbling and cheese was just starting to brown. Another twenty minutes and he'd take it out to rest awhile before serving. There were some things in life you just couldn't rush, he thought, no matter how badly you wanted to.

Kieran came tearing back down the hall, almost losing his balance when he reached the slick linoleum floor.

"Grandpa!"

Wendell cringed. "What?"

"What's the difference between hair and fur?"

"How the hell should I know? Does it matter?"

Kieran scowled. "Of course it *matters.*"

"Well then, stop bothering me and go look it up."

"Wikipedia!" the boy cried and ran off again.

Wendell was emptying the dishwasher when Kieran returned a few minutes later, a shoebox in his hands. He took a seat at the table, opened the box, and carefully lined the lid up along the table's edge before proceeding.

"Hair and fur are the same thing," he said matter-of-factly. "Both are made from strands of a protein called keratin, the same thing that makes claws, hooves, and Rhino horns."

"Is that so?"

"Yes," the boy said. "And that's why the fur I found this afternoon can go into my hair collection."

He took a plastic bag from the box and deposited a small clump of grey fur inside.

Wendell walked over to take a look.

"Fur, huh? Where'd you find that?"

Kieran took his time zipping the baggie shut and filing it away with the others. Then he lifted the top and set it carefully back on the box.

"In the woods."

"The woods? You were in the *woods?*"

Kieran made a face that Wendell had seen his older sister make dozens of times.

"Take a chill pill, Grandpa. It's no big deal."

The old man felt his temper flare.

"Don't be a sass mouth; I take enough damn pills. Now, when were you in the woods?"

Kieran's face fell.

"T-today. On the way home." A muscle in his face began to twitch. "I missed the bus."

Wendell ran a hand through his sparse hair, trying to stay calm. How many times had he told this kid to stay out of the woods? He might as well have been talking to a wall.

"Look here," he said, fighting to keep his voice even. "There are things in the woods that you don't want to mess with: snakes, raccoons, coyotes—"

"I know," the boy said, placing a hand on the spot where his cheek continued to jump. "Mom told me."

"Did she tell you about the traps? 'Cause there are folks who don't like those critters and they put traps in the woods to catch them."

Kieran blanched. "I-I didn't know that."

"Well, now you do. And that's why you should never go into the woods by yourself."

The boy looked crestfallen, his small body sagging under the weight of his grandfather's disapproval. Wendell sighed. How much danger was out there, really, he wondered, and how much was his imagination?

"Tell you what," he said. "The next time you feel like poking around in the woods, you tell me and the two of us'll go together. Fair enough?"

Kieran nodded, still cradling his cheek.

"Now, go put away your hair collection and wash up. Dylan and McKenna will be home soon, and you need to set the table."

As the boy slunk off, Wendell shook his head. That right there was the reason he kept pushing Renee to find a husband. The boy needed someone who'd take him outdoors—to hunt or fish or just to explore the natural world. An old man with creaky joints and a bad back was no substitute for a father who could give Kieran the confidence he needed to overcome whatever struggles he was going through. If Wendell could see that plainly, why couldn't his daughter?

He walked back to the dishwasher, feeling a surge of anger toward his ex–son-in-law. When things had gotten tough, Greg had just sauntered off without a thought or care about how his younger son would fare. Kieran might have his problems, but he was a good kid. He didn't deserve to have a mother who was never home and siblings who thought it was his fault their father had left them.

He noted the time and suffered a moment of unease— Renee should be arriving at the restaurant. This was the third blind date that Wendell had arranged for her, and he hoped it would go well. After two unsuccessful tries, his daughter's willingness to accept his matchmaking assistance was beginning to wane. For all their sakes, he hoped the third time would be a charm.

CHAPTER 2

Renee Richardson sat in the parking lot outside Bubba Pig, waiting for a single man to show up and go inside the restaurant before she did. She'd read about it in a dating book once: Showing up early made you look desperate. Of course, any woman whose father set her up on blind dates pretty much had to be desperate, but there was no sense advertising the fact.

A Chevy truck pulled into the parking lot, and a couple in matching shirts and Lee jeans got out, their breath leaving trails in the dark as they ran for the front door. Renee restarted her car's engine and blasted the heater, trying to keep her feet from freezing.

When Butch suggested they eat at Bubba Pig, she'd assumed the name was ironic, picturing a hip, local riff on Southern cuisine, but Bubba's looked like the real deal. Not that she minded; sampling regional specialties was one of the best things about moving to a new area. But if she'd known the place was so casual, she'd never have worn a skirt and strappy high heels. Good lord, it was cold!

Renee turned the engine off and looked at the time; she'd been sitting there for ten minutes and hadn't seen even one single man arrive. If she didn't go in soon, her teeth would be chattering so hard she'd bite her tongue off as soon as she said hello. Might as well go in, she told herself. Even pathetic was better than frozen. Besides, what if Butch had somehow gotten in there without her noticing? She checked her reflection in the mirror, locked the car, and headed inside.

There was no one in the waiting area, no single man at a nearby table looking her way. Renee bit her lip and wondered what to do. Maybe he was running late, she thought. She took out her phone and checked: no text, no message. Had she gotten the date wrong? No, she was sure it was tonight. Oh, God. What if he'd stood her up? A few of the patrons were giving her curious glances. She felt her face start to flush.

Cut it out, she told herself. You have as much right to be here as they do.

Renee lifted her chin, trying to look more confident than she felt, and began to study her surroundings. Inside, Bubba Pig was even more modest than it had appeared from the outside. The dining room was filled with Formica-topped tables and slat-back chairs, and a row of stools crowded the counter where you could watch red-faced cooks in white aprons work their magic. Judging by the tea-colored stains in the ceiling and four overhead fans—blessedly still at the moment—Bubba's had taken a fair number of beatings from the weather over the years, but a collection of ceramic pigs (pigurines?) on a shelf by the front window lent it a certain playful charm.

Plus, the place smelled incredible.

A sign by the cash register said, *Seat Yourself,* so when two more minutes went by with no date in sight, Renee decided she would. It was better than standing there being gawked at, and if Butch didn't show up, she could have dinner on her own, and no one there would be the wiser.

As she stepped into the dining room, Renee caught the eye of a passing waitress. With a booster seat in one hand and a tray piled high in the other, the woman was moving among the tables as deftly as a fish in a stream.

"Can I help you?"

"I'm just taking a seat." Renee pointed to the empty table. "My date should be here soon."

If he comes.

"Are you Renee?"

"Yes," she said, surprised. "I am."

"Your man's waitin' at a table over yonder," the waitress said, indicating the spot with a nod. "I'll be over to take your order in a minute."

The dining room, it turned out, was shaped like a capital L, which meant that Renee was halfway to the table before she saw Butch. Standing in the far corner, waving his arms like a shipwreck survivor, he had a napkin tucked into his shirt neck and a spot of barbecue sauce on his chin. As she made her way past tables full of hungry diners, she tried not to let her disappointment show. A divorcée with three kids probably wasn't his idea of a dream date, either, she told herself. Under that portly, bald exterior, Butch might just be a great guy.

"You must be Renee," he said, yanking the napkin out of his shirt.

"That's me," she said, smiling bravely.

She stuck out her arm, expecting to shake hands, and found herself yanked forward onto Butch's waiting lips.

"First kisses are always awkward," he said, by way of explanation. "I prefer to just get 'em out of the way. Don't worry, though. I don't kiss and tell."

Renee stood there, stunned, wiping barbeque-flavored grease from her mouth. Was this a deal breaker? she wondered. Good lord, she'd just gotten there.

Oh, fine. One wrong move and you're ready to write the guy off? Come on, give him a chance.

Butch sidled back to his seat and flapped his napkin at the chair across from him.

"Go on and sit down. Hope you don't mind I started in on the appetizers. I been waitin' on you awhile now."

Renee nodded and took a seat. *Now who looks pathetic?*

The waitress came by and took their orders. Mindful of her tardiness, Renee ordered the first thing she saw with the word "chicken" in it, after which Butch—not satisfied with the basket of fries and "pig wings" he'd just consumed—ordered the Bubba special: a half-rack of ribs, pulled pork, fried corn on the cob, slaw, greens 'n' beans, and an extra helping of hush puppies. As he set down his plastic-covered menu, Renee found herself mentally reviewing her CPR training.

"So," Butch said, folding his hands on the table. "Wendell's your pa."

"Um, yeah," she said, trying to square such an endearing term with her cantankerous father. "I guess he and your uncle—"

"Enoch. Old Testament. He's a pistol."

"Right." She nodded. "Anyway, I guess they thought the two of us might enjoy a night out together. Since we're both, you know, single."

Butch leaned across the table, his eyes narrowing.

"Can I ask you a personal question?"

Renee shrugged. "Sure, I guess so."

"What happened to your hair?"

She reached up and gently patted her coif.

"Why? Is it sticking up somewhere?"

"No. I mean, why the pink?" He pointed. "There, in the front."

"You mean my bangs?"

"Yeah. I've never seen that before. Did you do that on purpose?"

Renee took a deep breath, feeling her smile tighten around the edges.

"Why? Does it bother you?"

"I guess not, but in general, I like my girls' hair natural." He leered. "All of it, if you know what I mean."

"Oh," Renee said, reaching for her water glass. "Thanks for telling me."

She took a sip and looked around. Dinner, she thought, could not come fast enough.

Once the food arrived, however, things improved dramatically. Renee's chicken was tender with just the right amount of smoke, the collard greens and field peas were a revelation, and the fried corn on the cob was not the batter-dipped monstrosity she'd feared. Even better, with his mouth full, Butch was fairly tolerable company. Their blind date might not have been the best night of her life, but it certainly wasn't the worst. As they waited for dessert to arrive, Renee thought she might even be willing to see him again.

"So, three kids," he said, wiping his mouth.

Renee nodded, trying to stay calm. Here it comes, she thought. Dating as a young woman might have been awkward, but dating as a single mother was downright terrifying. Trying to kindle a romantic fire between two adults was hard enough, but adding kids was like tossing on a wet rag.

"Yep," she said. "Dylan, McKenna, and Kieran."

He frowned. "How old?"

Renee sat back. Butch's attitude had suddenly become

businesslike, his questions short and to the point. It was as if their date had suddenly morphed into a job interview.

"Well," she said, "Dylan's seventeen—he's a senior at Bolingbroke High—and McKenna is *very* thirteen, if you know what I mean."

She chuckled, hoping to lighten the mood a bit.

"And Kieran's my baby. He's nine."

Butch frowned.

"Is he the one with the problems?"

The question surprised her.

"Pardon me?"

"Uncle Enoch says the kid makes funny faces and has 'issues' at school," he said, his fat fingers making air quotes. "Is he just not right in the head?"

The waitress came by and Renee waved her off.

"I don't really think that's any of your business."

"Well, it is if you expect to see me again."

Butch picked up a toothpick and pointed it at her.

"Most single mothers just spoil their kids rotten. Not you gals' fault, of course. Kids need a man around the house to keep them in line."

Renee blinked. In spite of the pounding in her chest, she felt strangely calm.

"If you ask me," he continued, "a few good swats on your boy's backside would put a stop to that nonsense. You keep coddling him and calling him your baby, you'll just make the problem worse."

"You think so?"

"I do."

He grinned and stuck the toothpick between his teeth.

"Well," she said. "*I* think it's time for me to go."

She stood up and put on her coat.

Butch scowled.

"Oh, come on. Don't be like that. Sit down."

The diners on either side of them were craning their necks. Renee licked her lips and fought to keep her voice steady.

"No. I think it's better if I go."

She grabbed her purse and turned toward the door.

"No wonder your husband left you," Butch sneered. "You don't want a man. You're just looking for a meal ticket!"

Renee cringed as every head in the room turned toward them. Determined to hold on to as much dignity as she could, she took a deep breath and started across the room.

"Go on then," Butch shouted after her. "What do I care? I only went out with you as a favor to your pa."

CHAPTER 3

Monday was the slowest day of the week at Winona's House of Beauty, which meant that every hairdresser with a following avoided it. Walk-ins and infrequent customers weren't the sort of clients you could build a career on, and most of them were bad tippers, to boot. Nevertheless, a new hire couldn't afford to be picky, and Renee had faith that, given a chance, she could convince at least a few of them to come back and ask for her again. Starting out in a new town was never easy, but she was determined to succeed.

When Renee and her family had moved from Camden to Bolingbroke, South Carolina, the culture shock was almost overwhelming. Social groups could be hard to break into, and differences that seemed minor to her could determine whether and how you were admitted. Renee's mode of dress—bright colors and short skirts—was considered unorthodox for a woman of thirty-eight, as well, and Butch wasn't the only one who'd found her pink bangs peculiar. Nevertheless, Winona had been happy to have her, and Renee's books were filling up quickly—due in large part to recommendations from the salon's most influential customer, Savannah Hays.

Savannah was in the salon that morning, her feet propped up on the coffee table while she waited for her pedicure to dry. A popular interior decorator who trafficked in some of the juiciest gossip at Winona's, Savannah was a green-eyed brunette with a generously endowed figure and the sultry look of an actress from Hollywood's Golden Era. She'd been one of Renee's first clients at the salon and her effusive praise of the "new girl" had been a godsend. As much as Renee appreciated the woman's patronage, though, she was careful not to incur her wrath. In Savannah's mouth, even the sweetest-sounding criticism could draw blood.

That day, the object of Savannah's scorn was a woman who'd hired her to decorate her new home in Indian Land, an upscale community in Lancaster County. According to Savannah, the woman had more money than taste and was determined to spend every last penny making the place as drab and uninteresting as a mental hospital. Renee—who had a new client, Debbie, in her chair—kept her eyes on her work but, like every other woman in the salon, couldn't stop herself from listening in.

"I don't mean to be ugly here," Savannah announced to no one in particular, "but a carton of yogurt has more culture than she does. I walked that woman through our showroom—you know, to get a feel for what she wanted—and I promise you, there wasn't one interesting thing in there that she didn't turn up her pert little six-thousand-dollar nose at, bless her heart."

Knowing looks and murmurs of disapproval ricocheted around the room as Savannah delivered the coup de grâce.

"Where did she think we were, *IKEA?*"

Renee felt her cheeks redden as she put the final touches on Debbie's hairdo. What was wrong with IKEA? she wondered. The majority of her own furniture had come from the Swedish big-box store. Vowing never to let Savannah through her front door, she grabbed a can of hairspray off the shelf and set her client's hair in a cloud of lacquer.

"There," she said. "All done!"

Renee handed Debbie a mirror and turned the chair so she could examine her hair from the back.

"What do you think?"

Debbie's eyes lit up and her cheeks flushed with pleasure.

"It's beautiful! Savannah was right; you *can* work magic with difficult hair."

Renee smiled modestly and removed the drape. Debbie Crowder had walked in that day looking as apprehensive as a field mouse, her fine, ash brown hair in a style that hid, rather than accentuated, her heart-shaped face and lovely grey-blue eyes. Convincing her to make a change had been tough, but it was the kind of challenge Renee loved. Now, seeing those eyes sparkle made it all worthwhile.

"Your hair isn't difficult," she said. "You just needed the right cut"—she hesitated—"and maybe some better products."

It was the part of her job that Renee liked the least: the pressure to sell hair products to her clients. Every salon did it, of course. High-end brands were a lucrative revenue stream for both the shop and the hairdressers, who made a commission on each one they sold. Nevertheless, the financial incentive was troubling. Since her divorce, Renee's finances were precarious, and when bills piled up or her child support checks were late, it was hard not to wonder if her recommendations were based on her clients' needs or her own.

Debbie was still admiring herself in the mirror.

"Well, it's just perfect, Renee. How much do I owe you?"

Renee felt a twinge of dismay as she quoted the standard fee for a cut and blow-dry at Winona's. The amount was low for the area and only about a third of what she'd been making in Camden. The cost of living in Bolingbroke was less than it had been up north, but once Winona took her cut, it meant that Renee was pretty dependent upon tips to make ends meet.

"Well, it was worth it," Debbie said, reaching for her pocket-book.

She handed Renee the exact amount for the haircut, then took out two more dollars.

"And here's a little something extra for you."

But as she offered Renee the money, Savannah's hand shot out of nowhere and slapped Debbie's hand.

"*What* do you think you are doing?"

Debbie recoiled, her fingers still clutching the two singles.

"I *told* you," Savannah said. "As one of my *personal* referrals, that sort of thing is unnecessary. Why, with all the business I've sent her way, I'm sure Renee would be *ashamed* to take more of your hard-earned cash." She flashed Renee a dangerous smile. "Isn't that right, dear?"

Renee swallowed, caught between the desire to set things straight and the fear of losing Savannah's favor. The truth was, the woman had sent her a lot of clients, most of whom tipped generously when Savannah wasn't around, and she and Debbie could always clear this up later, if need be. At any rate, it wasn't worth quibbling over two bucks.

"Of course," she said. "Savannah's been very good to me."

"That's right," Savannah purred. "And if you still feel like throwing those two dollars away, Deborah Jean Crowder, you can buy me one of those giant candy canes they're selling down at the Piggly Wiggly. It's for charity."

Debbie's shoulders slumped as she tucked the money back into her wallet, her grey-blue eyes downcast. Renee felt her lips tighten. The loss of her tip wasn't half as upsetting as seeing the effect of Savannah's high-handedness on her client's confidence. Whatever lift Debbie's new hairdo might have given her had wilted under the heat of Savannah's rebuke. As the two of them walked out, Renee took a deep breath and tried to slow her pounding heart. One day, she thought, Savannah was going to go too far, and Renee would no longer be able to hold her tongue. For now, all she could do was hope that she'd be in a better place, financially, when that day came.

It was time for lunch, and Renee's station had to be cleaned before she went on break. She picked up a clump of Debbie's fine, mouse brown hair, stuffed it into a small plastic bag, then swept the rest of the cut hairs into a dustpan and threw them away before slipping the bag back into her pocket. She had twenty minutes to bolt down her lunch and get ready for her next client.

Winona's niece, Sissy, was in the break room, taking a load of towels out of the dryer.

"Hey, Renny. How's it going?"

Renee hid a rueful smile as she hunted in the refrigerator for her Tupperware container. Sissy had been mispronouncing her name for so long that she no longer bothered to correct her.

"Oh, fine," she said, extracting a blue plastic box from the second shelf.

"I heard what Savannah said about your tip. That wasn't nice."

"It's okay," Renee said. "It'll all work out."

She popped a corner of the container, set it in the microwave, and pressed the "reheat" button.

Sissy plopped an armload of towels into the laundry basket and set it beside the table.

"Do you mind if I set the folded ones here?"

"No, go ahead. I don't need that much room."

"That's what I thought," the girl said, setting down the first folded towel.

When the timer went off, Renee grabbed a fork and started stirring the food in her container. Sissy raised an eyebrow.

"What you got there?"

Renee picked out a bite of food.

"Leftovers," she said, putting it in her mouth.

"Kinda looks like puke. No offense or nothin'."

Renee shook her head. Sissy was a good soul, but the filter that kept most people from blurting out the first thing that occurred to them had not taken root in her brain.

"Well, in fairness, it's a combination of three different meals," she said. "But my kids would probably agree with you."

The tower of towels was getting precarious. Sissy pushed it aside and started a second one.

"How are your kids?"

"Fine." Renee took a swig of Diet Coke. "Dylan's coach thinks he'll be offered a football scholarship to Clemson—"

"Ooh!"

"—and McKenna's found some nice girls to hang out with after school."

"And how's your little fella, Kieran?"

Renee swallowed hard. How was Kieran, the troubled, brilliant, "problem" of the family?

"He's okay," she said. "I'm having a conference with his teacher after work. Maybe I'll know more then."

Sissy shook out another towel.

"I read where the things kids eat can affect the way they act sometimes. Junk food and such can make 'em kinda crazy."

Renee kept her eyes on the food in front of her. Sissy meant well, but this wasn't a subject she wanted to pursue. She knew her son was different, but all kids were a little strange when you came right down to it. It was a phase, that was all. Kieran would grow out of his odd behaviors the same way he'd grown out of short pants and thumb-sucking.

"Yeah," she said. "I've read that, too."

For a few minutes, the only sound in the break room was the snap of the towels as they were shaken out and folded. Then Sissy said:

"How was the blind date? Was he as nice as your daddy said he was?"

Renee shook her head.

"I don't think Dad and I have the same ideas about who I'd be interested in," she said, still stung by Friday night's humiliation.

She swallowed, feeling her stomach clench as she relived the last few minutes of her disastrous date with Butch.

"A few good swats to your boy's backside would stop that nonsense right away."

As if Kieran's facial tics were simply a way to gain attention! Renee ground her teeth, feeling an unreasonable anger at Sissy for reminding her of that awful evening.

"That's too bad." Sissy sighed. "I wouldn't mind if my daddy helped me find someone."

"Believe me," Renee said as she got up from the table, "it sounds more appealing than it is."

She washed her Tupperware in the sink and grabbed a fresh apron.

"Oh!" Sissy said. "Before I forget . . ."

She went over to her cubby and took out a small brown paper bag.

"I saved these for you."

Renee opened the bag and saw the hair-filled plastic bags inside. She looked up and smiled.

"Thanks, Sissy. I'm sure Kieran will appreciate it."

"No problem. Just, um, make sure he doesn't tell anybody where he got them, okay?"

"Don't worry. I'll remind him."

She reached into her pocket and took out her cell phone.

Sissy frowned. "What are you doing?"

"Texting my dad," Renee said as she headed for the door. "I want to remind him that I'm going to be late for dinner—I mean supper—tonight."

"Lucky. My daddy would've let us all starve before he'd've cooked us a meal."

Renee tucked the phone in her pocket and went back to her station. Sissy was right, she thought. She was lucky to have her father around to help her. It was, however, a decidedly mixed blessing.

CHAPTER 4

Kieran sat outside the principal's office, swinging his legs in the too-tall chair as he waited to talk to the school counselor. Mrs. Dalton had told him to go see the lady in the principal's office and that she and his mother would talk about it that night, but she hadn't said what would happen once he got there. Was the counselor nice? he wondered. Would he have to take a test? He hoped it wouldn't take too long. It was almost time for lunch, and he didn't want to run into Cody again.

He put his right hand into his coat pocket and fondled the piece of dog fur he'd taken from his hair collection. Rubbing the wiry strands between his fingers seemed to work a kind of magic on Kieran, giving him the same calm feeling that he'd had when he was with the dog. He wished it hadn't run away. If it had followed him home, maybe his mom would have let him keep it. Then he'd have someone to play with after school instead of just hanging out in his room alone.

Kieran closed his eyes and rubbed the fur harder, wishing

that his mother would let him walk home from school so he could see if the dog was still there. If it was, maybe the two of them could do fun stuff together, like play pirates or build a fort. He opened his eyes and sighed wistfully. And if that happened, he thought, maybe she would even let him keep it.

The principal's office door opened, and a woman in a blue dress stepped out.

"Hey there." She smiled. "Are you Kieran?"

He nodded.

"I'm Dr. Joan. Why don't you come on in so we can visit awhile?"

Kieran took his hand out of his pocket and followed her inside.

There were two leather chairs in front of the principal's desk—one on the left with a manila folder on it and one on the right that was empty. Dr. Joan took the folder off the left one and sat down. Kieran took a seat in the other and looked around. He'd never been in the principal's office before, but he knew some kids who had. They told stories on the playground about what happened in there—none of them good.

"So," she said. "How are you today?"

"Okay, I guess."

"Do you know why you're here?"

He shook his head.

The counselor frowned and checked the folder, then mumbled something and set it aside.

"Kieran, Mrs. Dalton tells me that you like to count your steps when you're walking around the school. Is that true?"

He squirmed in his seat.

"I don't really like it," he said.

"But you do it because you have to?"

He stared at her for a moment, then nodded slowly.

"Is that also why you make faces sometimes or cough when you don't have a cold?"

Kieran swallowed. No one had ever asked him about *why* he did those things before; they'd just told him to stop. He nodded again.

"And how does it make you feel when you count your steps or make faces?"

He ducked his head. "Bad."

Dr. Joan wrinkled her brow. "Bad like a stomach ache or bad like a bad person?"

"Just bad." He glanced away. "People make fun of me. They call me a freak."

"Does everybody call you that or just a few?"

Kieran fidgeted, unsure what to say. If he told her it was Cody Daniels, would she tell the principal? Things were hard enough at school; he didn't want to make things worse. He shook his head.

"Just some. I can't remember who."

She nodded. "So, there are some people who make fun of you and some that don't."

"I guess."

"And that bothers you?"

He gave the counselor a searching look. Was she making fun of him? No, Kieran decided. Adults just liked to ask dumb questions like that. He nodded.

Dr. Joan opened the folder again and starting writing. While he waited for her to finish, Kieran continued his survey of the room. There were trophies in a glass case and a shelf with a football helmet and a bobble-headed tiger on it. He saw something moving on the floor and saw a bright red ladybug crawl under the principal's desk. Mrs. Dalton said that people used to like ladybugs because they were cute and ate stuff nobody wanted, but now they were just pests.

The counselor looked up, her pen poised.

"I have just a few more questions for you and then you can go. All right?"

He shrugged. "Okay."

"When did you first start counting or making faces or funny noises?"

"I don't know."

"Well, was it when you lived in your old house or after you moved to Bolingbroke?"

"In my old house."

"And how much would you say, on average, that you count?"

Kieran frowned. "You mean, like how high?"

"No. I mean, how often do you feel the need to count things? Would you say you do it every day or a couple of times a week?"

"Every day, I guess."

"More than once a day?"

"Yeah."

"More than five or six times in a day?"

Kieran licked his lips. He'd never noticed how many times a day he counted or wrinkled his nose or made noises. Sometimes he didn't even know he was doing it until someone told him to cut it out. Mostly, he just hoped it would stop and then tried to forget about it when it did. He shook his head.

"Maybe," he said. "I'm not sure."

"Have you ever started washing your hands and found that you couldn't stop?"

Kieran rubbed his hands together.

"No." He paused. "Maybe."

Dr. Joan wrote something else in the folder.

"What about opening or closing doors?"

Kieran felt a whisper of panic. He could almost feel himself opening and then closing a door, over and over . . .

"No." He shook his head. "I don't do that."

She nodded.

"All right, let's stick with the counting, then. Is there anything that makes you want to do that?"

"I don't *want* to do it. I just *have* to."

"Of course," she said. "I'm sorry. What I should have said was, is there something that makes you feel as if you *have to* count things?"

He shrugged, thinking about the steps he'd been counting on the way to the office.

"When I'm nervous, I guess. Or scared."

Like now.

There was a feeling like a tickle in his cheek; the kind he got right before he made a face. Dr. Joan was writing something in her folder again. Kieran tried to wipe the tickle-y feeling away, hoping she wouldn't notice.

She looked up and smiled.

"Would you like to stop doing the things that people make fun of?"

Kieran nodded again.

"Well, that's good," Dr. Joan said. "Because I think I can help you. Would you like that?"

"Yes, ma'am."

"Good. Now, I see that Mrs. Dalton is going to speak to

your mother about this tonight. If she agrees, then we'll put your name on the list, and I'll send a release form to your parents."

"Not *parents*," Kieran said. "Just my mom."

"Oh. Well then, I'll send it to your mother."

He glanced over at the door.

"Can I go now?"

"In a minute." Dr. Joan closed the folder. "When you feel like you have to count or make faces, is there anything that helps you stop? Something you can think of or do that makes the bad feeling go away?"

Kieran thought about that.

"Sometimes I think about stuff my grandpa tells me."

"What does he tell you?"

"Well, if I get scared because I've lost count, he reminds me that it's okay to start over."

"That's nice." She smiled. "It's good to have a grandpa like that."

Kieran nodded.

"And if I've had a bad day at school, he says, 'Don't let those little shits get to you.' "

"I see." Dr. Joan cleared her throat. "Is there, um, anything else that helps you? Other than the things your grandfather says?"

"When I talked to the dog." He reached into his pocket. "When I was with him, I forgot to count or make faces. It was nice."

"I'll bet it was," she said. "I'm glad you have a pet like that to talk to. Dogs can be especially good at helping children deal with their anxieties."

She closed the folder and stood up.

"Well, I think that's all the questions I have for you today, Kieran. Thank you for coming by to see me. Hurry on back to your classroom now; it's almost time for the lunch bell."

Kieran headed back down the hallway in a daze. Dr. Joan had said that a dog would help him stop counting and making faces! When his mother heard that, she'd have to let him get one, wouldn't she? And when she did, he thought, he knew exactly which dog he wanted. He almost couldn't believe his good luck.

Then the lunch bell rang, and suddenly every door in the hallway flew open as hungry students poured out of their classes and headed for the cafeteria. Kieran began pushing his way through the crowd that moved against him like an on-rushing tide. This was what he got for daydreaming, he told himself. Why hadn't he been paying attention?

The crowd had thinned some by the time he reached his classroom. Kieran grabbed the brown bag from his cubby and hurried out the door. As he made his way back the way he'd come, he kept his head down and willed himself to be invisible.

He was almost to the cafeteria when he heard a door slam open behind him and the sound of menacing laughter fill the hallway. Kids on their way to lunch were jostled as the group of sixth-grade boys tumbled out of the room, shoving each other and making rude comments to the girls.

Hearing Cody's distinctive bray, Kieran started walking faster. He was almost past the lockers now; just another few feet and they'd be close enough for the lunch monitors to see them. If he could just stay out of Cody's reach for a few more seconds . . .

"Out of my way, freak!"

CHAPTER 5

Renee chewed an antacid as she sat in the hallway outside Kieran's classroom, waiting for his teacher, Mrs. Dalton, to call her in. This meeting was in addition to the regular parent-teacher conferences that were held twice a year, and bolting down her dinner had done nothing to settle either her stomach or her jitters. Was Kieran in some sort of trouble?

She heard voices coming from the other side of the closed classroom door but couldn't make out the words. That was good, she thought. Nothing worse than having to air your dirty laundry in public. If Mrs. Dalton did have a problem with Kieran, Renee preferred that it not be broadcast to the world at large. He'd had enough trouble back at his old school. She didn't want the people in Bolingbroke to take against her son before they'd even given him a chance.

Renee looked down at the snippets of hair that clung to her skirt and brushed them away, only to find that they'd reattached themselves to her leggings. She shook her head ruefully. It seemed like the perfect metaphor for her life: Every time she

He felt a hand on his shoulder, then a shove, and before he knew it, he was slamming into a locker, the clang of the metal door ringing in his ears. Kieran staggered, dropped his lunch, and watched helplessly as Cody and his minions trampled it underfoot.

thought she had a problem solved, it just cropped up somewhere else.

The solid sound of bootheels on the concrete floor caught
her attention. A tall man with salt-and-pepper hair was walking toward her, his cowboy boots echoing in the hallway. In a
dress shirt and a bolo tie, jacket, and Levis, he looked a bit like
the Marlboro man—all he needed was a Stetson to complete
the look.

Their eyes met and he returned her smile.

"Waiting for someone?" he said.

She threw a thumb over her shoulder.

"Conference with the teacher. You?"

"Killing time while I wait for a friend." He indicated the
chair next to hers. "Mind if I join you?"

"Feel free."

As he took his seat, the man reached up as if to doff a
nonexistent hat, confirming Renee's suspicions. The revelation made her curious. Raising livestock was only a small part
of the economy in Bolingbroke. Either the outfit was an affec-
tation or, like Renee, he was new to the area.

"Conference with the teacher, huh? You don't look like
you're even old enough to have a child in school."

Renee shook her head at the false flattery.

"I'm plenty old," she said. "And I've got three kids, not one."

"Hmm. Maybe it's the hair." He pointed. "I like the pink."

She reached up and touched her bangs self-consciously.

"I'm a hairdresser. Comes with the territory."

"Well, it looks good on you," the man said. "Maybe I'd
look better with pink hair."

Renee raised an eyebrow.

"Now you're just making fun of me."

"Not at all. The truth is, I could use a lift. But where are my manners?" He stuck out his hand. "I'm Travis Diehl."

She took his hand and felt calluses on the meaty palm.

Who knows? she thought. Maybe he is a real cowboy.

"Renee Richardson," she said. "Nice to meet you."

"Same here," Travis said, stretching his legs out in front of him.

Renee brushed some more hair off her skirt and saw him glance at her left hand. Was he checking for a wedding ring? He wasn't wearing one himself. She bit her lip, feeling a girlish thrill at the thought that this handsome man might find her attractive.

"So," he said, "three kids. They all go to school here?"

"Nope, just the youngest. The oldest is in high school; the other's in middle school."

"Boys or girls?"

"Two boys, one girl."

"That's nice. In our family, it was just me and my brother. I would have liked to have had a sister."

Renee laughed. "I'll have to tell my brother that. Maybe he'll trade you."

Why did I say that?

She glanced down, feeling foolish. Trying to make small talk with a strange man made her feel as awkward and off-balance as a newborn colt. She looked back over her shoulder at the closed door, wondering when Mrs. Dalton would wrap things up.

"You have an interesting accent," Travis said. "I take it you're not from Bolingbroke."

She shook her head. "We moved here from Camden in August."

"Is that so? I wouldn't have pegged you for a Jersey girl,

but then I'm no expert." He sighed. "Camden's a lovely town. I'll bet you miss it."

"You know Camden?" Renee said, feeling a pang of home-sickness.

"I do. I went to school not far from there."

"Really? Which one?"

"Princeton."

Renee swallowed. Suddenly, the chances that Travis Diehl was a real cowboy seemed remote.

"Wow. Princeton, huh?"

"Went there on a football scholarship," he said. "Still, my grades were good. I might have gotten in without it. What about you?"

"Me?" She laughed. "I went to Rowan. It was cheap and close to home."

In spite of her flippant attitude, his smile showed real interest.

"Rowan's a teacher's college, isn't it?"

"Used to be." She sighed. "No, I studied graphic art. The most useless major in the world, right?"

He shrugged. "Not if you love it. Seems to me the world would be a dismal place without art."

Was this guy kidding? Everybody knew how worthless an art degree was. Renee found herself wanting to goad him, to provoke the kind of ridicule she'd gotten from others—including her ex-husband—over her poor choice of major.

"You know what an art major says at his first job? 'You want fries with that?'" She laughed. "Believe me, it was stupid."

"It doesn't seem stupid to me. Not if you loved it."

Renee glanced away, feeling rattled. Okay, maybe it hadn't been stupid, but it had certainly been foolish of her to get an art degree—everyone else knew that, why didn't he?

Travis cocked his head, trying to catch her eye.

"I take it you never became a graphic designer, then."

She felt the corner of her mouth twitch.

"Actually, I did. We'd had Dylan by then, and I worked at home part time doing work for a print shop. It wasn't much, but it paid a few bills, and it kept me from falling too far into the mommy trap."

Thinking about those years made her feel wistful. Maybe if she hadn't gotten pregnant when she did things would have been different. She and Greg might have had time to get to know each other before they got married. Or maybe they wouldn't have gotten married at all. Still, she wasn't sorry. If she hadn't married Greg, she'd never have had her kids. Renee wouldn't have changed anything if it meant that she wouldn't have them.

Travis looked thoughtful.

"I have great respect for my friends who are artists. It's not easy trying to make a living at it, and most never do. But if it's in you to create art, then I think you've just got to find a way."

Renee nodded and looked away, swallowing the lump that suddenly rose in her throat.

"So," he said. "When did you become a hairdresser?"

"Hmm? Oh, after my divorce. It was part of our settlement; my ex agreed to pay for a year of training so I could get a job. Doing hair was something I could learn fast and make some decent money at."

"I should think a degree in art would come in handy, then."

"It does," she said. "But it's not like it's necessary. Most of the girls I work with barely made it through high school."

He nodded. "So what brought you here?"

What was this, she wondered, Twenty Questions? Still, he

seemed genuinely interested, and Renee found that she was enjoying his company.

"The cost of living, mostly. Plus, my mother died last year, and Dad was at loose ends. After my divorce, he suggested that the four of us move closer to my brother and buy a house together."

"So, you live with your father?"

She made a face. "Sounds lame, doesn't it?"

"Actually, I think it's kind of nice." Travis smiled. "How's it working out?"

"Pretty good. The house we bought is on a slope, so it has a lower floor with a separate entrance in back. Dad can come and go as he pleases, and I've got privacy when I need it." She felt her cheeks warm. "Not that I do very often."

Renee brushed a few more hairs off her skirt, trying to think of a way to get off the subject of her family. The fact was, in spite of their differences, she was having a good time talking to Travis Diehl. After the horrible date with Butch, the last thing she wanted was to scare him off by telling him about her kids. Or more specifically, Kieran.

She heard the door behind her open. A man and woman stepped out of Kieran's classroom and hurried away, their eyes averted. Renee looked up and saw Kieran's teacher standing in the doorway, smiling.

"Mrs. Richardson? You and your husband can come in now."

"Oh. No, he's not—"

She turned back and gave Travis an apologetic look.

"I'm so sorry."

He shook his head.

"It's fine," he said, waving her on. "You go on now. I've kept you long enough."

Renee stood up and walked into the classroom.

"Sorry for the wait," Mrs. Dalton said as she closed the door.

"That's okay," she said, taking a seat.

If only it had been a little longer.

Mrs. Dalton sat down across from her and took out her grade book.

"Thank you for coming down here on short notice. I know we're all busy with the holidays coming up, but there's been an interesting development around here that I wanted to talk to you about."

"Something to do with Kieran?"

"Yes."

"He's not in trouble, is he?"

The teacher smiled.

"No, not at all. In fact, Kieran's one of my favorite students. He's obviously very bright, and he behaves himself as well as he can in the classroom."

Renee frowned.

"What do you mean, 'as well as he can'?"

The woman colored.

"Oh. I just mean . . . you know . . . the counting and the facial tics can be distracting. And sometimes . . . well . . . the noises, but they don't generally disrupt our classroom activities."

"What about the other kids? Is he making any friends?"

"As far as friends go, it's still a bit early. It always takes a while for a new student to fit in." She cleared her throat. "The playground monitors tell me there's been some mild teasing at recess, but there's not really much I can do about that."

Renee squeezed her hands together, remembering the taunts Kieran had endured at his last school and the bullies whose parents she'd confronted when things got out of hand. Why couldn't they just leave him alone?

"Kids are so cruel."

Mrs. Dalton made a noncommittal gesture.

"I think most of them just lack social skills. They see someone who's acting differently, and they point it out."

Renee took a deep breath and nodded. There was no sense arguing about it. Mrs. Dalton had a lot of other kids to keep an eye on; it was probably just easier for her to think the best of them.

"So, if Kieran's not a problem, why am I here?"

The woman brightened, setting her folded hands on the desk.

"A gift of one hundred thousand dollars has been given to the school, to be used to help students like Kieran who have emotional or learning disabilities."

Renee frowned. "Who says Kieran has a disability?"

"Well, I thought . . . I mean, the things I mentioned . . ." Mrs. Dalton looked flustered. "I'm sorry. Has no one ever mentioned that your son may have OCD? Our counselor tells me he has all the classic signs."

"That's ridiculous," Renee snapped. "He's just a kid. He makes faces and funny noises, and yes, sometimes he counts out loud, but that doesn't mean he's *sick*."

The teacher held up a placating hand.

"Hold on. No one's suggesting that Kieran is sick," she said. "But if he does have a disability, I think it's important that you at least consider this opportunity. Receiving this donation now means that we'll be able to hire a full-time psychiatric aide to help any of the children who need it before their symptoms become problematic."

"No." Renee shook her head. "I will not allow Kieran to

be labeled. I've seen how this works: A kid seems a little different and the next thing you know, he's on medication so he doesn't disrupt the classroom. I'm not going to let you turn him into a zombie just to make your job easier."

Mrs. Dalton was visibly struggling to control her temper.

"I'm sorry you feel that way. Obviously, I made some assumptions here that I shouldn't have, and that's my fault. However, I would like to point out that no one is talking about medicating your son. The funds that are being donated are only to be used to help children like Kieran make the most of their time in school and to learn coping strategies for the years ahead. You're under no obligation to enroll him in the program, but I would strongly urge you to consider it. The longer Kieran goes without some sort of help, the harder it'll be for him to deal with it later."

Renee sat back and lifted a hand to cover her eyes. She supposed she'd known for a long time that something was wrong, but she'd told herself it was temporary. Something Kieran would grow out of in time. Greg's way of dealing with it had always been to tease Kieran or to punish him for what he believed was willful behavior. It had caused a lot of stress in their already shaky marriage, and when things fell apart, he'd blamed the breakup on the problems with their youngest child. But it was a lie, and they both knew it. With or without the added stress, their relationship wouldn't have survived. She took a deep breath and lowered her hand.

"I'm sorry," Renee said, reaching into her purse for a tissue. "I shouldn't have yelled at you. This is just a lot to take in."

"Of course. I understand."

She wiped her eyes, thinking about the couple who'd just left, their eyes downcast, scurrying away like they didn't want to be seen, and hoped that Travis Diehl would be gone by the time she left. She didn't want him to ask her what had happened. She crumpled up the tissue and sniffed.

"So," she said. "This gift. What does it mean for Kieran?"

"Well, the first thing would be for him to have a formal evaluation with the district's psychologist. Then, of course, she'd want to interview you and your husband to see what behaviors you've observed at home."

Renee glanced at the door.

"You know that man outside wasn't Kieran's dad, right?"

"I gathered that; I'm sorry if I made things awkward for you. I knew that you and Kieran's father were divorced. I just thought perhaps he'd come—"

"Greg doesn't come to anything that has to do with Kieran," Renee said. "He's remarried now, too, so unless the poor kid becomes a star athlete, I don't expect he'll ever see his dad again."

Mrs. Dalton looked down at her grade book.

"I'm sorry to hear that."

"Don't be. Believe me, we're all better off without him."

Renee forced herself to smile. She hadn't meant to sound so bitter. It wasn't this poor woman's fault that Greg was such a lousy father.

"So, this evaluation," she said. "When will that take place?"

"It depends on how many candidates are identified for the program, but our principal is anxious to get things moving. The school psychologist has offered to clear her schedule for us, too, so it could be as early as the first week of January."

"And after that?"

"We'll see what she recommends. If Kieran does appear to have OCD, he'll be enrolled in the program for further evaluation and therapy."

"But not drugs, right?"

Mrs. Dalton paused. "My understanding is that drugs will not be the first choice in this program, but I'm sure it all depends upon the child and how well he or she does in therapy. However, no child is going to be forced to take medication. It'll be up to each individual family to make that decision, if and when the time comes."

Renee took a deep breath and fought to keep the tears from flowing again.

"Well, that's that then. Thanks for letting me know."

She grabbed her purse and was almost out of the chair when Mrs. Dalton reached for her hand.

"Can I just mention one more thing before you go?"

Renee laughed cheerlessly and sat back down.

"Oh, great. You mean there's more?"

"Yes, but it's good news this time." The teacher smiled. "I know this has been a shock, and I know how worried you must be."

"You got that right."

"But you should also know that your son is very smart, and I've asked that Kieran's IQ also be tested. Unless I miss my guess, he should easily qualify for our gifted and talented program."

Renee closed her eyes and felt a tear run down the side of her face.

"Well, that's something anyway," she said. "Thanks for letting me know."

The temperature outside had dropped by several degrees. As Renee stepped out of the building, she saw her breath come out in puffs of white. There'd been no sign of Travis Diehl when she left the classroom and none outside, either. Probably for the best, she thought. Even if he had been interested, he'd probably have changed his mind once he found out

why she was there. Who wants to take on someone else's problems?

She thrust her hands into her pockets and hurried across
the parking lot, feeling wistful about what might have been.
Travis Diehl had seemed like a nice guy. It was too bad she'd
never see him again.

CHAPTER 6

"Hugh? I'm home!"

There was no answer, but that didn't mean no one was home; his brother didn't always respond even if he did hear someone calling him. Travis hung up his coat and heard music coming from the living room. He picked up the bag of Bojangles' chicken he'd bought for supper and went to investigate. As he'd suspected, Hugh was playing Tetris on his XBox.

He stepped between his brother and the screen.

"Hey! I'm home," he said. "Have you eaten yet?"

Hugh shook his head, craning to see around the body in his way. Travis pointed to his watch.

"Ten minutes. Finish your game and come eat."

Travis headed into the kitchen and set the bag on the counter, then went to call Max inside. The Irish wolfhound dashed into the room, his nails scrabbling for purchase on the wooden floor as he wiggled a happy greeting. Travis bent down, dodging sloppy kisses and patted the big guy's back.

"Whoa," he said, running his fingers through the coarse grey fur. "Did you lose another collar?"

He walked over to the pantry and got out a chew bone.

"You're getting to be an expensive habit," he said as Max caught it in midair, "you know that?"

While Max ran off to enjoy his treat, Travis set the table and started fixing the rest of their meal.

The meeting with Hank had gone well. A dozen kids had already signed up for the program at school and another half dozen were considering it. After all the hassle he'd gone through to get the ball rolling, it was exciting to see things finally moving forward.

He felt the phone in his pocket vibrate and took it out. It was a message from Savannah.

Dinner tonight? I made fried chicken.

Travis texted back.

Sorry, didn't see this in time. Thanks anyway.

Seconds later, another text came through.

Going to The Growler later. Wanna come?

Travis shook his head.

Another time. Hugh and I are staying in tonight.

He hit "send" just as his brother walked into the room.

"Who are you texting?"

"Savannah Hays."

Hugh made a face.

"What does *she* want?"

"Nothing."

Travis set the phone down and opened the refrigerator.

"Was Max's collar missing when you got home?"

"Dunno," his brother said, reaching for the Bojangles' bag.

"Did you wash your hands?"

Hugh stomped over to the kitchen sink and turned on the water.

"That's the second collar he's lost this month," Travis said as he took out a bagged salad. "I'll have to check the fence; maybe he caught it on a nail again."

With the salad on the table, Travis poured the drinks and said grace.

"How was work today?"

Hugh shrugged and bit into a piece of chicken. For the last three months, he'd been working at a nonprofit that hired programmers to do contract work for some of the big tech companies in the Raleigh-Durham area. Finding his brother a job hadn't been easy—it wasn't everyone who wanted to deal with people like Hugh—and Travis was proud of his brother for sticking with it. He only wished his folks had lived long enough to see how well their younger son was doing.

"The meeting at school went well." He smiled. "You know, you forget how small an elementary school is until you go back as an adult. I remember when we were there; we thought the place was enormous."

When there was still no response, Travis decided to just concentrate on his meal. This was what it was like most nights in their house: brief, one-sided conversations punctuated by the occasional outburst when Hugh got upset about something. It wasn't a bad life, but there were times when it felt awfully lonely. It was hard not to feel as if something, or someone, was missing.

If only Emmy could see how well Hugh is doing.

Travis shook his head. No. She'd made it clear that he had to make a choice. He could honor his wedding vows, or he could keep faith with his family. In the end, it wasn't even the promise he'd made to his parents that had torn the two of them apart so much as his wife's unwillingness to compromise. How could he have lived with Emmy if he couldn't live with himself?

Poor Emmy. She hadn't realized when she married me that there was another man in on the deal.

"I met a woman while I was there," he said. "Her name was Renee, and she had *pink hair.*"

Hugh glanced up. "Really?"

"Yeah. Not all of it, just her bangs, but they were like cotton candy pink. Really bright."

"I like cotton candy."

"I know you do. I think you would have liked her, too." Travis smiled at the recollection. "She was very nice."

Renee had been nice, he thought. One of those people who just seemed to put other people at ease. Between running his parents' business and starting up the Diehl Foundation, it had been months since Travis had had a casual conversation with a woman. He'd been sorry when she had to go.

Hugh reached for another piece of chicken.

"Why was her hair pink?"

"Hmm? Oh, she's a hairdresser. I guess they color their hair sometimes to show people what they can do."

When supper was through, the two of them cleared the table and walked into the kitchen for their nightly ritual: Travis at the sink, scraping and rinsing the dirty dishes, and his brother putting them in the dishwasher. Hugh was a master at getting everything to fit.

People like Hugh needed structure and predictability to function, and it was just one of many routines that kept everything running smoothly. It made life neat and orderly, but Travis knew that not everyone wanted to be bound to doing the same thing day after day. It was why he'd been reluctant to get involved with anyone else since the divorce. What was comforting to one person might feel like smothering to someone else.

Maybe that was what he'd liked about Renee and her pretty pink hair, he thought. There was something carefree about that arc of color sweeping across her forehead, something that had shocked him a bit, knocking him out of his day-to-day mind-set and making him feel as if there was more to life than the sort of Groundhog Day existence he'd been living since his parents died.

Hugh closed the dishwasher and looked at him.

"Trav?"

"Hmm?"

"They make blue cotton candy, too. Could she make my hair blue?"

"I'm not sure." He grimaced. "You sure you want blue hair?"

Hugh thought about that.

"No," he said. "Pink is better."

"I agree, but unfortunately I don't know where she works. I was going to ask her if she wanted to get a cup of coffee, but then she had to go, and I didn't get a chance."

Travis took out a dishtowel and started wiping down the counter.

"I don't know. Maybe I should have left her a note or something." He shrugged. "What do you think?"

He looked up, but Hugh had already gone.

With the dishes done and the kitchen clean, Travis grabbed his phone and headed to his office to do some work. Hugh was back in the living room, as sociable as a stone, with Max lolling on the floor at his feet. Travis took a seat at his desk, turned on the computer, and started writing an email to his lawyer.

Now that there were candidates for the school program, the stakes had gotten higher. He'd have to make sure that the funds to pay for testing the kids and hiring a therapist were in place before they were actually needed, and every step of the way would have to be documented and justified, lest they run afoul of the IRS. There were days when having to jump through so many hoops made him want to throw in the towel, but if it saved even one family from the kind of struggle his own parents had gone through, it would be worth it. And if it helped him ease the pain of their loss, Travis thought, so much the better.

He reread the email, then hit "send" and sat back, listening to the Tetris theme song as it drifted out from the living room. At thirty-six, Hugh was still childlike in some ways, and his ability to give himself over to a virtual world was one of the few things about his brother that Travis truly envied. What would he give, he wondered, to be able to let go of the responsibilities in his life for a few precious hours, without worrying that everything would fall apart?

His phone rang, and he checked to see who it was.

Savannah—again.

Travis sighed, feeling a pang of guilt as he let the call go to voice mail. It seemed as if Savannah Hays had known he was coming back to Bolingbroke even before he did.

Within days of his mother's funeral, she'd shown up at the house with food and an offer of help, and Travis, overwhelmed with grief and loss, had been grateful for her kindness. Savannah's knowledge of the people and places in Bolingbroke had been a boon as well, as he struggled to get himself plugged back into a community he'd left years before. But when it became apparent that Savannah had more on her mind than friendship, he'd found himself pulling back. With the trauma of his divorce still fresh, he simply wasn't ready for another serious relationship.

Since then, they'd had the occasional cup of coffee or drinks with the gang down at The Growler, but the more that time went on, the surer Travis was that things with Savannah were never going to work out. As beautiful and accomplished as she was, Savannah was very insecure, and with Hugh to look after and five thousand employees at Diehl Industries counting on him to save his parents' company, Travis had neither the time nor the energy to make her happy. Even so, he thought, they might have been able to make it work, but for one thing: Travis wanted children—adopted or his own, it didn't matter—and Savannah did not. Once she'd made that clear, pursuing a relationship seemed not only pointless but cruel; he wasn't going to change his mind and neither was she. Since then, his commitments had kept him busy enough that the two of them seldom crossed paths, but as things settled down and he became open to the idea of dating again, he was finding it harder and harder to keep his distance. Savannah could be as seductive as a siren, and just as hard to resist.

He heard scratching at the door, and Max pushed his way into the room. Getting a therapy dog had worked wonders for his brother, giving him confidence and nurturing the sort of social skills he needed in order to get a job. But lately, Hugh had been resistant to taking Max with him to work, saying he felt stigmatized for needing an animal's help. So, with Travis busy at work and Hugh away at his job, Max now spent most of his days alone. Perhaps that was why he kept trying to get out of the yard, Travis thought. Maybe some canine instinct was telling him he still had work to do. Or maybe, he thought, Max was just looking for a playmate.

Max padded over and set his head on Travis's lap.

"So," Travis said, stroking the dog's broad head. "No collar again today. What are you doing with them?"

He dug his fingers into the fur around Max's neck, trying to find a reason for the disappearing collars. Was something hurting him there? A rash or a cut that bothered him enough to make him want to get rid of anything touching it? Or was he just making mischief while everyone was at work? Whatever the reason, Max needed to cut it out. There were too many ways to get hurt out there for him to keep wandering off the property.

As his hands passed over the big dog's shoulder, Travis felt a small crusted patch on his skin.

"What's this?" he said, grabbing his reading glasses off the desk. "Are you hurt?"

Travis leaned forward and parted the fur, examining the spot where he'd felt the scab. Sure enough, a chunk of fur had been yanked out, leaving a bald patch and a pea-sized crust of dried blood behind. He touched it lightly, and Max's shoulder quivered.

"What on earth have you been doing?"

Max rolled his eyes upward, a look that seemed both sorrowful and apologetic, and Travis patted him gently.

"I know," he said. "It's hard being by yourself all day. Tell you what. I'll see if I can stay home one day this week."

He winced.

"No, not this week—too many meetings. Maybe this weekend. No, I'm meeting with the trustee on Saturday morning and there's the award ceremony at the Jaycees." He sighed. "And the board meeting the week after that, and then Hugh's visit at the group home and Christmas party—"

Travis groaned. He'd almost forgotten about Christmas. He'd have to get a tree and take the decorations down from the attic. Then there'd be presents to buy and wrap and Christmas dinner to fix—all the things that Emmy and his mother used to do that were now his alone to handle. He felt his stomach begin to churn. With everything else on his plate, when was he going to find the time?

If only he could delegate some of the work to Hugh, he thought, but the guy was useless. He couldn't drive, which meant that Travis had to either arrange for someone else to give him a ride or take Hugh himself, and letting him "help" with the shopping meant that it took twice as long to get it done. And because Hugh was always off in his own little world, he wasn't even someone you could talk to.

He felt Max's weight shift and looked down as the dog set a gentle paw on his arm. It was something he'd seen Max do hundreds of times whenever Hugh was in distress. Travis smiled.

"You understand, don't you, Max? You always seem to know just what to do."

He took a deep breath and sat back, embarrassed by his brief slip into self-pity. The fact was, Travis had it a lot easier than most family caretakers did. He might have more responsibilities because of his brother, but he had more resources, too—more, certainly, than his parents had had when Hugh was born. Plenty of people who were dealing with special needs relatives had no way to give them the help they required. That was why he was funding the special education program at their old elementary school. He wanted those other kids to have the same chance that Hugh had been given to make something of their lives.

He turned off the computer and headed down to his bedroom with Max following close behind. Trying to tackle everything at once was a recipe for disaster, Travis told himself. Christmas would arrive in its own good time, but the award ceremony was that weekend. If the Jaycees were going to make him their guest of honor, the least he could do was to look presentable.

Max jumped up on the bed and started circling his favorite spot. Travis's mother had said it would spoil Max to let him sleep on the bed, but Travis hadn't seen any evidence of that. Besides, Max was part of the family; you didn't make family members sleep on the floor.

He opened the closet and checked to see if his best suit needed cleaning. No, it was fine, and his favorite tie was spotless. Then Travis ran a hand through his hair. How long had it been since he'd had a trim? A few weeks, at least. He should probably get a haircut, too.

A haircut!

A slow smile spread across his face. If he found out where Renee worked, he could drop by and see if she could do it for him. Then, if things went well, maybe he could ask her out for that cup of coffee. He got into bed, pleased that he'd thought of an excuse to see her again, and reached for his book. Beside him, Max settled deeper into the bedclothes and sighed contentedly.

CHAPTER 7

The rich aroma of her father's lasagna greeted Renee when she walked through the front door. There was no one in the living room, but she could hear the television on downstairs and the singsong cadence of teenage gossip coming from McKenna's room. As she hung up her coat and headed for the kitchen, she felt her mouth begin to water. After the day she'd had, she was ready for a little comfort food.

The lasagna was on the stove under a double layer of aluminum. Renee peeled back the foil and frowned. Wendell's lasagna recipe made enough for a small army. Where was the rest of it?

Dylan, she thought. The kid was a bottomless pit.

She cut a modest slice of layered pasta and put it in the microwave to reheat, then grabbed a fork and took her plate over to the table. Dylan was hunched over an open textbook.

"Mind if I join you?"

He shook his head and moved the book out of her way.

"McKenna's in her room," he said. "Kieran's downstairs with Grandpa."

She blew on a bite of lasagna.

"You the only one with homework tonight?"

He shrugged. "Dunno."

Renee nodded, chewing thoughtfully. Wendell was good about getting the kids to do their homework. Dylan was probably just doing some extra credit, making sure he kept his grades up. It was amazing how quickly kids learned when their coaches held the line.

"You're taking McKenna to the dentist tomorrow, right?"

"Yeah."

"You think she remembers?"

"Probably not."

She took another bite.

"I'll remind her before I go to bed."

"Kieran wants to know if he can walk home again."

Renee let out a pained sigh.

"Oh."

When she heard that Kieran had walked home from school on Friday, she'd been afraid this would happen. It wasn't a terribly long way to go, but Kieran could get lost in his own thoughts, and she worried that if he found himself in a strange neighborhood, he might not be able to find his way home. Now that he'd done it successfully, though, that argument wouldn't work.

"I don't know," she said. "I'll have to think about it."

Renee finished her dinner and went to check on McKenna. The door to the girl's room was ajar; she rapped on it lightly and went inside. McKenna was lying on the bed, talking on the phone, with her feet propped up against the wall. When her mother walked into the room, she put her feet down and rolled onto her side.

"Hold on a sec." She put the phone to her chest and gave Renee an impatient look. "What?"

"You get your homework done?"

"I didn't have any."

"Nothing to make up?"

McKenna rolled her eyes. "No."

"You've got an appointment with the dentist tomorrow. Dylan's going to pick you up from school, so don't get on the bus."

"I *won't*. Geez, give me some credit."

Renee felt her lips tighten. This level of insolence was rare, even for McKenna. Was she really that peeved, or was this little act just for show?

"Who's on the phone?"

The girl's face fell. "Tierney."

So that was it. According to McKenna, Tierney was the most popular girl in school, the one all the other girls wanted to be and all the boys had a crush on. Gaining admittance to Tierney's ultra-exclusive circle of friends had been high on McKenna's to-do list since the day they'd moved in.

Renee pointed to her watch.

"Finish up and get ready for bed."

McKenna nodded and rolled back over as her mother closed the door.

"It wasn't anybody," she heard her daughter say. "Just my mom."

Downstairs, Kieran and Wendell were sitting on the couch, watching the television with the lights off. The bluish light drained the color from their faces, casting weird shadows that made them look like ghouls. Renee switched on the lights.

"That can't be good for your eyes," she said.

"Mom," Kieran protested. "We were making it like a movie theater."

"Well, I'm sorry, but it's time for bed."

Kieran crossed his arms, blinking furiously.

"Grandpa said it was okay."

She looked at her father.

"It's National Geographic," he said, as if that overruled any notion of bedtime. "It's educational."

"Yeah," Kieran said. "There was this shark and he came right out of the water and grabbed a seal like *this!*"

He jumped to his feet, demonstrating the maneuver.

"Grandpa said it probably chomped that sucker right in *half.*"

Renee raised an eyebrow.

"He did, did he?"

Wendell grabbed the remote and turned the TV off.

"Your mother's right. It's time for bed."

"Aww," the boy said, clinging to his grandfather's arm. "Can't I just stay up a little longer? We didn't even get to the good part yet."

"We'll watch it another time," Wendell said, patting his back. "Go on. Do as your mother says."

Kieran slid off the couch and crawled slowly across the floor, going up the stairs on all fours. When he reached the landing, Renee turned back and looked at her father.

"Dare I ask what 'the good part' is?"

Wendell shrugged.

"It's mating season. He wanted to know where the baby seals come from."

Renee was surprised. She'd have thought Kieran was a bit young for that, but maybe not. All three of her kids were growing up so fast. Dylan would be in college next year, and

McKenna seemed more like a young woman every day. She supposed she'd been hoping that Kieran would stay her baby a bit longer.

"Thanks for making dinner, Dad. The lasagna was great."

"You're lucky there was any left. Dylan must have eaten half of it." He stood up, taking a few seconds to work out the kinks in his back, and gave her a hug. "How was your day?"

She shook her head.

"I'll tell you about it in a bit. Let me get the kids in bed first."

An hour later, Renee walked back downstairs to find her father standing over the stove in his kitchenette. They'd converted the downstairs into a one bedroom apartment, and so far things seemed to be working out well, but there were times when she worried that buying a house together had been a bad idea. Wendell had already raised two kids, and except for a few aches and pains, he was still spry, still had all his marbles. These should have been his golden years, she thought. Instead, he was taking care of her.

"Kieran wants a dog," she said, taking a seat at the table. "Apparently, someone named Dr. Joan said he needed one."

Wendell nodded. "The counselor at school. He told me."

"And . . . ?"

"I said he could ask, but that you'd probably say no."

He took two mugs down from the shelf, added a large spoonful of Hersey's syrup to each, and poured in some hot milk. Then he topped them off with Bailey's Irish Cream and brought them to the table.

"Here you go. Good for what ails you."

"You're spoiling me," Renee said. "You know that."

"It's a father's prerogative," he said, taking a seat across from her.

She took a sip and felt it blaze a trail of warmth into her core.

"Wish I'd had this on the way home. It's freezing outside." Renee warmed her hands on the mug. "Thanks, Dad. I needed this."

Wendell took a sip and smacked his lips.

"I think you should reconsider."

"About the dog? Dad, please."

"The counselor's right; it might be good for Kieran."

"Yeah, well, Dr. Joan doesn't pay the bills around here. The answer is no."

A brief silence fell while the two of them savored their drinks. Renee knew her father had more to say on the subject of dogs, but for the moment, at least, he was willing to let it drop.

"What was the meeting at school about?" he said. "Anything serious?"

She swallowed.

"They're starting a program at school for kids with learning disabilities. His teacher thinks Kieran should be in it."

"What kind of learning disabilities?"

Renee shook her head. Talking to Mrs. Dalton had been hard, but this was worse. Wendell and Kieran were as close as father and son—closer, when you considered how distant Greg was. She wasn't sure how to tell him that his grandchild might be . . . flawed.

"The school counselor mentioned something about OCD."

"Oh, that." Wendell shrugged and took another sip of his hot chocolate.

She stared. "Wait a minute. You mean you're not surprised?"

"Why should I be?" he said. "The kid makes faces and funny noises and counts every goddamn step he takes. If that's not obsessive, I don't know what is."

Renee found herself at a loss for words. Was she the only one who hadn't seen what was going on?

"Why didn't you say something?"

"Why should I? Your eyes are as good as mine. I figured you didn't want to talk about it."

She slumped over the table, head in hands.

"Geez, Dad. I feel like an idiot. Here, I've been telling myself that Kieran's oddball behaviors were just kid stuff. You know, something he'd grow out of. If I'd realized it was serious, I would have—" She felt her chin start to tremble. "I mean, I should have *done* something, right? Instead of just letting him suffer."

"Who says he's suffering? It could be a lot worse. He could be washing his hands a hundred times a day."

She looked up.

"Oh, God. Don't say that, Dad, please. Don't even think it."

He shrugged and took another sip.

"So, what are they going to do?"

Renee wiped her eyes.

"They have to set up an appointment for Kieran to meet with a psychologist."

"And then?"

She shrugged. "Therapy, I guess. They've got some do-gooder who's donated the money for everything. I guess it'll depend on how much he or she is willing to pony up."

"So, that's that?"

"For now, I guess. Yeah."

Wendell noted her nearly empty mug.

"More?"

Renee nodded. "Maybe just a little."

He got up and started reheating the milk.

"So, how was the rest of your day?"

She smiled, grateful for the change of subject.

"Not bad. I had a few walk-ins and another referral from Savannah Hays."

She took the last swallow of her drink.

"I can't figure that woman out. On the one hand, she's sent a lot of customers my way—which I really appreciate—but then she tells them they don't have to tip me because they're her referrals, so I'm working harder for less money."

Wendell took her mug back to the stove for a refill.

"Can't you tell her that?"

She shook her head.

"Savannah's sort of the queen bee around there. I don't feel like getting stung."

"Mmm."

"How about you?" she said. "How was your day?"

"Same as always." He set their mugs down and took a seat. "I went down to Clint's, shot the breeze with the boys. Not much doing there."

She gave him an apologetic look.

"I'm sorry things didn't turn out better . . . you know . . . with Butch. You kind of stuck your neck out for me."

"Don't worry about it," he said. "There's lots of fish in the sea. We'll find someone."

Renee nodded. She knew he meant well, but it was embarrassing having her father out trying to scare up dates for her.

"Look, I appreciate the help, Dad, but you don't have to find me another husband. I'm a big girl."

"I know that," he said. "But you've got a job to do and three kids to raise. I don't think you've even *met* a man on your own since we moved here."

"That's not true," she said. "I met one tonight."

Wendell gave her a skeptical look.

"No you didn't."

"Yes I did. He was at the school when I was waiting for Kieran's teacher."

"What's his name?"

"Travis Diehl, and he was very nice."

Her father's eyes narrowed. "Did he ask you out?"

"Well, no," she said, deflating a bit. "I think he might have, but then Mrs. Dalton called me in and . . ."

She sighed, feeling the loss of what might have been settle over her.

"I don't know, maybe he wouldn't have. I mean, the guy went to Princeton. Why would he want to go out with someone like me?"

"What do you mean? You're smart enough."

"Anyway, I probably just misread the situation."

Renee set her mug down and shook her head.

"Sometimes it just seems . . . I don't know . . . like I'm going to be alone forever."

Wendell arched an eyebrow.

"Well, there's a happy thought."

"Sorry," she said. "Just having a pity party, I guess."

Renee took their empty mugs to the sink to be washed. It was the impending holiday that was making her feel this way, she thought. Christmas had always been the bright spot in the year for her: the carols, the lights, the tree—even the snow was magical. But this year, the kids would be missing their dad, and the thought of everyone just hanging around the house, getting on each other's nerves, was too much to bear. Thank goodness Jack and his family had agreed to come; she could always count on her brother to cheer her up.

She grinned. It would be fun playing Saint Nick again. Renee suspected that Dylan and McKenna had spilled the beans to Kieran, but Lilly and Grace were sure to be avid Santa watchers, and she knew she could count on the others to play along. She'd bought candy canes for their stockings, too, and if the kids forgot theirs, she had extras in the attic. Now, if Jack and Wendell could just go two and a half days without a fight, everything would be darned near perfect.

"I heard from Jack today. He said they'd love to come for Christmas."

Wendell had taken the newspaper out and was doing a Sudoku.

"Hmm. I'll bet he did."

Renee took a deep breath and tried not to let her father's lack of enthusiasm dampen her spirits.

"Who knows? With all this cold weather we've been having, we might even get a white Christmas."

"God, I hope not." He filled in a square. "Can you imagine getting snowed in with that bunch?"

She turned off the water and looked at him.

"Dad, please don't fight with Jack this year. Christmas is going to be hard enough without the two of you going at it."

"That's up to Jack," he said. "But for your sake, I'll try."

CHAPTER 8

Savannah stood in the dark, listening to Brad Paisley on the sound system as she scanned the barroom for familiar faces. The Growler had something of a split personality, attracting two different crowds depending on which night you showed up. Fridays and Saturdays, the place was packed with young executives drinking George Dickel and Mexican Cake at the bar, fine-tuning their pickup lines before they approached the lovely belles who congregated around the tables. Every other night of the week it was rednecks, karaoke, and Bud Light.

She spotted three members of the usual crowd sitting at a table in back. In Bolingbroke's social hierarchy, these weren't really "top tier" gals, but they were good for a laugh, and Savannah found the lack of competition relaxing. She caught the waitress's eye and ordered herself a Cosmo, then headed for the table. She might be slumming, she thought, but that didn't mean she had to lower her standards.

Angie was the first to spot her. She stood and waved her arms while Charity and Verna scooted their chairs over to make room.

"Hey, y'all," Savannah said, taking a seat. "Sorry I'm late."

"Hey," said the others.

Angie looked around.

"We were just asking ourselves if you'd be here before the karaoke started."

"Whatever for? I told you I would."

"Where's Travis?" Charity said, glancing toward the door. "I thought you said he was coming this time."

"It's his brother, bless his heart," she said. "Hugh had another one of his fits, and Travis didn't think he should be left alone."

"That Hugh is a strange one." Angie gave an involuntary shudder. "He always gave me the creeps when we were little."

The waitress came by and set down the Cosmo. Savannah fished out the orange peel and took a sip.

"So," she said. "Anything exciting going on around here?"

Angie threw a sidelong glance at the woman on Savannah's right.

"Verna thinks she's got a fish on the line."

Savannah grinned at the chubby redhead sitting beside her. Verna was blushing clear up to her roots.

"Why, Miss Vee," she said, slapping her hand. "Who's the lucky fella? Point him out to me so I can take a gander."

Verna shook her head and gave the others a warning look, to no avail.

"He's at the bar," Angie said. "Second one from the right. He and Vern have been sending eyeball telegrams since we walked in."

Savannah started to take a look, and Verna grabbed her hand.

"Nooo," she hissed. "I don't want him to know we're talking about him."

"Don't worry," Savannah murmured. "I am the *soul* of discretion."

She picked up her cocktail napkin and dropped it on the floor.

"Oh, dear me," she cried. "I'll just have to pick that up."

"Good one," Angie snickered. "I'm sure he won't suspect a thing."

Savannah reached down and took a glance at the man Verna had her eyes on. Leaning against the bar with his knees apart and his crotch aimed in their direction, he had a bottle in one hand and a look of carnal intent that aroused an unexpected throb of animal attraction in Savannah. He was muscular—wiry rather than pumped—with broad shoulders and pale blue eyes that contrasted nicely with the kind of tan that came from years spent in the out-of-doors. The man was no Travis Diehl, of course, but he was a giant step up from the ponytailed lowlifes and fat-bottomed truckers Verna usually hooked up with.

"Very nice," she said, setting her napkin back on the table. "Should be a fun evening for you. *If* you can reel him in."

"Oh, snap, Vern," Angie said. "Sounds like Savannah is doubting your prospects."

Verna smirked.

"Seems to me she's got troubles of her own in that department."

A knowing look passed between the other two as they struggled to hide their amusement.

"I told you," Savannah said through clenched teeth. "He had to stay home and keep an eye on Hugh."

"Yeah, right."

Verna sat back with a satisfied grin.

Savannah's lips tightened. How dare they treat her as if she was a nobody going nowhere? Back in high school, these girls would have given their eyeteeth for a single word from her, never mind an hour of her company. Why did she even bother trying to inject a little fun and excitement into their bland little lives? she wondered. This crowd wouldn't know a good time if it smacked them in the head.

Savannah took another sip of her Cosmo. This never would have happened if Travis had just come with her that evening. It had been months since the two of them had been out together, and she was tired of fending off people's inquiries with tales of burdensome workloads and previous engagements. Whether or not anyone believed her, they'd at least accepted that there was a solid foundation under their relationship, but it seemed that people were starting to detect cracks in the façade. If Savannah didn't shore things up fast, there were other women in town—some with a real shot at winning him over—who might get the idea that Travis Diehl was up for grabs.

"What's the deal with that brother of his anyway?" Angie said. "Is he just simple or what?"

Savannah shook her head, trying to keep her voice under control.

"I haven't asked what-all is wrong with him, but Travis has told me he's autistic."

Now that they were on safer ground, she felt the tension in her face begin to ease. Being a source of information about the Diehl family made it look as if she was still part of their inner circle.

Charity leaned forward.

"I heard his wife didn't want to take care of the brother, and that's why she left him."

Savannah nodded sadly.

"He doesn't like to talk about it, of course, but that's the story his mother shared with me."

Angie looked at her doubtfully.

"You sure *you* want to take that on?"

"Well," Savannah said, "Hugh's got one of those therapy dogs now, and he has a job, too, so we're hoping to move him into a group home soon. Before the wedding, certainly."

"Yeah," Verna drawled. "When *is* the wedding?"

Savannah turned and gave her a frozen smile. Verna was just being pissy because she'd made that comment about reeling in the man at the bar. Well, it wasn't Savannah's fault if she didn't want to hear the truth, which was that it was a lot easier for a gal like Verna to flirt with a man than to get him up off his backside to do something about it.

Poor Verna, she thought. Poor dumpy, dull, stringy-haired Verna would never know how easy it was to make a man do what she wanted. Since her divorce, Savannah had had dozens of men pursue her—men she'd given far less encouragement to than Verna had given that guy at the bar. The little lump would never even understand how much *more* fun it was to be the fish rather than the fisherman. A girl could have all sorts of fun holding out for more bait. *Would you cancel a meeting for me? Of course I would. Fly off on a "business trip" together? No problem. Leave the wife and kiddies? Just say the word, Savannah, and I'm all yours.* Verna should be careful who she was talking to.

A spotlight hit the stage and the KJ stepped up to announce the start of that night's karaoke competition. Savannah scribbled her song selection on a slip and handed it in with the others' when the waitress came by.

"What are you going to sing tonight?" Verna said. "'Lover Come Back'?"

"How about 'When You're Gone'?" Angie said.

Charity giggled. "Or maybe 'Need You Now'?"

Savannah frowned. What on earth were those ninnies going on about? They knew songs about lost love weren't her style.

Come to think of it, the three of them had been acting strangely ever since she got there, slipping each other sly looks like guilty kids putting one over on the teacher. Even Verna, whose backbone was about as stiff as a plate of grits, had been sassy to her—it was irritating. After Travis declined her invitation, Savannah had been hoping to soothe her ego with these hangers-on. Instead, they seemed determined to bring her down to their level. It just didn't make sense. Unless . . .

Was something going on with Travis that she didn't know about, some change in his feelings for her that had gone unnoticed?

Savannah took a sip of her Cosmo and considered the possibility. It seemed unlikely. Granted, they hadn't seen each other in a while, but that was only because he'd been busy settling his mama's estate and keeping the business running. And though marriage itself hadn't been discussed, they were both free now; it was only natural that they'd finally do what they should have done years ago.

She glanced at the others, still chattering like magpies as they looked through the songbook, and realized that something must be seriously wrong for them to oppose her so openly. They might talk big, but Savannah knew those three were cowards. The only thing that could make them this brave was knowing that she was heading for a fall, and the only thing that could bring her down like that, she thought, was losing Travis Diehl.

The realization sent adrenaline coursing through her body. Savannah clutched the drink in her hand as a white-hot fury engulfed her. Did someone somewhere actually think they could take Travis away from her? He'd gone away to college, yes. He'd even moved away and married someone else, but she always knew he'd come back to her. And now that he had, now that happily ever after was within her grasp, nothing was going to spoil it. Travis was *hers,* and if anyone tried to take him away, she was going to make that person very, *very* sorry.

She'd have to move quickly. If she was going to nip this problem in the bud, she needed more information, and she wasn't going to find it in a karaoke bar.

Savannah put her hand to her forehead and grimaced.

"Oh. Oh, no."

Charity sobered. "What is it? Are you okay?"

"Yeah," Angie said. "We were just having a little fun."

"I think I'm getting a migraine," Savannah moaned. "It must have been something in the Cosmo."

She took a deep breath and let it out slowly.

"Just let me sit here a second. Maybe it'll pass."

"You want a glass of water?" Angie said.

Savannah wretched pitifully and shook her head.

"It doesn't help. I'm sorry. I think I'll just have to go home and go to bed."

"Hey, sure. We understand. You need a ride or anything?"

Savannah swallowed hard and reached for her purse.

"No," she said as she took out her keys. "It's all right. You guys stay here and enjoy the karaoke."

She lifted her gaze to the man at the bar and saw him come to attention as she gave him a knowing smile.

"I think I've found someone to take me home."

CHAPTER 9

Berenice Judson was one of Renee's favorite clients. A strawberry blonde with an ample figure, a sweet face, and a booming voice, Berenice had a way of giving Renee and everyone within earshot the giggles. The two of them were the same age, both with three kids and aging parents who occasionally drove them crazy, and—now that Jack had accepted Renee's invitation—both were anticipating the arrival of out-of-town guests. Renee didn't normally discuss personal problems with her clients, but she was willing to make an exception for Berenice.

"So, your brother Jack and them decided to brave another holiday with Mr. Grumpy, did they?"

Berenice was sitting with her arms akimbo under the black drape, looking like a giant bat who'd swooped into the salon for a cut and color.

"Just for two days," Renee said. "I figure he and Dad should be able to keep from killing each other that long."

"And what's-her-name, your sister-in-law, is she going to mind her p's and q's?"

"Who knows?"

Renee made another part in Berenice's hair and daubed some color onto the roots. It was hard to know what to expect from Megan. Before she'd had children of her own, the two of them had been pretty close, but after Grace and Lilly came along, her attitude toward Renee's kids—especially Kieran—had changed. If Megan would just stand back and let the three of them work things out on their own, she thought, they'd get along fine. Instead, she hovered on the sidelines, ready to get involved in even minor squabbles. The resulting tension was hard on everyone.

"Take my advice," Berenice said. "Hand the woman a drink when she walks through your door, and keep the glass full until she leaves—and pour one for yourself, too. Trust me, this is the voice of experience talking. When I make up my holiday guest list, Jack Daniels is the first person I invite."

Renee laughed. "I'll keep that in mind."

When Berenice was done, Renee cleaned up her station and headed into the back. She'd left ninety minutes open in her schedule to do her holiday shopping that day. If she was lucky, there'd still be a few parking places open at the mall.

Sissy was mixing a batch of highlighter at the counter.

"Hey, Renny! How's it going?"

"Fine," Renee said, dumping her mixing bowls in the sink.

"I got some more hair for your little guy."

She nodded her head in the direction of Renee's cubby.

"Had a gal come in needing to have her dreads cut off for work, so I saved one—thought he might get a kick out of it. You'll want to air it out first, though." She wrinkled her nose. "Pee-yew."

Renee plugged the drain and turned on the water, squirting in some dishwashing liquid.

"Thanks for thinking of him."

Sissy watched the bubbles rise.

"How'd the conference with his teacher go? He wasn't in trouble, was he?"

"No, no trouble. She just wanted to tell me about a new program at his school."

"What kind of program?"

Renee hesitated. She didn't really want to discuss it, but she'd taken Sissy into her confidence more than once when she needed a shoulder to cry on. It seemed churlish not to pass along some good news, for a change.

"Someone gave a grant to the school to help kids with learning disabilities," she said. "The counselor thinks it might be good for Kieran."

"That's great."

"Yeah. I just wish Greg could see how hard Kieran is trying. Poor kid blames himself for the breakup."

"Has your ex told you if he's coming to see the kids at Christmas?"

Renee nodded. "He says he can't make it."

"Why not?"

"Oh, you know. The weather's bad; he can't spare the time; the new wife's puking her guts out. I just got his email this morning."

"Guess that means you'll have to give them the bad news then, huh?"

"Yup."

Of course that's what it meant, Renee thought. That's what it always meant whenever Greg backed out of a commitment. Why should *he* have to be the bad guy?

She set the bowls out to dry, put her combs in the Barbicide, and checked the time. Renee had been planning to go easy on the gift-giving this year, but after reading Greg's email, she'd decided not to worry about the budget. If she couldn't persuade their father to visit them, she thought, at least she could give her kids what they wanted.

The door swung open, and Dottie popped her head in.

"Hey, Renee, you busy?"

"I'm just heading out to the mall. Why, do you need something?"

"No, but there's a guy out here says he needs a haircut right away and wants to know if you'll take him."

Renee and Sissy exchanged a look.

"A *man?*"

Dottie nodded. "He asked for you specially."

"Hey, if you won't take him," Sissy said, "I will."

Renee couldn't think who it might be, unless . . .

Oh, lord. It isn't Butch, is it?

"Let me see who it is, first."

She stepped over to the door to take a peek.

"He's over yonder," Dottie said, as if there might be more than one man in the waiting area.

Renee peered across the room, prepared to find the portly, balding Butch loitering by the front desk. Instead, she saw Travis Diehl, trying to act as if he didn't notice that every woman in the salon was staring at him.

Like a bunch of hens when a rooster struts into the barnyard.

"Well?" Dottie said. "You gonna cut his hair or not?"

"Yeah, sure," she said. "Tell him I'll be there in a minute."

"It took me a while to track you down," Travis said. "Since I didn't know where you worked, I just started calling every salon in town. In hindsight, doing it in alphabetical order probably wasn't the best idea."

"You're lucky you caught me," she said. "I was just walking out the door."

He smiled. "Then I guess it's my lucky day."

Renee frowned thoughtfully and lifted another section of hair. It might have been his lucky day, she thought, but that didn't mean it was hers. A man's haircut didn't pay as much as a woman's did, and she'd still have to find time to get to the mall. Still, she was flattered that he'd spent so much time trying to find her—even if it was just so she could cut his hair.

"What's the rush?" she said. "Got a big date coming up?"

"Something like that."

Of course he has a date. Stop acting like a teenager.

"To tell you the truth, though, I'd skip it if I could. It's just one of those things I get roped into every so often."

Renee put down her scissors and ruffled his damp hair, trying to get a feel for the overall shape. He had good hair for a man his age—which, judging by the amount of grey in it, she guessed was around forty-five, though he looked younger. It had just the right amount of wave and none of the whorls that could make a shorter cut hard to control. She checked the effect in the mirror.

"What do you think? I can take off a little more if you'd like."

"No," he said, turning his head. "It looks good."

"Okay, let's see what you think once it's dry."

A final few snips and a quick clean-up with the electric razor and she was done. Renee removed the drape, and he paid the bill, adding a generous tip. As she set the money in the till, though, Travis didn't turn away.

"Listen," he said, looking slightly abashed. "The truth is, I didn't come by just to get my hair cut."

"Oh?"

"I was hoping you might be free to have coffee with me sometime."

She licked her lips. "'Sometime'?"

"Now. If you're free."

Renee realized that the salon had become unnaturally quiet. She hated being put on the spot, and she was sure that Travis Diehl—a graduate of Princeton, for God's sake—would find her incredibly boring, but it was too late now to get her shopping done, and she had nothing else to do until her next appointment. Besides, it wasn't every day that a great-looking guy took the time and trouble to look her up.

"Hang on," she said. "I'll get my coat."

CHAPTER 10

Travis was inordinately pleased with himself as he drove Renee to the coffee shop. He'd almost told her about Mimesis the night they met, but she left before he'd gotten the chance. Once he found out where she worked, though, he decided just to take her there himself. Pat, the owner, held a showcase for local artists every Wednesday, and he'd already told her they were coming.

He glanced over at Renee. She was staring out her window, one hand resting on the door handle.

"You're not planning to jump out, are you?"

She turned back and smiled at him.

"Not really, but a girl can't be too careful." She pointed. "There's another Starbuck's."

"I know," he said.

"I thought we were going for coffee."

"We are. We're just not going to Starbuck's."

"So, where *are* we going?" she said.

Travis grinned.

"It's a surprise," he said. "But don't worry; we're almost there."

Two blocks later, he pulled over to the curb and stopped. Renee squinted up at the marquee.

"Mimesis?"

"It means, 'The portrayal of human actions or objects found in nature.' In other words, 'art.' The owner is a friend of mine."

"But . . . coffee."

"Don't worry, they have that, too." Travis got out and opened her door. "Come on. She's expecting us."

Renee stepped out and smiled at the quirky, colorful artwork in the window.

"Your friend's an artist?"

He shook his head.

"Even better—she promotes artists. I come here every week, and I'm sure I've never left without buying something."

He grabbed the front door handle and pulled.

"I'll tell you about it in a second."

Walking through the front door was like stepping into a different world, one full of warmth and color and suffused with the aroma of roasted beans and fresh pastry. Tropical plants basked under grow lights on either side of the bar, and club chairs, bistro tables, and a red velvet chaise offered a silent invitation to linger. At the top of the wooden staircase, a loft offered additional seating, but what was really different about Mimesis was the art displayed on its walls: watercolor and oil, gouache, giclée, charcoal, and crayon—every sort of medium, it seemed, was represented.

Travis glanced at Renee and saw her staring, wide-eyed.

"Well, what do you think?"

"It's amazing." She looked at him. "Why didn't I know this was here?"

"You're new," he said. "And with three kids and a job? Probably too busy to check out the local art scene."

She looked down. "Well, you've got that right."

A stocky woman with a nose ring and a T-shirt that said *Earth Without Art is just "Eh"* walked over.

"Hey, Trav," she said. "This your artist friend?"

"It is. Pat, this is Renee Richardson."

Renee smiled.

"Nice to meet you," she said as they shook hands. "But I'm not really an artist—not anymore."

"Oh, don't be so modest," Travis said, giving her a shove.

"And you, don't be a *nudzh,*" Pat said, shoving him back. "Artists are like wild animals. You have to coax them out of hiding."

She looked at Renee.

"You got a portfolio? Something you wouldn't be too ashamed to show me?"

"Um, well . . . It's in storage right now . . ."

"Good. Take it out, dust it off, and bring it in. If I think it'll work here, I'll book you in a showcase. If not, I'll see if I can find someone who will."

"I, um, thank you," Renee stammered.

"Now, get yourself some coffee and have a look around." Pat nodded in Travis's direction. "I'd comp you a drink, but I don't want to embarrass this guy."

She slapped Travis on the back and walked off to greet another customer while he and Renee got in line to place their orders.

"Well?" he said. "What do you think?"

She scowled. "You set me up."

"Come on. Would you have come if I'd told you where we were going?"

She shrugged and looked away.

"No, probably not."

"Then what's the problem?"

Travis ordered a caffè Americano, and Renee asked for a nonfat latte. They found a table and sat down to wait.

"I guess I'm just not sure why you did it," she said. "I mean, we hardly know each other. You don't even know if my stuff's any good."

"Don't worry. If it isn't, Pat won't take it just for me."

"No," Renee said, looking around. "I can see she's done a good job curating these pieces. I doubt she'd put her reputation in jeopardy. I just—"

Travis could tell she was feeling overwhelmed. From his perspective, asking Pat to meet with Renee wasn't a big deal. The two of them were old friends, and he knew she wouldn't give someone a showcase if they didn't have the chops. But something about the way Renee had looked when she talked about making art that first time had touched him, especially since it was obvious that she'd pursued it in spite of her husband's opposition. If he could help her find an outlet for her work, why not?

"It makes me happy," he said. "I like helping my friends."

Travis heard their names being called and went up to get their drinks. When he sat back down, he saw Renee examining a watercolor next to their table.

"This is really beautiful," she said. "It looks like the woods near my house."

He nodded. "There's a lot of beauty in this area. When I moved away, there wasn't a day I didn't miss it."

She had a sip of her latte.

"You never told me why you left Bolingbroke."

He blew on his coffee and took a swallow.

"Princeton, remember? Football scholarship."

"But why go all the way to New Jersey when Clemson's an excellent university with a better football team?"

Travis glanced out the window and drank some more coffee, wondering what to say. Renee was right—they hardly knew each other—and until recently, some of the reasons he'd left had been a mystery even to him. Talking about his family was difficult, too; even more so now that his parents were gone.

"There were problems at home. Nothing serious, but I felt I needed to get away from everything for a while. The scholarship gave me an excuse to get out of Bolingbroke without making it look like I was running away."

"Why'd it take you so long to come back?"

He shrugged.

"Work, mostly. I got a job offer in Texas I couldn't refuse, but I always planned to return someday." He laughed. "Which usually means never, but in my case, I was serious."

She grinned.

"Never say never?"

"Right." He took a deep breath. "Anyway, I met a gal, fell in love, got married. Her family was in Texas, though, and she didn't like the idea of moving. We came back to visit every year, but even after her folks passed, she wasn't keen on the idea of making this place her home."

"And then your parents died."

Travis looked down as the realization struck him: Emmy was never going to move back. Hugh was just a convenient excuse.

"Actually," he said, "Daddy died first, but it was pretty plain that Mother wouldn't last long without him. When I told my wife it was now or never, she decided that 'never' suited her just fine."

"I'm sorry."

He tried to smile, felt it falter.

"Don't be. It's over now. Probably for the best, too."

They sat quietly for a few minutes after that, savoring their drinks, eventually pointing out the pictures in the showcase that each of them liked best. After his revelation about Emmy, Travis was grateful to have a break from answering questions. Acknowledging his ex-wife's role in their breakup felt freeing, even as it added a layer of bitterness to his memories of her.

"When I finally came back," he said, "after Daddy was gone, I moved into the old homestead." Travis gave her a sheepish smile. "I think that's why I felt a connection to you when you said were living with your father. Two grown kids living with a widowed parent."

Renee laughed.

"I don't know what your mother was like, but my dad . . ." She shook her head. "You know, you move away, you change. You think they've changed, too, but . . ."

"They do get set in their ways, don't they?"

"You're not kidding. It's like I never grew up. Suddenly, he's telling me how to drive, how to raise my kids . . ."

"I missed that part."

"And always—always!—trying to fix me up on dates."

Travis chuckled.

"Mother did the same thing."

"Yeah, well, after the latest disaster, I've decided no more dating," Renee said. "I'm officially off the market."

"For good?"

She looked down and her cheeks reddened.

"For now, anyway."

"You might get lonely," he said. "I know I do."

She shrugged and looked away, took another swallow of her drink.

Travis set his cup down and started turning it in circles on the tabletop.

"After my divorce—and the move back here—I was too hurt and too busy to even think about dating. Then Mother died, and I had her estate to settle. Gradually, everyone I knew went back to the lives they'd had before."

Travis paused and frowned at the coffee mug in his hands. *Why am I telling her this?*

"It's hard," Renee said. "Everybody's busy."

He nodded.

"I thought I'd start dating again, by and by, but now that I'm ready, it doesn't seem as if anyone in town is interested."

"That can't be true."

"It is! Remember the awards ceremony? I can't find anyone to go with."

She laughed. "I don't believe you."

Travis paused. Until that moment, he hadn't even considered asking Renee, but suddenly it seemed the most natural thing to do.

What the heck? he thought. Why not?

"Why don't you go with me?"

Renee shook her head.

"No, that's okay. But thanks."

"You see there? I've struck out again," he said. "What's wrong with me?"

"Nothing's *wrong* with you. It's just that . . . Well, for one thing, I have to work on Saturday. Plus, I've got nothing to wear."

"Excuses, excuses."

Renee glanced at her watch.

"And speaking of work, I'd better get back to the salon."

She grabbed her purse, and they headed out to the car. Travis got in and started the engine.

"You sure you won't come?" he said.

Renee sighed. "Look, I'll think about it, okay?"

"Okay, tell you what. I'll give you a call."

"Sure, fine, whatever."

"Good." He put the car in gear. "Just give me your phone number before you get out."

CHAPTER 11

Savannah parked her Camry in the driveway at Marissa Daniels's house and stepped out. It had taken two days to get an audience with her erstwhile best friend; two days of working her contacts and coming up empty-handed. The only person left in Bolingbroke who could tell her what she wanted to know was waiting for her inside.

The stately columns and alabaster portico of Marissa's home loomed overhead as Savannah made her way up the walkway. The gardener, blowing leaves off the front lawn, turned off the motor and waited for her to pass. She gave him a curt nod, then stepped up to the front door and rang the bell, noting with dismay the tacky Christmas decorations on the front porch. This was why she rarely took commissions from people she knew, she thought. Watching her hard work being destroyed bit by bit was just too painful.

She saw a flash of movement behind the leaded glass windows, and the door swung wide. Marissa stood on the threshold, decked out in a peach velour tracksuit and jeweled slippers, her blond hair looking like she'd just returned from the salon.

"Savannah, so good to see you," she said, taking a step back. "Do come in."

The two women exchanged a brief hug and kisses that barely grazed each other's cheeks.

"I won't stay long," Savannah said. "I know you're busy."

In truth, of course, it was *she* who was busy that day; Marissa Daniels had all the time in the world. With a gardener, a maid, a cook, and no job to keep her occupied, she had nothing to do until her kids got home from school. Nevertheless, Marissa's idleness had conferred on her a higher social standing than her old friend. It meant she'd married well and, unlike Savannah, had no need to work for a living.

The maid appeared and took her coat.

"When you've done with that," Marissa told her, "bring us some sweet tea in the parlor. Oh, and a few of GeeGee's petit fours, too, if you please."

She giggled.

"I swear, that cook of mine is going to turn me into a butterball."

Savannah looked back at her and smiled. She'd been taking in the grand entrance—the marble floor, the crystal chandelier, the subtle blend of peach and gold that culminated in a Gabryel Harrison still life at the top of the double staircase— pleased that the house she'd decorated hadn't yet been ruined by its owner's tasteless additions.

"Come on," Marissa said. "Let's go have us a chin wag."

She turned and padded out of the room, her ballerina flats as soft as a whisper.

"I was so surprised when you called, dear. Why, we haven't seen each other for *ages*."

That's because you decided I wasn't good enough for you.

Marissa tapped her chin thoughtfully.

"I believe the last time must have been when you were here, working on the house."

Working on the house. As if she'd been one of the construction crew.

They stepped into the parlor, and Savannah felt a pang. As she'd feared, it was already filling up with cheap tchotchkes and ugly, handmade decorations brought home by Marissa's children: Kendall, a quiet, sweet-natured, if not particularly bright girl; and Cody, a smart-mouthed bully who at twelve was a smaller version of his father. Thank God she and Donnie had never had kids, she thought. The world had enough problems without one more horrid little urchin running around.

Another unauthorized addition to the room had been hung on the wall next to the fireplace. Savannah walked over to take a look. It was a montage of photos from their high school days. There were the two of them: leading cheers at a football game, painting banners for homecoming, and dancing at the prom with Trey Daniels and Travis Diehl, the girls' outsized hairdos as Southern as pimento cheese. She felt her throat tighten. Who would have believed that a year later Travis would be at Princeton, and Savannah and Donnie Hiller would be arguing over who had left the cap off the toothpaste?

"Trey had a gal at his office put that together for me on my birthday," Marissa said, glancing over her shoulder. "Look at us, having a big time."

The maid walked in and set down a tray with two glasses of tea and an artfully arranged plate of cookies.

"GeeGee says Mr. Daniels told her to save the petit fours for him," she mumbled.

Marissa's lip twitched.

"Well, he is the *man* of the house," she said brightly. "If he doesn't think his wife and her *old friend* deserve them, then we'll just have to make do."

The maid padded out as they helped themselves to the tea and cookies.

Savannah took a sip.

"How is Trey these days?"

"Fine. Deer season started last week, and he's as happy as a pig in mud. I swear, I never met a man who enjoyed killing things as much as my husband does. If it isn't deer season, it's some other kinda season, and if nothing's in season, then he's out setting traps in the woods."

"Good. I've had two clients lose their cats to coyotes this year."

Marissa's shrug was noncommittal.

"I suppose every man needs a hobby." She motioned toward the sofa. "Have a seat, and tell me what's on your mind."

Savannah sat on the leather sofa, clutching her glass, and wondered where to start. After the abuse she'd taken at The Growler, she was desperate to discover who, if anyone, was trying to steal Travis Diehl's affections, but just begging Marissa to tell all wouldn't work. They might be "old friends," but they were no longer equals, and Savannah couldn't afford to reduce her status further if she wanted information. Marissa didn't do favors for people who couldn't return them.

"It's about Travis."

"Oh. Is anything wrong between the two of you?"

Savannah reached for a cookie. Was that an innocent question, she wondered, or had Marissa heard something? If she had, it couldn't be common knowledge, or she'd have heard about it at Winona's. As her gaze returned to the pictures on the wall, she was struck by the irony of the situation. There'd been a time when she, not Marissa, had been the key player in Bolingbroke's rumor mill.

Savannah was the mayor's daughter back then—the most popular girl in school, the person at the very center of everything. Even after her divorce, when some folks had taken Donnie's side, she never lost her place in the social pecking order. It seemed to her that she would always lead a charmed life.

But then her father got involved in a bad land deal, and not long after, he lost his bid for reelection. Suddenly, the party invitations dried up; old friends were "not at home" when she called; and instead of living comfortably under her parents' roof with a generous allowance, Savannah had been forced to get a job. She'd never gotten over the humiliation.

"Actually," she said, "I came to ask if you might have heard from him."

"*Me?*" Marissa simpered. "You mean he hasn't been in touch?"

"Of course he's been in *touch*," Savannah said. "But lately, he says he's been too busy to get together. The fact is, I've seen less and less of him since his mother's funeral."

"Dear me, that is a long time. But then, he did have to settle his parents' estate, and taking over the company has *got* to have been a nightmare."

"Well, he could at least *call*." Savannah gave her a frank look. "If I didn't know better, I'd say he was seeing someone else."

There. She'd said it.

Marissa settled back in her chair.

"Are you asking me if I've heard anything?"

"If you don't mind. I think I have a right to know."

"Hmm," she said, reaching for another cookie. "I'd have thought you'd keep better tabs on your man. You must be very busy at . . . work, these days."

Savannah felt her lips tighten. If Marissa thought she was going to sit there while she toyed with her like a cat with a mouse, she had another thing coming. She'd taken about all the crap she was going to from the girls at the bar.

She set her glass down.

"Look, let's just be honest. If you haven't got any information for me, then I should just go and let you get on with your day. Thank you for the tea and cookies," she said, standing. "I can let myself out."

"Oh, don't get your knickers in a twist." Marissa waved her down. "Who do you think you're talking to? I know everything that goes on in this town."

Savannah remained standing.

"And?"

Marissa leaned forward.

"It just so happens that Travis was seen having coffee with an eligible female this very afternoon."

Savannah felt the blood drain from her face. So, she thought, it was true.

"Who? Who was he with?"

"Sadly, I do not know the lady's name, but I'm told she's a hairdresser at Winona's, and my source referred to her as 'Pinky.'"

Savannah paused for a moment, then laughed out loud.

"'Pinky'? Oh, my goodness. You really had me going there for a second."

She dropped back down on the couch, patting her chest.

"That's just Renee Richardson. People call her that because she's got pink bangs."

"Richardson." Marissa frowned. "That name rings a bell. Do I know her?"

"I doubt it. She's new in town: divorced, with three brats, and as poor as a church mouse. Travis must have seen her in line and bought her something out of pity."

"Could be," Marissa said, "but when's the last time he had a cup of coffee with *you?*"

Savannah refused to be goaded. Travis and Renee? The notion was ridiculous. Still, if Marissa's source had seen them together, then other people must have, too. Better to put a stop to it before someone got the wrong idea.

"Fine," she said. "I'll take care of Renee. In the meantime, I've got another problem."

"Which is . . ."

"Every time I want to get together, Travis has an excuse for why we can't. If it isn't work, it's the foundation, and if that's not it, then it's something else. Last night, he told me he had to stay home and take care of his brother."

Marissa grimaced.

"Now, *that's* a problem. How on earth are you going to get rid of Hugh?"

"I'm not sure," Savannah said. "Once their parents were gone, I thought Travis would do the right thing and put him in a home, but it's been over a year now, and he's still living in that house."

"Maybe Travis wants to keep him." Marissa giggled. "You know, like a pet."

Savannah smirked.

"Well, I have a strict 'no pets' policy."

Marissa reached for another cookie. "Back in the day, that

sort wasn't even allowed in a regular school. They had their own places to go, and they were perfectly content. But now"—she rolled her eyes—"the schools waste all our time and money on *them* instead of giving normal children the education they need."

She paused, and her mouth opened.

"*That's* where I've heard the name Richardson. Has she got a boy at the elementary school?"

"I'm not sure, why?"

"There's a strange little boy with that name who's always making trouble for Cody. I've complained 'til I'm blue in the face, but Hank Fielding doesn't want to hear it."

Marissa set her glass back on the tray and began dusting the cookie crumbs from her lap—Savannah's cue that their visit was over.

"I'll let you know if I hear anything else," she said. "In the meantime, I think you need to tell Pinky to kindly leave Travis Diehl alone."

The maid appeared with her coat.

"Oh, I couldn't do that," Savannah said, and smiled. "I prefer to let other people do my dirty work."

CHAPTER 12

All was quiet as Kieran and the dog scoured the woods that afternoon, searching for the materials they'd need to build their fort. The fallen leaves, sodden with rainwater, no longer crackled underfoot as they made their way along the narrow paths, and the crow that had been quick to sound the alarm had finally settled down to watch them in silence. They'd found the perfect spot for their hideout the day before. Now, they were collecting sticks and branches for the walls.

Kieran spotted a broken branch and reached down to pick it up.

"I found a video on YouTube that showed how to make one," he said, testing the branch's strength. "It looked pretty easy."

While Kieran made his selection, the dog waited patiently, untroubled by the saddlebags that hung down at its sides. If he'd thought about it, the boy might have wondered why the dog was so willing to do what he asked, but finding it in the woods again the day before had been the answer to a prayer. He knew better than to question a miracle.

The stick in Kieran's hand was straight and strong, an inch thick and as long as his leg—perfect for one of the pickets against which he'd place the rocks and branches for the fort's walls. When he'd drawn out his plan the night before, he figured they'd need a dozen sticks like it, but getting them back to the clearing would be a problem. A load that large wouldn't fit in his small arms, and making multiple trips back to the clearing with only a few sticks at a time would have taken him all day. He'd considered making a travois, like his scoutmaster said the Indians used, but the long branches would have been too hard for the dog to pull over the tangled ground. Instead, he'd tied two of his mom's cloth grocery bags together and laid them over the animal's back. As the boy loaded his gathered sticks into the sacks, the dog accepted the extra weight with alacrity.

"That's the last one," he said, patting the dog's head. "Let's go."

They turned and headed back the way they'd come.

"This is going to be an awesome fort," Kieran said, imagining it in his mind's eye. "It'll be like our own private clubhouse. We can meet there every day, and when I'm not around, you can sleep there, too."

What the boy did not say was that he hoped the dog would come and live with him instead of remaining out in the woods. After all, even a well-built fort wasn't as comfortable as a house was, and if it got much colder outside, the dog might freeze to death without a more reliable form of shelter. Still, the two times he'd tried to coax it out of the woods, the dog had resisted, and Kieran didn't want to take the chance that it would run off and never come back. He was certain, though, that if the dog would only come home with him, it would want to stay, and with Dr. Joan on his side and Grandpa, too, he was sure his mother would change her mind and let him. He just had to keep the dog from getting away this time.

The clearing was on a patch of ground that was sheltered by the branches of a short leaf pine whose broad green canopy acted like a giant umbrella. All around it were saplings and brush, a few of which Kieran had tied together with twine to make a secret entrance—something he'd added to the plan after seeing one on YouTube. Once finished, he thought, their fort would be almost invisible.

Kieran ducked under the bowed saplings and held back the shrubbery "door" to let the dog enter the clearing. Even after the rain they'd had, the ground inside and its soft bed of pine needles were almost dry. The dog stood patiently while Kieran emptied the saddlebags and then the two of them took a well-deserved break. As the boy sat down, the dog began circling the ground beside him.

"I like it here," Kieran said. "It's peaceful."

Not like at home, he thought, where it seemed like everyone was angry about something. His mom and Grandpa were angry with Kieran's dad for leaving; McKenna and Dylan were angry at their mom for treating them like babies; and everyone was angry with Kieran for . . . well, for being himself. No one yelled at him, or even said anything about it most of the time, but he could feel it all the same. It was why he'd agreed to join the program at school. Maybe, he thought, if he could stop being the way he was, then everyone else would be a little less mad.

The dog had finally found the perfect spot. It plopped down next to Kieran and rolled onto its side, lifting its front leg a few inches in an inviting way. The boy reached out and began scratching its chest. Slowly, the dog rolled onto its back and closed its eyes, moaning happily.

"I almost didn't come in here that first time," the boy said.

"Mom and Grandpa always said it was dangerous in the woods, and Cody told me I'd never get out alive."

He scoffed.

"Cody's such a liar."

He reached for his backpack.

"I brought you something."

Kieran unzipped the top and retrieved the brown bag that had held his lunch.

"It's kind of squashed, but it's still okay to eat."

At the smell of peanut butter and jelly, the dog licked its chops. Kieran broke off a piece of sandwich, using the bag to keep from getting peanut butter and jelly on his fingers, and gave it to him.

"I had peanut butter on Monday, too, but Cody pushed me into a locker on the way to the cafeteria, and I dropped it," he said. "Then a couple of the other kids stepped on it."

Kieran reached up and touched the spot where his shoulder had hit the metal locker. When Mrs. Dalton asked why he didn't have a lunch that day, he'd lied and told her he left it at home. It didn't look like she believed him, but she just gave him the apple from her own lunch and told him to try and remember it next time.

The dog whimpered and sniffed at his hand. Kieran tore the rest of the sandwich into pieces and set them down on the bag.

"It must be nice to be a dog," he said as it bolted down the sandwich. "If somebody pushes you around, you can just bite them."

He glanced over at the spot where the sandwich had been seconds before. The pieces had disappeared, and the dog was looking for any it might have missed. It gave the brown bag an experimental lick.

"Hey, don't eat that!"

Kieran snatched the bag away and wadded it up.

"Grandpa sure makes good sandwiches," he said.

As the dog continued to sniff the ground next to him, Kieran stuffed the bag into his backpack. Then he took out the ball of twine he'd brought from home and started unraveling it.

"Did I tell you I met the school counselor on Monday? Her name was Dr. Joan."

Kieran casually set the ball of twine on the ground next to him and took out the pocket knife he'd hidden inside it.

"She asked if there was anything that made me not want to count anymore, and I told her it helps when I talk to you." He gave the dog a sidelong glance. "She said it was a good thing that I had a dog."

Kieran bit his lower lip. The dog was smacking its tongue against the roof of its mouth, trying to loosen the last of the peanut butter sandwich; it wasn't paying attention to what he was doing. Slowly, the boy spooled out a length of twine—one long enough for a collar and leash—then cut it off and slipped the knife into his backpack.

"Would you like to be my dog?"

He made a slipknot at one end and gently tugged the loop until it was large enough to go over the dog's head. Then Kieran slowly got to his feet. He didn't want the dog to panic and run off before he could put the makeshift collar around its neck.

"I'd have to ask my mom," the boy said. "But maybe if Dr. Joan talked to her . . ."

Sensing the boy's heightened anxiety, the dog scrambled to its feet. Kieran reached out and murmured reassuringly, but the element of surprise was lost. Before he could slip the loop around its neck, the dog was out of reach.

Kieran dropped the leash.

"I'm sorry," he said. "Please don't go. It's okay if you don't want to be my dog. I just—"

But the dog had made up its mind. Giving the boy a quick backward glance, it pushed through the secret entrance and ran away.

"Bye," Kieran said sadly. "I'll see you later, okay?"

CHAPTER 13

Renee felt almost giddy as she set the table for dinner that night. Seeing Travis Diehl at the salon had been surprising, and having him ask her out for coffee even more so, but she was still amazed that he'd taken her to Mimesis. It was so sweet of him and so unexpected. Whether she took Pat up on her offer or not, she'd been touched that Travis would be so generous to someone he barely knew. It was as if a whole new world of possibilities had suddenly opened up for her. Missing her trip to the mall had definitely been worth it, she thought, even if Travis did only think of her as a "friend."

Wendell was serving up dinner, watching her from behind the stove.

"What are you grinning about?"

Renee tried to deflect the question.

"Remember Debbie, the client Savannah told not to tip me? She came by the salon and left me a Christmas card with ten dollars in it."

He started scraping the mashed potatoes into a serving dish.

"Ten whole dollars, huh? That's what's got you all giggly?"

Renee shrugged, afraid that telling him about what had happened would undo some of the magic. Nevertheless, she knew her father. Once he sensed that something was going on, he'd hound her until she spilled her guts.

"Travis Diehl came in for a haircut and asked for me specially."

"A man at Winona's," he said. "Boy, that is news."

Renee opened the refrigerator.

"And he took me out for coffee at a cool place called Mimesis. They serve coffee *and* showcase local artists."

He smiled. "Ahhh."

"There's no 'ahhh' about it, Dad. He knew I had a degree in art, and his friend owns the coffee shop. End of story."

She walked back to the table and started pouring the milk. This was exactly what she'd been afraid of. Now that she'd put it into words, the whole thing felt diminished—even trivial—compared to the fairy tale she'd conjured up. In spite of what she'd been telling herself about just being friends, she'd been thinking of it as a real date. Embarrassed now, she felt compelled to downplay the whole episode.

"It was just two adults having a cup of coffee," she said. "I'll probably never see him again."

Wendell looked doubtful.

"If you say so."

"I do."

He put the vegetables into a bowl and handed it to her. "Why don't you call the kids, then? Dinner's ready."

Having dinner together was the one inviolable rule in the Richardson household, a chance for the five of them to talk about their days and share any news—good or bad—about what was going on in their lives. It was a tradition Renee remembered fondly from her own childhood, something she felt was worth preserving—especially when so much else in the world had changed. With computers, video games, and social media vying for everyone's time and attention, it was too easy for family ties to simply wither from neglect. Forcing everyone to spend at least a few minutes a day together felt like the least she could do.

Of course, that didn't mean that everyone else at the table agreed with her or even that the time they spent together was always pleasant. Depending on the season, Dylan sometimes showed up just long enough to shovel in some food before running off to practice or a meeting with his coach, and McKenna's resentment over not being able to use her phone at the table was always simmering in the background. And although Kieran and her father were seldom rude, their contributions were often little more than grunts between mouthfuls, which meant that Renee sometimes felt like the host of a bad variety show, trying to coax the best performance out of each guest. Nevertheless, most nights yielded at least a few nuggets of important information, and for that reason alone, she felt it was worth the effort.

Everyone was hungry that night and little was said before half the food and all of the rolls had been eaten. Dylan gave a terse summation of that day's classes while scooping up a second helping of mashed potatoes, and McKenna reiterated the need for a new pair of boots before her warm-but-unfashionable feet made her the laughing stock of Bolingbroke Middle School. Wendell's day was condensed into a single sentence, and after intense prompting from his mother, Kieran admitted that the walk home from school was uneventful. That left a few minutes for Renee to share her news.

"I heard from Uncle Jack today. He and Aunt Megan and the girls will be here on Tuesday," she said. "Isn't that wonderful?"

"Is it?" McKenna drawled.

"Oh, come on," Renee said. "It'll be fun. Remember when you were little, always wanting to play with the 'big girls'?"

"Don't remind me."

"Well, consider it payback time, then," she said. "Who knows? You might even enjoy it."

Kieran grimaced.

"I don't want them to come. Aunt Megan doesn't like me, and Lilly cries all the time."

"That's because Lilly was a baby the last time you saw her," Renee said. "And don't say Aunt Megan doesn't like you, she does. She was just stressed out the last time they were here."

Wendell shot her a look that Renee pointedly ignored. The fact was, Megan hadn't been very nice to Kieran the last time they'd visited, and it was anyone's guess whether it was the stress of a new baby or something more that had been the problem. Either way, however, Renee was not going to poison their relationship by letting Kieran think that his aunt was biased against him. If everyone would just put aside their preconceived notions, she was sure that they could all enjoy a wonderful holiday together.

"We'll all have to make some sacrifices," she said. "McKenna? Uncle Jack and Aunt Megan will be staying in your room, so you'll be sleeping with me and using the master bath."

McKenna groaned.

"And Kieran, the girls will be in your room, so you'll be

sleeping downstairs on Grandpa's pullout couch and using the bathroom down there."

"Yeah!"

Of course he was delighted, Renee thought. Sharing with Grandpa meant unlimited access to the television.

"I'm finished," Kieran said. "Maybe I be excused?"

She nodded. Kieran put his dirty dishes in the sink and ran off to his room.

"I don't want to sleep in your room," McKenna said, pushing a Brussels sprout around her plate. "Why can't they stay in a hotel?"

"Hotels are expensive, Mac, and we have the room," Renee said. "Besides, it'll be more fun if we're all under one roof."

The girl let out a pained sigh.

"Why do we even have people over if it's going to be such a hassle?"

"Be quiet," Dylan said. "It's only for a couple of days."

"Be quiet yourself," she snapped. "Stop trying to act like a grown-up. You're not *Dad*."

Dylan lowered his fork and looked at Renee.

"Have you heard from Dad yet?"

Renee took a deep breath. She'd been hoping to tell each of the kids privately when she tucked them into bed. She didn't like having to give bad news at the dinner table.

"I'm sorry, Dyl. Dad says he's not going to be able to make it here for Christmas."

Dylan nodded resignedly, perhaps expecting the worst, but McKenna exploded.

"*What?*" Her fork clanged onto her plate. "Why not?"

Renee shook her head.

"I'm sorry, sweetie, I know you're disappointed, but your

dad has a lot on his mind right now. It's a difficult time for him. Caitlyn's expecting a baby, and he doesn't want to leave her alone."

"Of course not." McKenna glanced in the direction of Kieran's room. "He doesn't want to take a chance on having another *damaged kid*."

"*McKenna!* That's a terrible thing to say."

"It's true," the girl said, tears welling in her eyes. "Everything was fine until Kieran—"

"Go to your room," Renee snapped. "Right now."

McKenna threw her napkin on the floor and ran from the table, sobbing. Everyone flinched as her bedroom door slammed.

Renee could feel the blood pounding in her ears. Yes, McKenna was being rude, but blaming Kieran for Greg's departure was something they'd all done at one time or another. All she'd done was say it out loud.

"I'll talk to her later," she said, "once she's cooled down."

Dylan licked his lips.

"Do you think Kieran heard her?"

"I don't know," she said. "But just for the record, your dad's leaving had nothing to do with Kieran. He'd been"—she swallowed, not wanting to say too much—"he'd been unhappy for a long time."

Dylan nodded and stared at his plate.

"May I be excused?" he said. "Coach wants us in the gym by seven thirty."

"Of course," she said. "Go on."

Dylan put his dishes in the sink and headed down the hall, feeling emotionally unsettled. The idea that Kieran had been responsible for their parents' divorce was stupid—he'd known they weren't getting along even before that—but McKenna's other accusation had stung. The truth was, since their father left, Dylan *did* feel as if he needed to be more of a grown-up. Sure, Grandpa was there, but he indulged the other two more than their father had and left the discipline to their mom. As time went on, Dylan felt less like a kid and more like the man of the house.

The door to Kieran's room was ajar. Dylan rapped on it with his knuckles and pushed it open. His little brother was sitting at his desk, looking through the shoebox that held his hair collection. Dylan shook his head.

What kind of kid collects hair?

"Hey," he said.

Kieran didn't look up.

"Hey."

"You missed the fireworks. Dad's not coming for Christmas, and McKenna threw a fit."

The boy shrugged. Either he hadn't heard what their sister had said about him or he was choosing to ignore it.

"I knew he wouldn't."

"Yeah," Dylan said. "Didn't surprise me, either."

He looked around. Kieran's room was so neat it was almost creepy. There was no art on the walls, no dust on the shelves; the books were all in alphabetical order, and the plastic animals had been grouped together by species. The kid didn't even throw his dirty clothes on the floor! And no one but Kieran was allowed to touch anything, either, which meant that he spent a lot of time keeping things just the way they were. If his little brother hadn't been so annoying, Dylan might even have felt sorry for him.

He checked his watch. If he wasn't at the gym soon, Coach would be making him run laps.

"Look, I want you to be nice to the cousins while they're here," he said. "This is going to be a tough Christmas for Mom. We owe it to her to be extra good."

When there was no reaction from Kieran, Dylan shrugged and walked away.

CHAPTER 14

Savannah's hands gripped the steering wheel as she drove to Winona's. All through that afternoon, even as she pretended to listen to her clients, she'd been thinking about Travis and Renee. She might have laughed when Marissa warned her that there was something going on between them, but that didn't mean she hadn't taken the situation seriously. By the time her last appointment was through, she'd worked herself into a snit.

After all I've done for her!

This was a betrayal of the worst kind, she thought. Renee was biting the hand that had practically fed her and her family since they'd come to town. Without Savannah's patronage, that woman would still be scrounging for work at the salon, sitting in the back room and hoping for a walk-in to come through the door so she could earn her keep. It took a special kind of person to stab someone in the back like that.

At least she hadn't given herself away to Marissa. If Savannah had let on that she was the least bit bothered about it, her old friend would have been quick to tell everyone in town. Then the vultures would really have started circling. If someone like that could turn Travis Diehl's head, they'd say, just think how much easier it would be for them. Well, it wasn't going to happen. If Renee thought she could just waltz into town and steal someone's man, she had another thing coming.

Savannah pulled into the parking lot, checking to make sure that Renee's car was gone before she got out. It was Winona she'd come to see—the only one in this situation whose interests aligned with her own. After all, it was her salon's reputation that was at stake. If the women of Bolingbroke got the idea that Winona would sit by while their men were lured away by one of her girls, she'd soon be out of business.

The salon was nearly empty when Savannah walked through the door. There were no customers in the waiting area, and most of the girls had left for the day. She glanced over at the two remaining hairdressers—Tammy doing a blow out and Sissy a haircut—and wondered if either of them knew about Renee and Travis.

Of course they did, she thought. Renee had probably crowed about it the second she came back to the salon, trying to make it sound as if the two of them might actually have a future together. Had these two believed her? Snickered when they heard the news? Savannah ground her teeth. It was too bad there was no way to get rid of them, too.

Don't get distracted. You've still got work to do.

Winona was tidying up the waiting area. Savannah wandered over to have a little chat.

"Hey, Winona."

Winona looked up and gave her a warm smile.

"Hey, Savannah. What brings you in here at this hour?"

"I was on my way home from work and thought I'd stop by to see if Renee had any openings next week."

"Well, Renee's already gone, but I can check her book for you, if you'd like."

Savannah pretended to think about it.

"No, that's all right. I'm not really sure what-all I need. I'll just call her in the morning."

She paused, then sighed reluctantly and assumed the pained expression of someone with a regrettable, if necessary, duty to perform.

"Actually," she said, "there's something I need to tell you."

"Oh?"

"I was talking to Marissa Daniels today. You know Marissa, don't you?"

"Yes, ma'am."

Of course you do. Her father's one of the richest men in this town, and her husband's the mayor.

"She told me that Renee and Travis Diehl were seen having coffee together during working hours. Did you know about that?"

Winona set the last of the magazines in a neat row.

"I don't get involved with my girls' personal lives. If you have a question about that, you'll have to ask Renee."

Savannah pursed her lips.

"I must say, I'm surprised," she said. "I mean, if you don't care that your employees may be fraternizing—"

Winona held up her hand.

"Stop right there," she said. "I told you, I do not get involved with such things."

"But your reputation—"

"No. If I'd seen something unprofessional going on—here, in my salon—I'd have put a stop to it, but when my girls walk out that door, what they do is no business of mine. If the gossips in this town want to judge me by something I've got no control over, then there's nothing I can do."

"Of course," Savannah said. "I just thought you should know, seeing as it was all Marissa could talk about."

Winona picked up a pillow and gave it a slap.

"If Marissa Daniels is that upset, I'm sure she'll tell me herself. I do see her here pretty much every week."

Savannah felt her lips tighten. She'd been counting on Winona to take her side and tell Renee she'd been out of line, but the stupid old woman didn't even seem to care. She took a shaky step backward.

"I've had a long day, and I truly am very tired," she said. "Would you mind if I set a spell before I get back on the road?"

"Of course," Winona said. "The girls should be here awhile longer. Can I get you a glass of water before I go?"

Savannah simpered.

"That would be lovely. Thank you, ma'am."

While Winona fetched the water, Savannah took a seat on the couch. The woman's stubbornness was infuriating, but if she wanted to bury her head in the sand, there was nothing Savannah could do about it. It did not mean, however, that she was giving up.

Who else could she enlist?

If it had been anyone else making moves on Travis, she'd have known plenty of people who would pressure that person to back off. But she and Renee didn't run in the same circles; the only common ground the two of them had was right where she was sitting. In order to get that little Jezebel out of the way, Savannah would have to find someone at the salon to help her.

Winona brought her a glass of water, then told the other two to lock up when they were finished and headed out the door. Savannah thought the woman's good-bye seemed a bit cool, but it hardly mattered. And, she thought, it might just have been her imagination. As the door closed on a gust of frosty air, she narrowed her eyes at the remaining two hairdressers, trying to decide which one would be more useful.

When Tammy's client was done, she settled her bill and walked out with Tammy hot on her heels, leaving no time for the two of them to have a word. That left only Winona's niece, Sissy.

Savannah thought about that. Sissy was like a big, friendly puppy, always sniffing around and sticking her nose into other people's business. If anyone knew what was going on between Renee and Travis, it was probably her. Unfortunately, Sissy was closer to Renee than any of the other hairdressers, most of whom had little patience for Winona's awkward, meddling niece. If Savannah was going to get any information out of Sissy, she'd need to find a way to persuade her to talk *and* keep her from blabbing about it to Renee. The question was: How?

Minutes later, Sissy's customer left, and the girl started cleaning up her station. Savannah watched as she wiped down the counter and put her combs in the Barbicide, shook out the drape, and put it in the hamper along with the towel she'd wrapped around her client's neck. Then Sissy grabbed the broom from a hook on the wall and started sweeping up the floor around her chair.

Savannah leaned forward and frowned. Sissy had taken a small plastic bag from her pocket and was bending down. As she watched, the girl picked up a handful of hair, stuffed it into the bag, sealed it, and stuffed it back into her pocket before sweeping up the rest of the hair and throwing it away.

What on earth was she doing?

Whatever it was, Savannah thought, it didn't appear to be something the girl wanted anyone else to know about. On a hunch, she got up from the couch and followed Sissy as she walked into the back room.

"What were you doing out there?"

Sissy nearly jumped out of her skin—a sure sign, Savannah thought, of a guilty conscience.

"Just cleaning up my station," she said with exaggerated indifference. "Why?"

"Because it looked to me like you were stealing your client's hair. Does your Aunt Winona know about that?"

It was a flawed argument, but Savannah was counting on Sissy's credulity to make it work.

The girl tried to laugh, but it caught in her throat like a hiccup.

"Who says I was stealing hair?"

"I am. I saw you, just now. You grabbed a handful of hair and stuck it in your pocket. Now, either you tell me what you were doing or I tell Winona that you're a thief."

For a few awkward moments, it looked as if Sissy would hold her ground. If she did, Savannah knew she'd have no choice but to back down. Taking hair might be a bit creepy, but there was probably nothing illegal about it, and Winona would certainly be disinclined to report her own kin. As the seconds ticked by, though, Savannah stayed firm. Finally, Sissy's brave front faltered. Her lower lip began to tremble.

"Why do you want to know?"

Seeing her fold so quickly made Savannah smile. This had been almost too easy.

"Because what you're doing is wrong—it might even be dangerous. You could be using that hair to make voodoo dolls."

Sissy gasped. "That's not true! I only took it because Renee asked me to."

"*Renee* asked you? Why would she do that?"

Now that the spotlight had been turned away from her, Sissy was eager to tell all.

"It's for her little boy," she said. "He collects hair. It's his hobby, like."

"His hobby is collecting *hair?*"

"Yeah." She shrugged. "He's sort of different, if you know what I mean, but he doesn't do anything bad with it."

Savannah felt her mouth open. What was it Marissa had said when she heard Renee's last name was Richardson?

"There's a strange little boy with that name who's always making trouble for Cody."

She licked her lips, smiling as a whole new world of possibilities opened up. Not only had she found a way to get Sissy to do her bidding, but she might have found a weapon against Renee, as well.

Sissy was beginning to look less cowed.

"You know, Renee says once you cut it off, hair's just trash, and nobody cares if you take their trash."

She might have a point, of course, but Savannah had no intention of giving in. If she was going to use the girl to send a message to Renee, she'd have to keep her in doubt as to the consequences of her actions.

"She's wrong. Haven't you ever seen one of those police shows? Hair's got DNA in it; Renee could be using it for all kinds of reasons. If anyone found out that you were helping her, you'd be in a whole mess of trouble."

Sissy flinched, too unsure of herself to question what she was hearing. It was exactly the sort of reaction Savannah had been hoping for. All she had to do now was offer the girl a way out of her predicament.

"Of course, you only took the hair because *Renee* told you to . . ."

"That's right," Sissy said hopefully. "I was just trying to help."

Savannah grimaced, as though pondering a perplexing moral situation.

"Yes, and it hardly seems fair to punish you for that . . ."

She sighed dramatically.

"I think the *best* thing to do would be to tell Winona and let her decide—"

Sissy mewled in agony.

"—but I'd hate to see you get in trouble for something that wasn't your fault." She shrugged. "Maybe we should just forget about it."

Sissy practically melted with relief.

"Thank you *so much*. Honestly, I mean it. I really, really appreciate it."

"Of course. I mean, you and I are friends, Sissy, and friends help each other out."

Sissy nodded earnestly. Having finally found a way out of her predicament, it was clear she was willing to do almost anything to pay her back.

"And now that I've helped you out," Savannah said, "I'm going to need you to return the favor."

CHAPTER 15

It was the last day of school before Christmas vacation, and Kieran was taking in his hair collection for show and tell. The students would be doing their science project in the spring, and he was hoping Mrs. Dalton would be impressed enough to let him do his on hair. He'd put new labels on all the bags and used cut out pictures from hair magazines to decoupage the box the night before. As he checked to make sure that everything was in order, he rubbed the dog's fur between his fingers for luck.

"Hurry up, Kieran! We're going to be late!"

At the sound of Dylan's voice, he felt an involuntary tic wrinkle his nose.

"I'm coming!"

Kieran put the dog fur back into its bag, closed the lid, and slid the box into his backpack. Then he hurried down the hall, counting his steps as he went.

Dylan and McKenna were waiting for him by the front door.

"Put your coat on," Dylan said.

"And stop counting," McKenna snapped. "It's embarrassing."

Kieran set the backpack on the floor and took his winter coat from the hook, briefly checking the patch job under the left arm. If anyone had noticed, they hadn't mentioned it.

Grandpa came out of the kitchen and handed each of them a sack lunch.

"I put a toothbrush in yours," he told McKenna. "You don't want to go to the dentist with crap stuck between your teeth."

McKenna snatched the bag out of his hand and stuffed it into her backpack.

"Got your hair collection?"

Kieran scowled. "It's a *science* project."

"Oh, right," Grandpa said. "I forgot."

Dylan opened the door, letting in a blast of frigid air.

"Let's get going," he said, urging the younger siblings outside.

"Shotgun!" McKenna cried as the two of them ran for the car.

"No fair," Kieran said, scurrying after her.

The two of them piled into the ancient Toyota as Dylan got into the driver's seat and started the engine. Kieran put on his seat belt, took out his hair collection, and set it gently down beside him. McKenna craned her neck around the passenger's seat and glared at the box.

"Do you just *want* to be bullied?"

"No," he said. "Of course not."

"Leave him alone," Dylan said, checking his mirrors.

She crossed her arms. "I'm just saying."

"I know what you're saying"—he put the car in gear and started backing out of the driveway—"just stop saying it."

"Fine," she huffed, and turned to look out the window.

Kieran swung his feet on the way to school, slipping in one or two "accidental" kicks to the back of his sister's seat along the way. Why was she always asking him stupid questions like that? She made it sound like he was doing stuff just to make her look bad.

He opened the lid of the box and looked at the bag with the dog fur inside. The dog didn't care about any of that, he thought. It hadn't even cared that first time, when Kieran cried; it just licked his face and put its paw on his arm to show him it was okay. If the dog was his, he thought, he'd always know that there was someone at home who didn't care about being embarrassed or think that everything bad that happened was his fault.

Middle school started earlier than elementary school, so they dropped McKenna off first. As they approached the drop-off zone, she checked her face in the mirror and did a quick touch-up of her hair. Since starting middle school, Kieran thought, his sister spent way too much time in the bathroom trying to look like all the popular girls in her grade. He made a face, hoping she'd see him behind her, but she ignored him.

As Dylan pulled over to the curb, McKenna snapped the visor back up and hoisted her backpack.

"Remember," he said. "You've got a dental appointment today."

"Like I could forget? Give me a break."

"You forgot last time, and Mom still had to pay."

"Yeah, sure. Fine. Whatever."

She got out and slammed the door, then ran toward a group of girls who were standing out in front. Dylan shook his head.

"She'll forget."

"Yup," Kieran said.

Dylan turned and looked back at him.

"You want to sit up here?"

"No. I don't want to move the box around too much. It gets everything all messed up and then I have to fix it."

As they pulled back into traffic, Kieran daydreamed in silence.

What should he name the dog? he wondered. As disappointing as it was that the twine leash hadn't worked, he wasn't giving up on the idea of taking the dog home with him, and in the meantime he was getting tired of calling it just "dog." He liked the name Rex, but he'd had a friend back in Camden with a dog named Rex, and he didn't want people to think that he'd copied.

Whatever name he picked would have to be a boy's name, though, because that's the kind of dog it was. He was glad, too, because if it had been a girl dog McKenna might have insisted on buying it a pink collar and dressing it in clothes like she used to do with her dolls. At least a boy dog would be spared that indignity. With luck, in fact, his sister wouldn't want to have anything to do with it.

When they got to the elementary school, Kieran gathered his things, carefully returning the box with his hair collection to his backpack. As he kicked the car door shut behind him, Dylan rolled down the passenger side window.

"You sure you don't want to come to the dentist with us?"

"I'm sure."

"You should take the bus, then. It's too cold to walk."

Kieran jutted his jaw stubbornly.

"Mom said I could walk home if I wanted to."

Dylan shrugged.

"You got the note for the office lady?"

Kieran patted his breast pocket.

"Yes."

"Her name's Debbie. Don't forget to tell her the note's from Renee Richardson."

Kieran let out a pained sigh.

"I *know.* Can I go now?"

Dylan pressed his lips together and gave him a hard look.

"Okay, get out of here," he said, then added: "Good luck."

Kieran hurried through the front door and turned right, heading for the principal's office—the same place he'd met with Dr. Joan. Principal Fielding wasn't in yet, but his secretary, Debbie, was at her desk, talking to a woman he'd never seen before. The woman had her hip on Debbie's desk and was leaning over as she spoke. Her blouse hadn't been buttoned all the way, and Kieran could see the top of her breasts. Before he could look away, the woman turned and gave him a smile that made his cheeks burn.

"Good morning, young man," Debbie said. "What can I do for you?"

Kieran shook his head, fighting the urge to wince, and reached into his pocket.

"This is for you," he said. "It's from Renee Richardson."

He took out the slightly crumpled envelope and set it on her desk.

She smiled. "Why, thank you."

The other woman was staring at him.

"You must be Kieran," she said.

"Yes, ma'am."

He glanced at Debbie, hoping for an explanation.

"This is Miz Hays," she said. "She's a client of your mama's, just like I am."

Miz Hays laid a finger on his backpack.

"That's a lot of books you've got in there. They must be heavy."

"No, ma'am. It's my hair collection."

"Well, bless your heart. Your mama's a hairdresser and you collect *hair*." She looked back at Debbie. "Isn't that just the cutest thing?"

Kieran smiled uncertainly. Was Miz Hays being nice, or was she just teasing him?

Debbie glanced up at the clock.

"The bell's about to ring, Kieran. You'd best be going," she said. "You don't want to be late."

CHAPTER 16

It was five days until Christmas, and the parking lot at the mall was packed. As Renee drove up and down the aisles, searching for an empty space, she could feel her frustration growing. Other than a few things to put in their stockings, she hadn't bought a single present for the kids. Who knew if there'd be anything left on the shelves by the time she got in there? She almost wished she'd done her shopping on Wednesday instead of having coffee with Travis Diehl.

Almost.

A woman up ahead was walking out to her car, keys in hand. Renee put on her signal and waited for the parking spot to open up. Doing her shopping now might be frustrating, she thought, but she wasn't really sorry she'd put it off. Having coffee at Mimesis was the first time in years that she'd done something just to please herself, and it had given her a more optimistic attitude toward the future. Whether or not she took her portfolio to show Pat, that alone had been worth it.

Her phone rang—a number she didn't recognize. Renee reached down and pushed the button.

"Hey, it's Travis. Are you busy?"

The woman in the parking lot started backing out of her space.

"Sort of. I'm at the mall, waiting for a parking spot. What's up?"

"Have you made up your mind about Saturday?"

Renee sighed. The short answer was no, she hadn't. Since he'd asked her, in fact, she'd been changing her mind on pretty much an hourly basis. This didn't feel like the right time to be making a firm decision one way or the other.

"Hold on a second."

As the other car drove off, she pulled into the space and turned off the engine.

"Okay, here's the thing," she said. "I'm really flattered that you'd ask me, but I have a long day at work tomorrow, and when I say I have nothing to wear, I'm really not kidding."

"What about the outfit you were wearing at the salon? That looked fine to me."

She shook her head in exasperation, smiling in spite of herself. He certainly was persistent.

"Maybe to you, but I doubt anyone at the ceremony would agree. Anyway," she said, reaching for her purse, "I don't have time to talk about it right now. I just got to the mall, and if I don't get in there fast, my kids will get nothing they want for Christmas."

"What a coincidence," he said. "I'm at the mall myself. Tell you what. Why don't I help you do your shopping while you think about it?"

Renee laughed.

"You've got to be kidding."

"No, I'm serious. Come on, you've got two boys, right? Believe me, I know all the stuff boys want these days."

Oh, for heaven's sake.

"Fine. Meet me in front of Belk's in five minutes. Good luck finding a parking place."

Inside, the mall was almost worse than the parking lot had been. Holiday music blared from unseen speakers, and anxious shoppers scampered from store to store while screeching, crying children waited in line to see Santa Claus. As Renee stepped into the crowd, it felt as though she was being pushed along by a strong, unseen current. There was nothing to do but go with it and try not to be overrun.

Travis was sitting on a bench in front of Belk, grinning at Renee as she approached.

"How'd you get here so fast?" she said, breaking free of the mob.

"Trade secret."

"Come on."

He pointed to the bags sitting on the floor behind him.

"You're not the only one with Christmas shopping to do."

She glanced at the bags and saw the names of some high-end stores.

"Generous guy. What'd you get?"

"Presents for the office staff and a couple for my brother, Hugh."

"I don't remember your telling me you had a brother."

"Didn't I?" he said. "I must have forgotten."

He reached down and picked up the bags.

"Okay. Where to first?"

Their first stop was at Claire's to get a pair of birthstone studs for McKenna's newly pierced ears, then off to Sephora for a ten-dollar gift certificate.

"Girls wear makeup in *middle school?*"

Renee rolled her eyes at him.

"Times change, Gramps."

"Hey, thirty-eight isn't old."

He frowned.

"What? How old did you think I was?"

"I don't know," Renee said, embarrassed that her surprise had been so obvious.

He ran a hand through his hair.

"It's the grey, isn't it?"

"No! Well, maybe, but it looks good."

"I was going for ruggedly handsome," he said. "But I guess 'good' will suffice. Where to next?"

Renee smiled at him, thinking that "ruggedly handsome" was just about right.

"GameStop," she said. "I need something for Kieran."

They stepped back into the surging crowd and emerged five minutes later in front of the electronic game store. As they walked through the door, Renee felt immediately overwhelmed by the number and variety of titles on the shelves.

"Did he give you a list?" Travis said.

She showed it to him.

"What kind of platform is he using?"

Renee gave him a blank look.

"The machine he plays the games on." Travis smirked. "Now who's the fogey?"

"Oh, that," she said. "Their dad bought the kids an Xbox."

"Okay, then. You take that half of the store; I'll take this half, and we'll see if any of these are left."

Renee headed down the first aisle, looking for any of the titles on Kieran's list. There were lots of different games, for different ages and different interests, and they all seemed to need different devices to play them on, but not a single title was one that her son had asked for. Thinking she might find something else that would interest him, she wandered over to the section marked *E for Everyone,* picked one at random, and started reading the description on the back.

Comic Mischief, Mild Cartoon Violence . . .

Travis walked up, shaking his head.

"Couldn't find a single one."

He looked at the cartridge in her hands.

"*Wipeout in the Zone?* That isn't on the list."

"I know," she said. "I couldn't find anything either."

She handed him the box.

"What do you think of this?"

Travis turned it over and started reading the description on the back.

"How old is Kieran?"

"Nine."

"He into dodgeball, stuff like that?"

She shook her head.

"Let's find something else, then."

He put the game back on the shelf.

"What does he like to do in his free time? Does he play sports? Have any hobbies?"

What did Kieran like to do? Renee thought. Collect hair? Count his steps? Neaten up his already spotless room?

"It's hard to say. He's sort of an odd kid."

He nodded. "Nine's an odd age."

She swallowed, feeling her stomach clench. Once she told Travis anything about her younger son, the only question would be how quickly the guy would run off.

Well, too bad, she thought angrily. Kieran was a good kid who was doing his best. If Travis Diehl—or anyone else— couldn't handle that, then they could go take a hike.

"He likes to count things," she said, feeling more than a little defensive. "And he—he collects things and enjoys keeping them in order."

Travis's face lit up.

"In that case," he said. "I know the perfect game for him. Come on."

Renee was stunned.

He actually smiled. Who'd a thunk?

Caught off guard, she had to hurry after him as Travis strode away. Where were they going? she wondered. They'd already left the "E" section. He wasn't proposing she give Kieran an adult game, was he?

He glanced back over his shoulder.

"Do you mind if the game is pre-owned?"

"Uh, no. I guess not," she said. "But I mean, it's a gift."

He stopped at the counter and told the clerk what he was looking for. As the man walked off, Travis turned and looked at Renee.

"Let's see what kind of shape it's in, then you can decide if you want it."

The clerk returned and handed her a box. Renee peered at the title.

"Tetris Evolution?"

"It's the perfect game for a kid who likes to put things in order. My brother Hugh plays it all the time."

Renee was intrigued. She turned it over. The box was in good shape, she thought, practically brand-new. If Travis hadn't told her, she'd never have known it was used.

"Are you sure it's appropriate for a nine-year-old?"

"Positive," he said. "There's no blood and guts, no questionable behavior. The theme song will drive you nuts after a while, but I could buy you some earplugs."

"It's perfect," she said. "Thanks. I owe you one."

"Great. How about coming with me tomorrow?"

Renee gave him an exasperated look. Why was he doing this? There must be dozens of women in Bolingbroke who would gladly go with him. She told herself she should just say no and put an end to it.

And yet . . .

And yet, she was flattered. More than that, she felt that maybe—just maybe—Travis Diehl thought that there was something special about her. Something he hadn't found in any of those other women. The idea made her feel warm and silly and scared, all at the same time.

"Well?" he said.

She shrugged and gave him a wry smile.

"All right, but I'll have to meet you there. If my last appointment runs late, I don't want everyone to blame me for delaying the guest of honor."

CHAPTER 17

The moment school let out, Kieran hurried toward the parking lot, trying to make it look like he was taking the bus home so he could throw Cody off his scent. By the time the first bus passed him, he was already halfway down the street, head down, shoulders hunched.

He was heading for the woods, hoping to find Rex. When Kieran had shown up the day before, the dog hadn't been there, and he was worried that he might have scared it off. He thought his plan might have worked if he'd been able to buy a real collar and leash, but there'd been no way to get those things without his mom finding out, and he didn't want her to say no without giving the dog a chance. As he hurried along, he held the piece of fur in his hand like a talisman. Even if Rex didn't want to be *his* dog, Kieran thought, he hoped they could at least be friends.

The box in his backpack was thumping painfully against his spine as he hurried down the road, breaking the boy's concentration as he tried to think of another way to lure the dog out of the woods. Kieran stopped and took out his hair collection, then slung the backpack over his shoulder and continued on. Better to carry the box in his hands, he thought, than to wind up with a bruised back.

It felt as if he'd been walking forever by the time Kieran passed the last house. The first time he'd gone into the woods he'd been running from Cody, and since then, the anticipation of seeing the dog had made him oblivious to the distance it was from school. Now, though, he almost dreaded the thought of getting to the woods. If Rex wasn't there this time, Kieran feared he might just be gone for good. He saw the place where they'd first met up ahead, but Rex wasn't waiting for him. As far as he could tell, there was no one around.

He heard a rustling in the bushes, and Kieran almost sobbed in relief. Rex *was* there; he hadn't run away. They could still be best friends, and maybe someday, the two of them would even walk the rest of the way home together. Clutching his hair collection tightly to his chest, he hurried forward to see how Rex was doing.

A dark silhouette stepped out of the woods.

"What took you so long, freak?"

Kieran held back a cry of dismay. How had Cody gotten there before him? He'd thought he was so smart, slipping away unnoticed, and all the time his enemy had been lying in wait.

Cody stepped out onto the berm, his hands balled into fists, and his face twisted into an ugly sneer. Kieran felt rooted to the spot. What good would it do to run? Cody was bigger and faster than he was. The only reason Kieran had outrun him before was because Cody had been afraid to follow him into the woods. Now, however, it seemed that fear had been overcome. As the bigger boy raised his fist, Kieran cringed, waiting for the blow to connect. Instead, Cody snatched the box out of his hands.

"What's this?" he said, tossing the lid on the ground. "Looks like a bunch of junk."

"Don't," Kieran said, reaching for the box. "Please. I've got everything in order."

Cody reached in, grabbed a handful of plastic bags, and squeezed them between his fat fingers. As one of them burst, Kieran flinched.

"This is nothing but *trash*," he said. "What are you doing with a box full of trash? Are you a *trash man?*"

Kieran felt tears welling as panic rose up in his chest. His hair! All the hair he'd collected since he was a little kid was being thrown on the ground like so much rubbish. He watched, horrified, as Cody took every bag out of the box, threw them all on the ground, and stomped them underfoot. He wasn't just getting the bags out of order, he was destroying them! Kieran balled his small fists in frustration, wishing he was bigger so he could give the bully what he deserved.

Cody saw the tiny bunched hands and laughed.

"You think you can hurt me?" He threw the box into the ditch. "Think again, weirdo."

He grabbed Kieran's coat and jerked him forward. He stumbled and fell. Kieran felt the gravel tear into his palms and wished he'd put on the gloves that were still in his pocket. He struggled to his feet and stood tall, his back to the woods, then closed his eyes and waited for the gut punch that was coming. His palms were bloody and his knees stung, but he refused to beg for mercy.

Cody took a step toward him, then paused and looked around.

"What was that?"

Kieran had heard it, too: the rustle of bushes followed by a low, menacing growl. He shook his head.

"I don't know."

Cody's eyes widened.

"What the—?"

Kieran heard something crashing through the bushes, then a huge grey shape launched itself out of the woods and landed in front of him. Cody scrambled backward as the dog stood, snarling and barking, the fur along its backbone stiff. Kieran was in too much shock to move. He could only stand, agape, as Rex stood his ground.

"Call your dog off!" Cody screamed. "Call him off!"

Kieran shook his head.

"I can't. He's not my dog."

"Then why's he coming after me?"

"I don't know," he said. "Maybe he doesn't like you."

"Yeah, well. I don't like him, either," Cody said, braver now that he'd put some distance between them. "You'll be sorry for this. I'm gonna tell my dad."

But the brave talk was just that and when the dog barked again, Cody turned and ran, skittering on a patch of ice as he scrambled away.

Kieran was amazed. Cody Daniels was actually afraid of something! He looked over at the dog, who'd begun to settle as soon as the bully ran off. The fur on its back flattened again, and the stiffness in its limbs relaxed. Issuing one final growl in Cody's direction, it returned to Kieran and nuzzled his hand.

Kieran beamed.

"That was *awesome!*"

CHAPTER 18

Wendell sat at the kitchen table on Saturday morning, drinking his third cup of coffee and fretting over this new wrinkle in his matchmaking plans. For the last five days, Renee had been giddier than a schoolgirl over someone named Travis Diehl. Every other word out of her mouth was, "Travis this," and "Travis that," and tonight, she was meeting him at some big to-do after work. Never mind that she'd sworn it was nothing serious, he thought. Wendell might be getting old, but he wasn't senile.

If only the boys down at Clint's had mentioned this Diehl character when the subject of eligible bachelors was being discussed, he'd be fine with it, but the man's name had never come up. Either those old guys had been holding out on him or this fella wasn't as available as Renee thought he was. Either way, he wasn't going to just sit by and wait for his little girl to get her heart broken again. Whatever it took, he was going to get the lowdown on Travis Diehl. The question was: How?

Wendell got up and started clearing away the breakfast

dishes while he worked on a plan. Asking the boys at Clint's for help would be tricky; Butch's failure had dampened their enthusiasm, and Wendell wasn't in the mood to jolly them up. Besides, who knew if that bunch even had any information to give? If they hadn't said anything about this Diehl character before, it might just mean they had nothing to say. Nevertheless, it was worth a shot, and if he did come up empty-handed, he could always head over to Joe's for a trim and a bit of friendly snooping. Lucky pennies could turn up in the strangest places.

He got dressed, told the kids he'd be back in a couple of hours, and headed out the door.

Midmorning was always a slow time at Clint's, and the parking lot was almost empty when Wendell arrived. A couple of the boys' cars were parked around back, though, and that was the important thing. He went inside to see what was going on.

The "boys" was a misnomer, of course. At sixty-nine, Wendell was one of the younger men who stopped by Clint's every day to palaver over a cup of coffee, a meal, or a friendly game of cards before picking up some items from the small grocery section in front. The eponymous Clint had passed away years before, and the place had changed hands several times, but the store had been a fixture in Bolingbroke for so long that changing the name would have been unthinkable. Its current owner, Maggie McRay, was a widow who'd bought the place with the proceeds from her late husband's life insurance.

Jim, Ted, and Bill were playing penny ante poker at their regular table in back, and Maggie was at the counter writing the dinner specials on a chalkboard, her lank grey hair pulled back in a haphazard bun. When Wendell came in, she looked up and pushed a wayward strand out of her face, giving him a smile as he walked by. He poured himself a cup of decaf from the self-serve carafe and took a seat at the table. Ted dealt him in without looking up.

"Just a couple of hands," Wendell said, setting a handful of change on the table. "Gotta get back to keep an eye on the grandkids."

The men checked their cards and anted up, then drew from the pile as needed. Wendell, who'd been dealt a pair of fours, threw three cards away, hoping for a full house, and settled for three of a kind. He tossed two pennies in the pot.

"I'll raise."

"I'll call," Bill said, tossing in another two.

Jim put down his cards. "I'm out."

Wendell grimaced. "Really? You can't risk two goddamn pennies?"

"Not with this hand. I'm on Social Security."

Two more pennies went into the pot as Ted equaled Wendell's bet.

"Call."

Wendell glanced at his cards again. Three fours wasn't great, but it wasn't awful, either, and losing a hand or two might even be a good thing if it put the others in a sympathetic mood. If he was going to find out who Diehl was, he'd need to have them on his side. He picked up another penny and tossed it in.

"Raise."

"Call."

"Call."

The cards went down, and Wendell's measly three of a kind prevailed. He pulled in his winnings, feeling out of sorts as Ted dealt another hand.

Maggie bustled over with a coffeepot and topped off Wendell's cup.

"Can I get you something else, hon?"

"Nope," he said, tossing in his opening ante.

She looked around. "How about the rest of you boys?"

"No thanks."

"I'm good."

"No thank you, ma'am."

As she walked away, Wendell considered his next move. The first time he'd mentioned his find-Renee-a-husband scheme, the boys had taken to it with enthusiasm, eager to make inquiries among their friends and relatives as to who might be in the marriage market. Since Renee's unfortunate date with Butch, however, their noses had been a little out of joint. Querying them about Travis Diehl might not be the same as soliciting the names of potential suitors, but it might be seen as covering familiar ground. Nevertheless, he was determined to find out who had set his little girl's heart aflutter, and he wasn't about to let a little resistance discourage him. He just needed an offhand way to introduce the subject.

The back room was quiet as the game progressed, the clink of pennies and murmured bids the only interruptions to Wendell's train of thought. On the weekends, Clint's did most of its business at mealtimes: before nine, when people stopped by for coffee and sweet rolls; around noon for a pre-made sandwich, a cup of soup, or a bowl of chili; and suppertime, for one of Maggie's hot entrées or to pick up fixin's for a meal at home. The rest of the time, the place was pretty much dead.

"Clemson's looking good this year," Bill said, raising the stakes by two cents.

"Yes, they do," Jim agreed, matching his bet. "Be something if they went to the Orange Bowl again, wouldn't it?"

"It would, indeed."

There was a collective sigh from the others as the memory of the Tigers' 2015 romp over Oklahoma was savored anew. As the only non-Clemson alumnus at the table, Wendell felt a prick of irritation that he was unable to bask in the team's reflected glory, which only increased his determination to bring the conversation around to something more personally useful.

"Any of you know a fella named Travis Diehl?" he said.

Jim rolled his eyes.

"Uh-oh. Here we go again."

Wendell drew back, offended that his intentions had been so quickly discovered.

"Can't a man ask a simple question around here without getting the third degree?"

"Any man but you."

The three of them chuckled.

"Well," he said, taking another tack. "What's wrong with asking a few questions about a man who's been spending time with my daughter?"

"When are you going to let Renee run her own life?" Bill said. "She's a grown woman. She doesn't need you sticking your nose in."

Wendell's face folded itself into a stubborn mask.

"She's not thinking straight," he said. "This Diehl character's got her head turned, and I don't want to see her get hurt."

The other men exchanged a look and shook their heads.

"It's your turn, Wendell. You in or out?"

He grabbed two pennies without checking his cards and

tossed them into the pot. Why had he even bothered to come down there? He'd have had more luck and less aggravation talking to a wall.

"Come on," Ted told him. "Do us all a favor and give it a rest. Better yet, leave Renee alone and find someone for yourself."

Wendell's scowl deepened.

"I've already outlived one wife, and I don't need another. I'm doing just fine on my own."

"Oh, yeah. You're *fine*," Bill drawled as the others nodded sagely.

"And even if I was looking," Wendell said, "where am I going to find a woman that'd have me? My retirement checks only stretch so far, and I'm about as good-looking as a horse's backside."

"He's got a point there," Jim said with mock seriousness.

"Doesn't mean you can't find a lady friend," Ted insisted.

"Oh, yeah, like who? Come on boys, let's hear some names."

Furtive glances ricocheted around the table.

"What about Maggie?" Bill said, sotto voce.

Wendell was nonplussed.

"Maggie who?"

"The gal who just poured your coffee, dummy. Haven't you seen the way she looks at you?"

"And she doesn't need your money, either," Jim added. "She owns this place."

Wendell glanced back at the counter and shook his head.

"She's too old."

"Not that old, and you're no spring chicken yourself."

Ted chuckled. "Wendell probably didn't even know she was a woman."

Maggie lifted her head and glared at them from across the room.

"I heard that, Ted Coburn!"

"All I'm saying," Bill continued, "is that you'd be doing the both of you a favor if you'd stop trying to help and let Renee find someone on her own."

Wendell hunkered down and studied his cards. These old farts were no help at all. They didn't see how times had changed. Men didn't go courting these days; they expected a woman to pay for half of everything and still put out on the first date. The thought of his baby girl being taken advantage of by a scoundrel like that made his blood boil. That's why she needed him to weed out the bad actors. Travis Diehl might be a good guy, but until Wendell had verified that fact, the man remained on probation.

When the hand was over, everyone laid down his cards. Wendell had won again. He'd been sitting there for twenty minutes and had nothing to show for it but a handful of pennies. It was time, he decided, to strike out in a different direction. He scraped his winnings off the table and bid the boys adieu.

A string of jingle bells tinkled merrily as Wendell pushed his way through the front door at Joe's. Joe's Barbershop was a serious place where men went for their grooming needs, not a girly, gossipy, home-away-from-home like Winona's. The walls were clad in wood paneling, and three red leather barber chairs stood like sentries along the left-hand side of the narrow room. Four mismatched chairs huddled in a corner on the right and well-thumbed copies of *Carolina Sportsman*, *Sports Illustrated*, and that day's *Charlotte Observer* were stacked in a haphazard pile atop a wooden crate with *Pepsi Cola* stenciled in blue and red on its side. After a quick look around, Wendell took a seat, relieved that none of the boys from Clint's was there. He needed an informed source with an open mind, not some damn naysayers.

When it was Wendell's turn, Joe tucked a strip of tissue paper around his neck and put a drape around his shoulders.

"What'll it be today, Mr. Evans?"

"How about thick on top and long on the sides?"

Joe chuckled.

"Same as always," he said, running a comb through Wendell's wet and dwindling mane. "How's the family?"

"Good," Wendell said. "It looks like Clemson's going to offer Dylan a full-ride for next year."

The barber nodded his approval.

"Can't do better than that."

"The younger ones are doing well, too. McKenna's the spitting image of her mother at that age."

"Mmm-hmm. Probably best not to tell her that."

Wendell laughed. "I wouldn't dare."

As snippets of hair began to fly from Joe's scissors, Wendell realized that he didn't have the luxury of time. If he was going to ask about Travis Diehl, he'd have to do it soon.

"I was hoping you might be able to help me with something," he said.

Joe smiled. "I will if I can. What is it?"

He heard a crash, and the clang of jingle bells made both men flinch. Wendell looked over and saw Maggie McRay trying to push the barbershop door open with a box of supplies in her arms.

As Joe put his shears down and ran over to help, Wendell scowled. He'd spent the entire drive over there trying to figure out how to broach the subject of Travis Diehl without having Joe accuse him of meddling, and now Maggie had spoiled the whole thing.

"Miz McRay!" Joe said, taking the box from her arms and setting it on the counter. "What are you doing carrying that heavy load?"

Maggie shook out her arms and wiped a sleeve across her forehead. In an oversized corduroy jacket, with her grey hair tucked up under a bucket hat, she looked as drab and shapeless as a burlap sack.

"Thank you, Joe," she said. "My delivery boy is out sick today."

She looked around and smiled warmly at Wendell.

"Oh, hello again."

"Hello," he said stiffly.

Wendell folded his arms under the drape and turned away. He refused to be civil to this interloper. The sooner she left, the sooner he could get back to work.

Maggie stood there awkwardly, glancing from Wendell to Joe and back.

"Uh, can I pay you for those supplies now?" Joe said. "I know we ordered some extra this time."

"Oh, no need," she said. "We can settle up at the end of the month like always."

She gave Wendell another glance.

"Well, I guess I'd better let you gentlemen get back to work."

"Thanks for bringing those things by," Joe said as he walked her to the door. "We'll see y'all later."

Joe was strangely quiet as he returned to the chair, deftly

turning away Wendell's attempts to restart their conversation. As a result, the haircut was almost finished before Wendell was able to bring things back around to where he'd left off. With only a few stray hairs to go, he decided to skip the nuance and blurt out the question he'd come there to have answered.

"Ever heard of a fella named Travis Diehl?"

The name, at least, had finally caught Joe's attention.

"Diehl. He the one who owns Precision Industrial?"

"I don't know," Wendell said. "Could be."

Joe turned toward his partner, Mack, who was busy sweeping up around the next chair.

"Didn't the Diehls have two sons?"

"I believe so, yes."

"Do you remember their names?"

"The younger one is Hugh," Mack said. "I used to see him around town with his daddy. Was the other one called Travis? Might have been. He moved away a long time ago."

"Seems to me he came back, though, didn't he?"

Mack's brow creased. "I believe I heard both boys were at their mother's funeral. I don't know if he's moved back here permanent."

Wendell looked at him.

"And you don't know for sure if the older one was called Travis?"

"'Fraid not," Mack said.

"Are there any other Diehls here in town?"

The man shrugged and shook his head.

"You know who could tell you? That gal who just left here. She knows pretty near everybody in town."

Wendell glanced toward the front door.

"Mack's right," Joe said.

He removed the drape from Wendell's shoulders and brushed away a few errant hairs.

"If anyone could have given you the lowdown on Travis Diehl, it's Maggie McRay."

He handed Wendell a mirror and gave him a stern look.

"Too bad you just chased her off."

CHAPTER 19

Savannah hung up the phone and threw herself down on the bed, pummeling the mattress until her arms ached. She'd tried, she'd *really* tried to give Renee a chance, to let her bow out gracefully without having to resort to any ugliness, but the woman refused to listen. When Sissy warned her not to mess with Travis, Renee had not only refused to be told "who she could and couldn't see," she'd announced that she was going out with him that night! Clearly, subtlety was not going to work.

She snatched up the phone and dialed Marissa's number. Sissy had told her that Renee and Travis would be attending a formal dinner that night—the kind the mayor and his wife would surely be going to, as well. Savannah pursed her lips. Why hadn't Marissa mentioned that to her on Monday? Surely, she could have taken her along as a guest. The phone rang five times before Marissa answered.

"Hey. Have you got a minute?"

"Well, I do, dear, but only just. Trey and I are going out, and I still haven't taken a shower. What's this about?"

"Are the two of you going to an awards banquet, by any chance?"

There was a lengthy pause.

"Why do you ask?"

"Will Travis be attending?"

"I certainly hope so," Marissa tittered. "He's receiving one of the awards."

Savannah closed her eyes and pictured her hands around Marissa's neck. Was the woman actually that clueless? Had it really not occurred to her that taking Savannah along to confront Travis in person might just have resolved the problem she claimed to be so concerned about?

"I take it your 'inside connection' let you down."

Savannah nodded, feeling tears starting to well again. *Everyone* had let her down: Renee, Winona, Sissy—even Marissa. If she lost Travis, too, there'd be no one left.

"She told me she delivered the message but that Renee didn't care."

"Did she also mention that Renee and Travis were seen shopping at the mall together yesterday?"

She gasped. "*Why, that little bee!*"

"I didn't see them myself," Marissa said, "but apparently things were *very* cozy."

Savannah patted her chest, feeling dizzy and breathless. How could she? How could *they*?

"I hadn't heard about that. She just said that they were attending some sort of soirée tonight, which is why I called. I thought you and Trey might be going."

Without me.

"Well, that's interesting," Marissa said. "I wonder if I might be able to help Renee see how ill-suited the two of them are.

I mean, the owner of Precision Industries and a hairdresser? Please."

Savannah nodded, somewhat mollified. She knew Renee was still feeling her way around the social circles in Bolingbroke. Perhaps a little instruction from the mayor's wife would show her where in the hierarchy she belonged.

"By the way," Marissa said, "did you ever find out if Renee had a son at Cody's school?"

Savannah frowned. What did this have to do with anything?

"I did," she said. "You're right, he's very strange. But—"

"Hold on a minute and listen to me. Travis's award is in recognition of his foundation's donation to the elementary school—money earmarked for children like his brother, Hugh . . . and Renee's boy. Trey thinks it's just awful, of course, but the Jaycees saw it differently."

"Oh."

"It's ironic, don't you think? I wonder if Renee knows."

"That Travis gave the money for the program?" Savannah said. "I doubt it. I spoke to Hank's secretary yesterday, and she told me that at this point, the whole thing is very hush-hush."

"So, you don't know for sure if her son is in the program?"

"Well, of course I do, dear. The list was sitting right there on her desk. All I had to do was ask for a glass of water and take a picture when she walked out."

Marissa laughed. "Why you imp! What are you planning to do?"

"Never you mind," Savannah said sweetly. "You just make sure that Renee knows she's not wanted at that party, and I'll take care of the rest."

"Oh, don't worry. It'd be my pleasure. The sooner she and that strange little boy of hers leave town, the happier we'll all be."

Savannah ended the call, feeling at least somewhat better than she had when she rang Marissa. She would have preferred, of course, to get an invitation to the ceremony. If she'd been able to go, she could have confronted Renee directly and put a stop to her meddling. Instead, she was being forced, once again, to work through intermediaries. This time, however, she wasn't going to just sit back and hope they did their jobs. If there was ever a time for her to take action, it was now.

She walked over to her desk and picked up the list she'd printed from the picture she took at school. It was still hard to believe how gullible Debbie had been. After going on about how important it was to keep the names of the kids and their families a secret, she'd left the list sitting right there on her desk while she toddled off to the water cooler. It was almost as if she'd been daring Savannah to take a look. Thank God for smartphones, she thought. If she'd had to write down all those names and phone numbers, she'd have been caught for sure.

She read down the list until she found a name she didn't recognize. Renee had told her once how few of the parents she'd spoken to at Kieran's school, but it would have been awkward if Savannah called someone that *she* knew. Chances were, they wouldn't recognize her voice on the phone even if she had, but it was safer just to put the odds in her favor.

Savannah dialed the number and got into character as she waited for someone to pick up. For her plan to work, she'd need to make sure her voice held the right note of concern. After all, she thought, she was doing this for the kids.

"Hello?"

"Oh, hello, Mrs. Patel. My name is Renee Richardson. We haven't met, but our sons go to school together, and I have some concerns I was hoping to share with you. Have you got a minute?"

CHAPTER 20

Travis Diehl wasn't the kind of guy who got nervous speaking to crowds. As captain of his high school debate team, and later, as community liaison for a major oil company, he'd spoken in front of audiences both hostile and partisan without breaking a sweat. Nevertheless, as he watched the crowd file into the hall that night, he was as jumpy as a cat. Maybe it was the surprise—he hadn't thought his gift to the elementary school was that big a deal—or maybe it was a delayed reaction to the loss of his parents, whose dream it had been to help kids like Hugh, but whatever the reason, the thought of getting up onstage in front of people he'd known since childhood had him sweating bullets.

He hoped Renee would get there soon. She'd sent him a text telling him she was running late but that she'd be there before dinner started, and Travis had replied that he would eat her dessert if she didn't. It was the kind of lighthearted banter that he and Hugh never indulged in; he hadn't realized until it happened how much he'd missed it.

Hank Fielding walked over, wearing a grin that said he

could tell that his old friend was on edge. Travis pointed an accusing finger in his face.

"I blame you for this."

"Oh, quit whining," Hank said. "This town's had it rough the past few years. It does our hearts good to have something to celebrate—even if it is you."

"Maybe, but if you hadn't told everyone in town about the money, I wouldn't be standing here like a bride on her wedding night."

"Well, if that's the way you feel, I'll give you the same advice my grandmother got on her wedding night: Don't worry, dear. It'll all be over soon."

"Oh, you're a big help."

Hank turned and surveyed the room.

"Like it or not, the fact is you deserve this award. Thanks to the Diehl Foundation, there are twelve kids in this community who'll have a chance to make the most of their schooling."

"Only twelve? I thought there were fourteen now."

"There were, but a couple of parents called me with questions this afternoon. Once that's cleared up, I'm sure they'll be back on board." He smiled. "This program is going to be a real testament to you *and* your folks."

"I just wish they were here to see it. They would have been so proud."

Hank laid a hand on his shoulder.

"I believe they are proud," he said. "Proud of you both for what you're doing."

Travis felt a lump rise in his throat. It had been a long time since he was a regular at church, but his faith was still strong, and he knew his folks were in a better place. Still, that didn't keep him from missing them or wishing they were still there in the flesh.

"Hugh's having a trial run at a group home, did I tell you?"

"No."

"I take him down there in the morning and pick him up on Christmas day. Not the best timing, but they're having a party on Christmas Eve, and they encourage the prospective residents to attend. Sort of a trial run to see how they handle the excitement."

"You think he'll be wanting to make it permanent?"

"He seems ready for it. My only real concern is for Max. The group home already has a therapy dog, and there's no room for another."

"What'll you do with him?"

"Oh, I'll keep him," Travis said. "He's good company, and Hugh will want to see him when he comes home to visit. My biggest problem right now is keeping him in the yard. The little booger's wriggled out of every collar I've put on him."

From the corner of his eye, Travis caught a flash of pink hair; Renee was standing just inside the door. He saw her bite her lip as she looked around, searching for a familiar face.

"Listen, I gotta go. Nice talking to you."

"Same here," Hank said. "I'll see you later."

Renee held her breath as she scanned the room, trying to find a woman whose outfit was as casual as hers. The two she'd already seen outside were so dolled up she'd had to summon her courage just to walk past them. Now that she was inside, however, it looked as if her wardrobe might not be too much of a liability. She spotted Debbie Crowder across the room, too, and smiled, relieved to find a familiar face. When it was time to pick a spot for dinner, maybe they could sit together.

Travis was coming toward her, wading through a sea of people who seemed intent upon slowing him down with congratulatory handshakes. When their eyes met, he gave her an apologetic shrug, and Renee shook her head. *It's fine,* she mouthed. After all, he was the one getting an award; he deserved their accolades.

"Sorry I'm late," she said as he joined her. "I had a client who just *had* to have her color done for a party tonight."

"It's fine," he said, giving her a quick hug. "You look great."

Renee felt her cheeks warm.

"Thanks."

"I'm glad you're here," he said. "I could use some moral support."

"You and me both."

He raised an eyebrow.

"Problem?"

"I don't know. It's just"—she looked around—"these are your friends, but I hardly know anyone."

Travis leaned closer.

"Honestly, I hardly know them myself. I've only been back in Bolingbroke a year, and I'd been gone a long time before that."

She shrugged.

"In that case, I guess we'll just have to stay calm and hope they don't bite."

He laughed. "Just keep your hands away from their faces."

The crowd parted as the two women Renee had seen outside walked in. They were both blond—one willowy, the other on the plump side—and both accompanied by men in formal suits who abandoned them at the door to make beelines for the bar. When they spotted Travis, the two of them headed over.

Of course, Renee thought, dreading their arrival.

"Hey, Travis," the plump one said, giving him a couple of air kisses. "How are you, darlin'?"

"Fine, Marissa," he said as the other blonde left dual lipstick smudges on his cheeks. "Hey, Laila."

"Who's your little friend?"

Renee could almost feel herself shrinking under the woman's gaze. Now that they were closer, she recognized her as one of Winona's regulars.

Travis made the introductions.

"This is my friend, Renee Richardson. She agreed to come and watch me make a fool of myself tonight." He winked at Renee. "And these ladies are Marissa Daniels and Laila Campbell. Marissa's husband, Trey, is our new mayor. Laila's husband is in real estate."

They shook hands.

"So pleased to finally meet you," Marissa said. "I've seen you at Winona's several times, but we've never had a chance to be properly introduced."

Renee felt Travis's hand lightly touch her back.

"Can I get you something from the bar?"

She nodded, suddenly sure she wouldn't make it through the evening without a drink.

"A glass of white wine, if they have it."

"Wine it is." He smiled. "Ladies? If you'll excuse me."

Renee watched him walk away, feeling a bit like Daniel in the lions' den.

"So tell me," Laila said. "Who stained your hair that *interesting* shade of pink?"

Marissa gave her a disapproving look.

"It's not a *stain,*" she said. "And I believe Renee does it herself, don't you, dear?"

"Oh . . . you're one of Winona's *girls.* Well, bless your

heart." Laila glanced toward Travis's retreating back. "How on earth did you meet our Mr. Diehl?"

Renee swallowed. This was exactly the reason she'd been reluctant to accept Travis's invitation. Their comparative social standing made them about as compatible as oil and water.

"I met him at my son's school," she said. "And later, he came by the salon for a haircut."

"And it looks *very good*, too," Marissa said. "We both remarked upon it when we came in, didn't we?"

Laila turned ever so slightly away from Renee and began fussing with her own hair.

"I wonder if I should drop by Winona's and see what she can do for me," she said. "Once my own girl's books began filling up, it seemed as if she just stopped trying. They do that, you know."

They do that? Renee was aghast. Was that how Laila thought of her, as one of *them*?

Marissa gave her friend a peevish look.

"Laila dear, I think I see Beau looking for you. Why don't you go and find out what the man wants?"

"Of course." The woman gave Renee a condescending smile. "So nice to have met you."

Marissa waited until the woman was out of earshot before turning back toward Renee.

"I am *so* sorry," she said. "I'm afraid Laila thinks entirely too much of herself."

"No, that's all right," Renee said. "I'm sure she's not the only one who's surprised that Travis invited someone like me here tonight."

"Oh, don't worry about them," Marissa said. "We're here for Travis. This award is a very big deal."

Renee nodded, feeling marginally less awkward. Marissa

was right: It was Travis's night. But maybe, she thought, it would be a turning point for the two of them, as well. They hadn't known each other a long time, but each time they saw one another it seemed as if their connection had deepened. Even better, she wasn't afraid he'd turn out to be another Butch. Any man who'd donate the funds for a program like the one at Bolingbroke Elementary had to be someone who understood the needs of kids like Kieran. And as soon as she had the chance, she was going to tell him how much it meant to her, personally.

Marissa looped her arm through Renee's and gave it a hug.

"I can't tell you how glad Trey and I are that those children are getting the help they need. With the economy like it's been, there are many families in our town who are struggling just to pay for food and housing, much less the expensive medication their children need."

Renee looked at her.

"Medication? I thought the program was about therapy."

"Well . . . I suppose it is, in a way. But you can't expect therapy to work if the children are unmanageable. Once they're properly medicated, it will be much easier to deal with them in the classrooms without disturbing the others. Bless their hearts, most of them just can't control themselves."

Renee slowly withdrew her arm from Marissa's grasp.

"You mean, the point of the program is to *medicate* the children?"

"I should think so. What do you think Travis Diehl has been doing for the last fifteen years?"

She shook her head.

"He told me he worked for an oil company."

"He did."

"But you just said—"

"Oh, you sweet thing. *Most* medicines are based on petroleum." She gave Renee a pitying look. "Did you not know
that?"

"No," Renee said. "I didn't."

She glanced toward the bar and saw Travis talking to Debbie Crowder. How could a man who was so kind and so thoughtful be so unfeeling when it came to kids like Kieran? No wonder
he hadn't wanted to talk about his award, she thought. Renee had
already made her objections known; as soon as Kieran joined the
program, they must have warned him. She'd even asked him
why he'd chosen learning disabled kids for his donation, and
instead of telling her, he'd changed the subject.

And I thought he was just being modest.

She felt dizzy, her mind a riot of conflicting emotions. She
thought she was falling in love with him, but how much did
she really know about Travis Diehl? Who was he, really?

"I'm sorry," she said. "I've got to go."

"But you just got here," Marissa said. "Is there something
wrong? Was it something I said?"

Renee shook her head.

"No. No, it wasn't you. I'm just—" She glanced across the
room. Travis was almost at the head of the line. If she didn't go
now, she'd be stuck there all night, trying to pretend that her
heart wasn't breaking. She had to go. She couldn't bear to talk
to him until she'd had time to think about what Marissa had
said.

I have to get out of here—now.

The line at the bar had been moving at a glacial pace since
Travis arrived. As it inched forward, he'd been monitoring
Renee and hoping she was all right. The people of Boling-

broke were as kind and generous as any group of humans on the planet, but they could be critical of newcomers, and he hoped she wasn't getting the third degree—especially from Marissa. She and Savannah Hays were best friends in high school, but his mother had told him there'd been an estrangement between the two, and he had no idea where things stood. Renee seemed to be getting on with her well enough at the moment, though, and as soon as he got their drinks, he'd go back and rescue her.

He was almost to the head of the line when a thickset man in a dinner jacket came over and slapped Travis on the back.

"Well, if it isn't the Prodigal Son," he said. "How you doing?"

"Couldn't be better, Trey."

Travis had known Trey Daniels since high school, but the two of them had never been close. Back then, most of their interactions had been through the girls they were dating—Trey with Marissa and Travis with Savannah Hays. Trey and Marissa married when they were in college, and Trey had worked at his father's construction company until becoming Bolingbroke's mayor the year before. From the looks of him, though, Trey Daniels hadn't been doing much construction lately. The man had the well-fed look of a lazy house cat.

"I was sorry to hear about your mama," he said. "She and your daddy were good people."

"Thank you," Travis said, freeing himself from a handshake that was too tight to be entirely friendly. "Hugh and I miss them both every day."

Trey frowned, working his mouth like a man who'd found a pit in his olive.

"How is that brother of yours?" he said. "Have you decided what to do with him yet?"

"Hugh's got a job doing computer programming for an outplacement firm in Raleigh. I'm not sure what you think I ought to *do* with him."

"Oh, a job, sure," Trey said, throwing Hank Fielding an annoyed glance as he joined them. "That's good, I suppose. As long as you keep him and that dog of his off the streets."

What was going on? Travis wondered. Had there been a problem with Hugh and Max that he didn't know about? He glanced at Hank, who gave his head a slight shake and looked away. He was about to ask for clarification when Trey held up a hand.

"Gotta go. My foreman just got here," he said. "Congratulations on the award. Maybe next time you'll give your money to a good cause."

As the man strode off, Travis gave Hank an open-mouthed stare.

"What the hell?"

"Don't mind him," Hank said. "You know how Trey is."

"No, to be honest I don't know how Trey is. I didn't ask anyone for this award. If he's got a problem with it, it's not my fault."

Hank raised his hands.

"It's okay, Trav. The man's just letting off steam. He thinks anybody who doesn't do what he'd have done in the same position is just plain wrong."

"Then he can keep it to himself," Travis said, watching Trey blunder his way through the crowd.

"Can I get you something, sir?"

He turned back and saw the bartender looking at him expectantly.

"Two glasses of white wine, please."

Debbie Crowder walked by and gave his sleeve a tug.

"Love your hair. We must have the same great hairstylist."

"Oh," he said. "Did Renee tell you?"

"No, Savannah mentioned it when she stopped by the office on Wednesday. I told her we'd better be careful, or Renee'll be too busy to see us anymore."

"Well, I'm sure she'd appreciate the compliment, if you want to tell her."

"Oh, is she here?"

He pointed toward the door.

"Over yonder, talking to Marissa."

Debbie looked over and frowned.

"Really? I don't see her."

CHAPTER 21

Renee rolled over in bed the next morning and picked up her phone: seven missed calls since last night and two messages, all of them from Travis. She set it back down on the nightstand and stared at the ceiling.

I won't talk to him. I can't—not now. Not until I know what to do.

She'd been thinking all night about what Marissa Daniels had said, trying to decide what exactly had upset her so much that she'd felt she had to leave. It wasn't just that the Diehl Foundation's program was aiming to medicate the children—Renee knew that some kids needed, and were helped by, their meds—it was that everyone involved had lied about it, even when they knew she had objections. Either Hank and Mrs. Dalton had been instructed to lie, or they didn't know they were lying because Travis had lied to them. And if he'd do that, how could she ever trust him to tell the truth to *her?*

The phone buzzed again. Renee glanced at the caller ID and checked the time; Travis was getting an early start. When the buzzing stopped, she threw her legs over the side of the bed and walked into the bathroom. She wasn't going to sit there all day, jumping like a flea whenever she got a call. In two days, Jack and his family would be showing up, and she had plenty of things to keep herself busy until then. If she left her phone at home, she might even have an hour or two without being reminded of Travis Diehl.

She took a shower and got ready to go before heading down the hall to eat breakfast. Her father was sitting at the kitchen table with a cup of coffee when she walked in.

"Eggs and sausage on the stove if you want it."

"No thanks."

She opened the refrigerator and took out the milk, noting the level on the side.

"How was the awards show?" he said. "Sounded like you came back early."

"My last client ran late. I was too tired to stay for the whole thing."

"Mmm."

She poured herself a bowl of Cheerios and ate it standing up.

"I'm heading down to the store after breakfast. We're almost out of milk, and we'll need stuff for lunches. I still haven't gotten a turkey for Christmas dinner, either, and I know there are some things that Megan feeds the girls that we don't have on hand."

Wendell snorted.

"When I was a kid, you ate what you were served at someone else's house."

"Yes, but that was back when dirt was young," she said. "Besides, the last thing I want to do is alienate my sister-in-law the second she walks through the door. I'm hoping this visit will be a chance to start over."

Renee gave him a significant look, the unspoken message being that she did not want a repeat of the outburst that had caused their families' thirteen-month estrangement, but her father was refusing to look at her. She decided not to push it. Whether or not he'd admit it, Wendell knew he'd been in the wrong. She finished the cereal and set her bowl in the sink.

"Well, I'm off," Renee said. "I'll see you in a couple of hours."

She put on her coat, grabbed her purse, and headed out the door.

Wendell watched the door close behind her, wondering what was going on. Renee had been tickled pink when Diehl asked her to that banquet, and now she was acting as if it had been nothing special. It was all he could do not to call up the SOB and demand to know what he'd done. He would have, too, if she hadn't reminded him of that argument with Jack. As hard as it was for him to admit, his son hadn't been entirely in the wrong that time, and Wendell had been sufficiently chastened to wait until he knew more about Diehl before going off like that again.

Which was why he was going to have a talk with Maggie McRay.

He heard a door open and footsteps coming down the hall. A sleepy-eyed Kieran walked in and sat down at the table.

"Morning, Grandpa."

"Hey, bud. You ready for some breakfast?"

"Uh-huh," the boy said, rubbing the sleep from his eyes.

Wendell set the crossword aside and served up the scrambled eggs and sausage his daughter had ignored.

"Your mother's out shopping," he said, setting the plate down, "and I'm going to have to leave here in a minute. Will you be okay with just your sister watching you?"

Kieran made a face.

"Where's Dyl?"

"Gone to the gym. He thinks he's Charlie Atlas."

"Who?"

"Never mind. Just eat your breakfast."

Kieran had gotten himself dressed by the time Wendell was ready to go. The kid had put his dishes in the dishwasher, too, and if the smell of peppermint was any indication, he'd taken a stab at brushing his teeth.

"Can I go for a walk while you're gone?"

"It's cold outside."

"Not that cold," Kieran said. "And Mrs. Dalton says kids need more exercise."

"Fine," Wendell said. "Tell your sister where you're going, and don't forget your gloves. I won't be gone long."

Kieran hugged him.

"Thank you, Grandpa."

"Save it," Wendell said, peeling the kid off his leg. "I already said yes, didn't I?"

Clint's was closed on Sundays, which meant that Wendell had to drive over to Maggie's house to talk to her. He would have preferred to do it at the store. The thought of being there alone, just the two of them, made him feel awkward. Since his wife's death, Wendell had felt uneasy being around women his own age. It sometimes seemed as if they were all on the make: batting their eyes or asking him over for tea—once, he'd been flat-out propositioned! That's why he'd never taken the ribbing from the boys seriously. If Maggie McRay had had any interest in him, he thought, he'd have known it.

Besides, when you came right down to it, why did any woman need a man? Financial security? Maggie owned her own business. Clever conversation? She talked to customers all day long. Prowess in the boudoir? At his age, things could be hit or miss. No, Wendell thought, it was just easier all around to think of Maggie as one of the guys.

Her house was all decked out for Christmas: a crèche in the front yard, a string of lights—unlit at the moment—along the eaves, and a pinecone wreath with a tartan bow on the front door. Wendell sat in his car, staring at the holiday display, and thought about what, exactly, he would say when he went inside.

How would she react when he asked her about Travis Diehl? Would she understand that Wendell meant well, that he was only trying to find out what sort of man the guy was so that he could protect his baby girl? Or would she accuse him of being a busybody and toss him out? Bolingbroke was a small town, and he was running out of informants. He knew that if he messed this up and said the wrong thing, he might not get another chance. The thought was making his palms sweat.

Maggie must have been working on the house when he rang the bell. She was wearing a man's coverall with the legs and arms rolled up to fit her smaller frame and a bandanna over her hair. There was a smudge of grease on her cheek.

"Oh, it's you," she said, her green eyes narrowing. "What do you want?"

Wendell swallowed and cursed his bad luck. Of all the days for her to be in a bad mood.

"I was hoping we could talk," he said.

"What about?"

"I have a question I need to ask you."

"Fine," she said. "Ask me tomorrow. Store's open at seven."

As the door began to close, Wendell panicked.

"I can't! It's, it's . . . *personal.*"

Maggie looked startled.

"It is?" she said, touching her hair.

He nodded.

"May I come in . . . please?"

"Oh! Of course," she said, stepping back from the door.

Wendell followed her into the living room, surprised at what a homey place it was. Not too girly, but fancier than he would have expected. There was a sofa on the left under the front window and a recliner on the right with a rocking chair beside it. Wendell chose the sofa. He figured he was shaky enough without sitting on something that might move underneath him.

"I wish you'd called me before you came over," Maggie said, still tugging at her bandanna. "I'm not really dressed for company."

"It's all right," he said. "This won't take long."

"So," she said. "What's on your mind?"

Wendell took a deep breath and tried to shake the feeling that the walls were closing in as he stared into Maggie's green eyes. He'd been rehearsing what to say all morning, but now that they were actually face-to-face, he wasn't sure how to begin.

He should leave, he told himself. Forget the whole thing. Maggie had already warned him about trying to play matchmaker for Renee, and she'd be stingy with information if she thought he was meddling. But darn it, Mack had said that if anyone in town could tell him about Travis Diehl, it was her. This might just be his last, best chance.

He gave her what he hoped was an ingratiating smile.

"I'm not sure how to say this. I'm afraid you'll think I'm being a foolish old man."

"Why, Wendell. I could never think of you as foolish. Or old," she added quickly.

Wendell frowned. Maggie's face looked flushed. Was she ill? "You okay?"

"Of course. Why do you ask?"

He shrugged. "No reason, I guess."

Perhaps it was a personal problem, he thought. The same thing that had made her cranky when she opened the door. Whatever it was, she obviously didn't want to discuss it, which was fine with him. The sooner he got to the point, the sooner he could get out of there.

"So," she prompted. "You had something you wanted to ask . . . ?"

"Right."

Ease into the subject, he thought. Try to be subtle.

"I suppose you meet a lot of people around town. Men, especially."

"A fair number, yes," she said.

"Right. That's right," he said, warming to the subject. "So, if you were to meet a man—someone new, perhaps—you'd just naturally be curious about him, wouldn't you?"

"I suppose."

"And you'd probably find that you'd developed some sort of feeling about him."

Her cheeks dimpled. "I certainly would."

"And because of that, you might be able to sense whether or not he was a good guy. Someone you could trust."

"Uh-huh."

Wendell willed himself to relax. He was almost there and

so far Maggie hadn't accused him of being a meddling so-and-so. This was going even better than he'd imagined.

"So," he said, "if someone were to ask you what you thought of that man, you could probably tell them, right?"

"Tell who what?"

"Whether or not the man was honorable. Someone they could trust."

Maggie seemed perplexed.

"You lost me."

Wendell shook his head in frustration. He'd made it plain enough. Why did she have to be so thick? Well, fine, he thought. He didn't have the whole goddamn day. Time to just lay it out there.

"Renee's in a tizzy over some character named Travis Diehl, and Mack said you could give me the lowdown on him."

The green eyes flashed.

"Goddammit, you're doing it again, aren't you? Trying to set your poor daughter up with this man. Why don't you just leave her alone?"

"No, I'm not," Wendell said, backpedaling desperately. "I haven't even met the man. I just want to find out more about him before Renee goes off and gets her heart broken."

Maggie closed her eyes for a moment, shaking her head.

"Fine. What do you want to know?"

That's more like it.

"Well, first off: Is he single?"

She opened her eyes and sighed heavily.

"His Aunt Winn told me after the funeral that he'd married a gal in Texas, but it didn't work out. As far as I know, they're divorced."

"What else?"

She looked at him sharply.

"What do you mean, 'What else?' I'm not the goddamn *FBI.*"

"Come on, Maggie," he wheedled. "Help me out. What else can you tell me about the man?"

She folded her arms.

"He played football down at the high school; seemed like a good kid: good grades, never got into any serious trouble that I knew of. Got a scholarship to Princeton or Yale—one of those. His folks belonged to the Methodist church, but I don't know if he does. The father was killed by a drunk driver a little over a year ago, and his mother passed in June. He's got a younger brother name of Hugh who's a little off."

"What do you mean, 'off'?"

She shook her head.

"Not sure. If you met him, you'd know. The family never discussed it and I didn't ask."

Wendell nodded. This was all good information. Nevertheless, the fact that Diehl was divorced was bothersome. If he was such a great catch, why had his wife turned him loose?

"So, you've met him, right?"

"Many times."

"How does he seem to you?"

Her mouth was pinched.

"What do you mean, how does he seem?" she snapped.

"I mean, if you were a woman, would he be someone you'd be interested in?"

Maggie's face reddened.

"If I were a woman? *If?*"

She got up and marched to the door.

"Get out!" she said, throwing it open.

"What?"

"You heard me."

He stood up.

"Now, don't get all huffy, dammit. All I wanted was—"

"Exactly," she said, pointing at him. "That's *all* you wanted. Now that you've got what you wanted, *git!*"

Wendell stepped outside and flinched as the door slammed behind him. What on earth had gotten into her?

CHAPTER 22

The cold air made Kieran's eyes water as he hurried down the street. Grandpa said he wouldn't be gone long, and the boy knew he'd come looking for him if he wasn't home when he got back. He hunched his shoulders and glanced furtively back at the house. In spite of the hat, gloves, and heavy jacket, his teeth were beginning to chatter, but Kieran wasn't worried about the cold. He'd be plenty warm once he got to the fort.

It had turned out even better than the one on YouTube. The walls were almost as high as Kieran's belt, and the secret entrance was so good that if you didn't know where the fort was, you could barely see it. If Cody Daniels ever came looking for him, he'd probably walk right by without even noticing.

Kieran slipped a hand into his pocket and patted the slice of meat loaf he'd brought with him, feeling the gravy squish a little in its plastic bag. He hoped that Rex would like it. With nothing to eat but a peanut butter sandwich, he thought, the dog must be starving.

Unless Rex already has an owner.

He pulled his coat tighter around himself and shook his

head. Rex couldn't have an owner, he thought, otherwise why would he be in the woods? And if he belonged to someone, wouldn't he be wearing a collar? As Kieran wrestled with the unwelcome notion that the dog he loved was someone else's, he felt a tic begin to tug at his cheek. Everything had been so good since he found Rex. He didn't need so much time to get his room right, and if he started to count steps, just picturing Rex's calm gaze helped him to stop. He didn't worry so much about Cody Daniels anymore, either, now that he had a friend to protect him. If things went back to the way they were before, it would be unthinkable. Therefore, he wouldn't think about it.

At the end of the block, Kieran turned left and felt the tension in his shoulders begin to ease. He was out of sight of the house now, and the edge of the woods was only half a block away. The thought that he might see the dog again gave him a warm feeling inside. Somehow, he was sure that this was the day that Rex would follow him home. They wouldn't have to meet in the woods anymore, he thought, and the two of them could spend as much time together as they wanted. And Kieran would be really responsible, too. He'd feed Rex and clean up after him and brush him without anyone ever having to ask.

Not that he'd be selfish about it; the rest of the family could do stuff with Rex, too. Mom could pet him, and Dylan could throw balls for him to fetch, and McKenna could feed him scraps from the table. At night, the dog would sleep in his room, but while Kieran was at school, he could keep Grandpa company and protect the house. If only Rex would trust him and come out of the woods, he thought as he left the pavement, life would be just about perfect.

Kieran knew something was wrong as soon as he stepped

into the woods. The brush on either side of the trail had been trampled, and a broken sapling lay on the ground, knifelike pieces of green wood protruding from its stump. The boy swallowed, remembering his grandfather's warning about critters in the woods. A fox or coyote couldn't do this kind of damage, he thought, but a bear could. As he peered into the dimly lit interior, he wondered if something large and dangerous was looking back.

He took a deep breath and, remembering his scout training, began searching the area, looking for anything that might give him a clue as to what had happened. It didn't take long. A dozen yards ahead, a glimpse of red and yellow caught his eye. Kieran knew what it was before he'd even picked it up. He shook off the muddy footprints that had nearly buried it.

A potato chip bag.

The boy shivered as a different kind of chill gripped him. Someone had been there! Someone who didn't know or care what the woods meant to Kieran and Rex had stomped around and treated their sanctuary like a garbage dump. His heart skipped. What if they'd found the fort? Though it hurt his pride to admit it, Kieran knew the hideout wasn't invisible, and the thought that someone might have destroyed all the hard work that he and Rex had done made him ill.

He'd just taken a step, determined to see what, if anything, had happened to the fort, when he heard a noise off to his right: a wild thrashing of brush followed by a heartrending whimper of agony—the sound of an animal caught in a snare. He narrowed his eyes and peered into the gloom. Whatever it was, it was too far away for him to see.

Kieran turned toward the sound and quickened his pace. Remembering how the dog had skirted the poison ivy that first day, he knew it couldn't be Rex—Rex was too smart to let himself get caught in a snare. Still, he had to be sure. If it wasn't Rex, it might still be some other dog—or even a cat—that had been caught. He couldn't just turn his back and walk away if someone's pet was in trouble.

He heard the sound again—louder this time, but still too far away for him to see where it was coming from. Kieran told himself to stay calm and not to panic, but as he stepped off the trail, a sense of foreboding crept over him. Seconds later, he was crashing heedlessly through the undergrowth, the sound of his own mad scramble making it impossible to tell which way the sound was coming from. The boy paused, trying not to breathe, and listened. The woods were silent. The noise—whatever it was—had stopped.

Then he heard a muffled growl—closer this time—followed by the sound of more desperate thrashing. Kieran felt as if he'd been punched in the gut. There was no mistaking what it was this time.

"Rex!" he screamed, his young voice breaking. "Rex, where are you?"

Tears blurred his vision as he stumbled toward the sound. Kieran saw a patch of dappled light and movement up ahead: some sort of hairy man doing a strange dance. He wiped his eyes on his sleeve and looked again, trying to make sense of what he'd seen. Then the picture came into focus and Kieran gasped. It was Rex, dangling from a rope around his neck. His back paws, barely touching the ground, were the only thing keeping him alive. From the torn foliage and claw marks on the ground, Kieran could tell that the dog had been fighting the noose, struggling to break free, and from the animal's staggering, exhausted movements, he knew it had been a long time.

He tore off his gloves and threw them on the ground.

"It's okay, Rex," he said, reaching for the folding knife in his pocket. "I'll get you out of there, just hold on."

He stepped forward warily. Kieran didn't think that Rex would hurt him on purpose, but an injured animal was dangerous. If the dog bit or clawed him, they'd both be in trouble. As he opened the knife, he swallowed hard, trying to make his voice sound as calm as possible.

The dog began to prance on tiptoe, its yellow eyes showing white along the edges as they rolled in Kieran's direction.

"Shh, it's all right," the boy said. "Try to hold still."

He did a quick survey of the snare, trying to find the best way to cut the dog loose. The rope had been tied to a sapling that someone had bent over the trail and held down with a stake just large enough to keep it from snapping back up until an animal disturbed it. Kieran had seen snares like that in his Boy Scout Handbook, but they were for catching smaller animals, not something as large and heavy as a dog this size. Why hadn't Rex been able to break the sapling and get free?

Then Kieran saw the sapling, broken and lying on the ground nearby. So, it hadn't held. Then why was Rex still caught? Following the rope higher, the boy found his answer. When the sapling had sprung back, Rex must have leapt up, leaving enough slack in the rope for it to catch on the branch of a sturdier, mature tree—the branch from which it now dangled. As Kieran's gaze traveled from the branch down toward Rex, he gasped.

He was wearing a collar.

The sight of the leather strip around the dog's neck staggered him. After all this time, he thought, why had someone put a collar on him? Was it the person who set the snare, or had Rex belonged to someone else all along? In that instant,

Kieran felt as if his dreams had died. Nevertheless, he thought, he couldn't let Rex die with them.

In spite of its exhaustion, the dog was continuing to struggle, and Kieran knew he'd never be able to get close enough to cut the rope near the noose. He'd have to shimmy up the tree and cut it there. Taking a moment to search the trunk for likely hand and footholds, he tucked the knife back into his pocket and started up.

It didn't take long. Kieran's knife was sharp, and Rex's struggles had frayed the rope to half its original thickness. A few minutes of determined sawing and the dog was free. As the rope fell, Rex collapsed in a heap on the ground. Kieran shimmied back down the trunk and hurried over to take a look.

The hair around the dog's neck had been worn away, and the nails on its back paws were torn and shredded from hours spent scuffling on the ground, trying to stay upright. There was blood on the collar, but Kieran couldn't see much more than that. As he came closer, the dog opened its eyes and let out a piteous moan. The thought of what might have happened if he hadn't gotten there in time sent chills through Kieran's body.

"It's okay," he said. "You're free now."

He reached forward tentatively and set a hand on the dog's back, patting it gently. The animal closed its eyes and seemed to sigh in thanks. Kieran glared hatefully at the collar. If it hadn't been for that, Rex might have gotten himself free.

"I'll bet that thing hurts, huh?" he said, moving his hand closer to the dog's neck. "Would you like me to take it off?"

Kieran's fingers shook as he touched the collar, waiting to see what the dog would do. When it didn't try to bite him or cry out in pain, he started gently pushing the leather through the buckle.

"Here," he said. "Let's just see what your neck looks like without it."

As the collar opened, Kieran grimaced. The skin on Rex's neck was raw and bloody; not something that would heal on its own. He'd have to get him to a vet or the wound might become infected. Kieran folded the collar, stuffed it into his pocket, and looked around. He had to get Rex out of there, but how?

He stepped back and patted his thighs encouragingly, hoping Rex would be able to stand up and walk out on his own, but the dog didn't move. Kieran even took the meat loaf out of his pocket and waved it in front of his nose, hoping to entice him onto his feet, but the animal refused. The boy began to despair. Rex was too big for him to carry, and he had no way of caring for it by himself. He had to get help.

He bent down and gave the dog a solemn look.

"You stay here, boy," he said. "I'll be right back."

CHAPTER 23

It was the coldest December Bolingbroke had seen for half a century. Roads were slick, icicles hung from the rooflines, and forecasters on the television were giddily predicting snow. As Travis drove his brother to Charlotte that morning, though, he wasn't thinking about the prospects for a white Christmas. He was thinking about Renee.

Why had she run off without telling him why she had to leave or even good-bye? And more importantly, why wouldn't she answer his calls? If there'd been some kind of emergency, surely she would have said so, but Marissa told him that Renee had gotten no call and received no message from anyone.

"One minute, we were just chatting like old pals," she said. *"Then she looked over at where you and Hank were talking at the bar, and she just . . . bolted."*

Travis had left messages on her phone, hoping she'd return or at the very least let him know she was okay, but as the evening wore on, he gave up trying and assumed that once things were settled, she'd let him know what had happened.

Instead, she'd left him in the dark, and now the concern he'd felt was turning to anger.

What the hell was going on?

It didn't help that this was the day he had to drive Hugh to the group home. His brother had been in a state since he woke up, pacing the floor and mumbling to himself. Travis had anticipated that there'd be a certain amount of anxiety surrounding this visit, so he wasn't really surprised. What he hadn't counted on was that Max would choose this morning to run away. Hugh had let him out to do his business when they first got up, but when it was time to leave, the dog was no longer in the yard.

At least he has a collar on, Travis thought. If anyone finds him, they'll know who to call.

Hugh was sitting in the passenger's seat with his shoulders hunched and his head bowed, staring at his fingers.

"You okay?"

Hugh shrugged.

"I'm sorry I let Max out."

Travis shook his head.

"I already told you: Max's running off had nothing to do with you. If you hadn't let him out of the house, I would have. It's what we always do in the morning, right?"

Hugh nodded and looked out the window.

"Don't worry," Travis said. "Chances are, Max will be at the house when I get back. Just go and have a good time like we talked about."

Hugh chewed his thumbnail.

"You're not mad?"

"No. I'm not mad. I'm just a little upset about last night. A friend of mine had to leave early, and I haven't heard from her, so I'm a little worried."

"Trav?"

"Yeah?"

"Can we stop at Starbuck's? The sign said there's one at the next exit."

Travis stifled a yawn, grateful for Hugh's keen eyesight. After the night he'd had and with ice on the roadways, he needed to be wide awake if he was going to make it to Charlotte and home again safely.

"Good idea," he said. "I could use one myself."

Hugh stayed in the car while Travis went in and ordered. Standing at the counter, waiting for his name to be called, brought back memories of having coffee with Renee. She'd just cut his hair, and he'd been congratulating himself for taking her to Mimesis. As enjoyable as it had been, talking with her at the school, it wasn't until she was called away that he realized just how much he'd liked *her*. So much so that he'd had a hard time concentrating as he sat in Hank's office afterward. His mind kept drifting back to Renee and regretting that she'd left without his getting her number. Since then, there hadn't been a day that she wasn't on his mind, and he was certain she felt the same way about him. That's why her odd behavior was so maddening. What had changed?

Whatever it was, he thought, there'd better be a good reason for it.

Max was still missing when Travis arrived home. He checked with the neighbors on either side, but they hadn't seen him, nor had the woman who lived in the house behind his property. He slipped on a pair of boots and his parka and started walking the area, calling the dog's name and peering into the places a dog might hide. An hour later, he was back home, calling the vets in the area to see if anyone had brought in an injured dog. No luck there, either.

Travis walked the perimeter of his property, checking to see where Max had gotten out and to find out if he had, once again, left his collar behind. He found the spot under the fence where the dog had dug his way out, but at least there was no collar. If the worst happened and Max had been badly injured or—God forbid—killed, there would at least be some way to notify him.

A car pulled up to his next door neighbor's house as Travis walked by. As soon as it stopped, the doors flew open and a family of five tumbled out, the three children scrambling toward the front door where their grandparents waited with open arms. Watching the scene unfold, he felt his throat constrict. As much of a relief as it would be to have Hugh out of his hair for a while, the thought of being alone so close to Christmas was depressing.

He wondered what Emmy was doing. Had she found someone else, or was she—like he was—alone? He should call, he thought, then shook his head. Their last conversation had ended in a fight, and things had been said on both sides that he knew he regretted, even if she didn't. The truth was, he knew the two of them were better apart and that there were sound reasons why things hadn't worked out, but there was something about being by himself at Christmastime that made him feel almost homesick. Without Emmy, without his parents or even Hugh, he felt emotionally adrift in a vast sea of indifferent humanity.

Travis felt his phone vibrate, and his heart leaped. Finally, he thought, thrusting a hand into his pocket. Whatever Renee's excuse was, he'd already forgiven her.

He glanced at the caller ID, and his face fell.

"Hey, Savannah."

"Hey, Trav. How you doing?"

"Fine," he said, scanning the area. "Just out looking for Max. Stupid dog ran off this morning, and I can't find him."

"Oh, dear. Anything I can do to help?"

"No thank you, but I appreciate the offer."

He turned up the driveway toward his house, the anticipation of the warmth inside making the outside feel all the colder.

"So," he said, "what's up?"

Savannah sighed dramatically. A sure sign that she was feeling sorry for herself.

"Have you got any plans for Christmas Eve?"

"Not at the moment, why?"

"Neither do I, and it's making me feel awfully blue. If you don't get a better offer, would you mind if I came over there and spent it with you? I just don't think I can face it alone."

If you don't get a better offer?

Travis could certainly identify with the way she was feeling. Hadn't he just been dreading Tuesday night? Given his parents' deaths and Hugh's absence, his own mood was understandable, but it wasn't like Savannah to be so unsure of herself. If his mother was right, though, and she and Marissa had had a falling-out, then maybe there were others keeping their distance as well. As hard as it was to believe, he thought, Savannah Hays might just be as lonely as he was. For the first time in his life, he found that he actually pitied her.

"Of course," he said. "I'll see you then."

CHAPTER 24

"Hurry, Grandpa, hurry!"

Kieran capered like a spooked horse as he led his grandfather toward the place where he'd left the dog. Wendell grumbled and pushed another broken branch out of his way. The boy had been hysterical when he came home, crying and pointing as he jabbered on about an injured dog in the woods. *The woods, for God's sake!* He'd barely had time to put his coat back on and grab his car keys before the boy pulled him out the front door. For now, he'd just do what Kieran wanted, but once this crisis was over, the two of them were going to have some very strong words.

"Slow down, will you?" Wendell gasped.

As he struggled forward, he searched the ground in front of him for trip hazards and poison ivy. The weak December sunlight was quickly fading, and the heat radiating from his face had fogged up his glasses.

"Where the hell is it?" he said. "I can't see a goddamn thing in here."

"He's up there, see?" Kieran said, pointing. "Where it's lighter."

Wendell shook his head and pushed on.

Of all the damned fool things . . .

Another few yards and they were at the edge of a clearing, in the middle of which lay what looked to be a moth-eaten grey rug—the shaggy kind that was popular back in the sixties. Then Kieran ran up to the rug and it moved: A large, mis-shapen head rose up from one end and an enormous whip of a tail at the other. Wendell lunged forward, his heart pounding.

"Stop! Don't let it bite you!"

The boy shook his head.

"No, Grandpa. Rex and I are friends, see?"

Kieran squatted down and started patting the giant head as the large tail thumped the ground. Wendell stopped and squinted at the foggy scene.

"Well, I'll be damned."

He took off his glasses and wiped the lenses clean, then stepped up for a closer look. The dog turned its head and regarded him with solemn yellow eyes.

"What are we going to do?" Kieran said.

Wendell surveyed the area—the hairless stripe around the dog's neck, the bloody noose, a broken sapling tied to a severed rope, the destruction left by an animal desperate to get free—and despaired. The animal had been fighting for its life, probably for hours. There was no way it could walk out of there on its own, and he was reluctant to try and carry an animal that might turn on him. No, he thought. Better to call Animal Control. If the dog survived the night, they could pick it up in the morning. If not, then they'd have to be content to let Nature take its course. It would be a hard lesson for Kieran to learn, but it wouldn't be the last in this life.

The dog had settled its head back on the ground, content to let Kieran pet it, and Wendell grimaced. It wasn't going to be easy convincing the boy to leave it behind. It seemed very gentle for such a large animal, and surprisingly calm, given its circumstances. It seemed to have formed some sort of bond with Kieran, too; something he wouldn't have thought possible, given the boy's odd behaviors.

Wendell frowned. *What odd behaviors?*

Thinking back, he realized that Kieran hadn't counted a single step since they'd left the house, nor had Wendell seen any tics or heard any unusual sounds from the boy. This, in spite of his obvious agitation. And now, there he was, sitting on the cold ground, his pants crumpled and soiled, as calm and accepting of the situation as the dog was. Wendell felt tears sting his eyes as a sudden determination came over him. Injured or not, there was something about this dog that had freed his grandson—at least temporarily—from the prison of his disorder. An animal who could do that deserved his gratitude—and his help.

He took a deep breath. Finding a veterinarian on a Sunday would be impossible, and the family couldn't afford the emergency clinic's fee. His friend Ted Coburn, however, was a retired vet, and Wendell thought he might be willing to take a look. Even if he couldn't treat the dog himself, perhaps he could let them know how badly it was injured. He just had to figure out a way to get the animal back to his car without getting either his grandson or himself hurt.

Wendell stepped back and pursed his lips, trying to estimate the animal's weight. If it had been a beefier breed, like a Rottweiler, it would have been too heavy for him to carry, but this one was mostly fur, its body long and lean. Wendell was no weightlifter, but he had no problem carrying bags of manure through the yard for his vegetable garden. If Kieran could cradle the dog's head and shoulders, he figured the two of them could grapple the thing out to the car and drive it over to Ted's place.

"Come on, bud," he said. "Let's see if we can get this guy out of here."

If someone had shown up with a strange dog at his door, Wendell thought, he'd have been speechless. Ted Coburn, however, acted like it was an everyday occurrence. When Kieran told him where he'd found the dog and what had happened to it, Ted had quickly sized up the situation and brought out a scaled-down gurney that he kept in his garage for just such occasions.

"I still see a couple of old clients on the side," he confided, by way of explanation.

The three of them wheeled the dog inside, through the house, and onto a sunny back porch where Ted's wife sat knitting in front of a space heater. It wasn't until Ted dragged a lamp closer to the gurney and turned it on that she even bothered to look up.

"This is Wendell and his grandson, Molly. They found a dog half-hung in the woods."

Molly smiled pleasantly.

"Would you gentlemen like some sweet tea?"

Kieran shook his head.

"No, ma'am."

"I'm good, thanks," Wendell said.

"Very well." Molly smiled and went back to her knitting.

Ted was examining the dog's neck.

"These abrasions look bad," he said, "but they're not really serious. I can give you some salve that should clear them up.

What I don't know is, what kind of damage may have been done to the structures below the skin. He can move his limbs, so it's probably a safe bet that the spine is intact, but hanging there would have put a good deal of stress on the spinal nerves. He may be experiencing weakness or tingling in his legs or other parts of his body; I just don't know."

Kieran's face was the picture of despair.

"You mean Rex might be paralyzed?"

The man's face softened.

"I don't think it's likely, son. Rex is moving his tail and legs, even if he's not ready yet to stand. With a little rest and some anti-inflammatory medicine, your dog will be back on his feet in a day or two."

Kieran gave the man a guilty look.

"He's not my dog," he murmured.

"Kieran found him when he was playing in the woods," Wendell added. "He just thinks he looks like a Rex."

Ted gave the dog an appraising look.

"You're right; he does look like a Rex. Do you know who the owner is?"

"No idea." Wendell looked at Kieran. "He wasn't wearing a collar when you found him, was he?"

Kieran swallowed, feeling the edge of the dog's collar pressing against thigh, and shook his head.

"Well, that's not unusual," the vet said. "Lots of people around here don't bother, especially if they let their dogs roam. It's too easy for an animal to get it caught on something. Chances are he's been chipped, but I haven't got a reader here at the house. Most vets have one in their office, but with Christmas this week, a lot will be taking time off. If you don't find Rex's owner by the time he's back on his feet, you can take him down to the Humane Society to get the chip read."

"We'll do that," Wendell said.

"Meantime, I'll call around and see if anyone I know has a patient reported missing."

He opened a wooden cabinet behind him and took out a small silver tube.

"Here's some ointment for the neck," Ted told him. "The instructions are on the label. And I'll trim up those back claws before you leave."

Molly looked up from her knitting.

"The dog is welcome to stay with us," she said. "Ted and I have an empty kennel out back."

"That's right," the vet said. "We've got the room, and it'd be no trouble."

Kieran gave his grandfather a panicked, pleading look.

"No, that's okay," Wendell said. "I think we'll just take him home with us."

Ted cocked an eyebrow.

"You sure your daughter will be okay with that?"

"Oh, sure. Renee won't mind at all."

Renee lugged the last of her groceries up the front walkway and shouldered the door open. The stores had been crowded with harried shoppers that day, all of them trying to do their Christmas shopping before time ran out, and she'd been shoved and jostled more than once as she'd made her way down the aisles. Nevertheless, it had been a relief to get away from the incessant calls and messages from Travis Diehl, and as she set her bags down on the counter, she felt almost, *almost* relaxed. Getting away from the house had been the right thing to do.

As she set the turkey in the refrigerator, Renee heard muffled voices downstairs. She'd noticed when she drove up that

Wendell's car had moved, the engine ticking as it cooled, and she suspected he and the kids had been out shopping for presents. No doubt, another bottle of eau de cologne would be under the tree this year.

Kieran came charging up the stairs, his footsteps reverberating throughout the house.

"Mom! Mom!"

He ran into the kitchen, his hair mussed and his clothes shedding a potpourri of dirt and leaves. Renee stared in horror at the muddy footprints on her clean floor.

"Take your shoes off! Look at the mess you're making."

"But, Mom! You have to come and see."

"In a minute," she said. "First, the shoes."

As she turned him around, Renee got a closer look at his outfit.

"What have you gotten into? Is that tree sap?"

Kieran wriggled from her grasp and ran for the front door as Renee stared aghast at the damage to her house. She'd just finished mopping that floor. Now she'd have to do it again before Jack's family got there.

She heard the *thump-thump* of Kieran's shoes as they hit the tile entryway, then the muffled sound of a coat being shed. In seconds, he was back.

"Can you come now, *please?*"

"Okay, all right," she said. "Keep your shirt on."

She checked the bags to make sure there was nothing more that needed to be refrigerated or frozen.

"What is it you want me to see?"

He shook his head.

"I can't tell you. It's a surprise."

Renee gave her son a skeptical look and followed him down to Wendell's apartment, trying not to think about the trail of dirty footprints on her just-cleaned carpet. Cleaning a house with children in it, she thought, was like drinking water from a sieve.

Wendell was standing in the middle of the room wearing an expression that was somewhere between self-satisfied and apologetic, a look that said: I'm sorry, but I'm not *really* sorry. Renee was about to ask what had happened when her father stepped aside and pointed toward the couch.

"I can explain."

At first, all she saw was a grey shape against the brown leather. Then the shape moved and two yellow disks appeared. Renee took a sharp breath and stepped back.

"What is it?"

"It's a *dog!*" Kieran said, tugging her arm. "He got caught in a trap and I found him but I couldn't pick him up so I got Grandpa and we took him to Doctor Ted's house to get medicine for him and his wife said the dog could stay there but Grandpa told her you wouldn't mind so we brought him *home.*"

Renee looked at her father.

"Oh, he did, did he?"

Wendell shrugged.

"Molly was just being polite."

She closed her eyes and lifted her face heavenward. Their guests would be arriving in less than forty-eight hours, and she still had to finish cleaning, put the tree up, get it decorated, *and* do a full day's work at the salon. The last thing she needed was a strange animal in her house.

Lord, give me strength.

"Come on," Kieran said, urging her forward. "He won't hurt you. He didn't even try to bite me when I cut him down from the tree."

Renee stared.

"What tree? *Where were you?*"

The boy shrank back.

"I–In the woods," he said, darting a glance at his grandfather.

Wendell cleared his throat.

"We've already discussed this," he said. "Kieran knows he shouldn't have gone in there alone, but when he heard the dog and realized it was in trouble, he knew there might not be time to get a grown-up to help."

He gave Kieran an encouraging nod.

"Isn't that right?"

"Yeah," the boy said. "Uh-huh. That's what I did."

Renee's eyes narrowed. She knew when she was being played, but she also knew that if Kieran had actually saved this animal's life, it was something to be praised, not censured. Her youngest had always had the kindest heart of her three children, and she wasn't about to punish him for following it. Once this crisis was over, they could have another talk about the woods.

She took a step closer to the couch and saw the dog's yellow eyes widen in apprehension.

"What happened to its neck?"

"It got hurt when he tried to get out of the trap," Kieran said.

Renee looked at her father.

"Basic peg snare," Wendell said quietly. "The rope caught on a higher branch and pretty much hung him. I'm surprised he made it."

She grimaced. "Poor guy."

Renee felt her resistance weakening. The poor dog looked pitiful lying there. She knew that if she had been been the one to find him, she'd have done the same thing. All they could do now was to keep the animal comfortable until its owner showed up.

"Have you contacted its owner?"

Her father shook his head.

"He wasn't wearing a collar, but Ted's certain he's been chipped. He's going to ask around and see if anyone's heard of a missing dog. If the owner doesn't turn up, we can take him down to the Humane Society after Christmas and have them read it."

"*After* Christmas?" she said.

"It's only three days."

"Three and a half. We can't keep this thing until *then*."

Wendell's face darkened.

"Why the hell not?"

Renee struck her forehead in exasperation.

"Dad, do you even *hear* yourself? Jack and Megan will be here *tomorrow night*. We can't have a dog running around all over the house."

"He's not *running around*," Wendell countered. "Look at him; he can't even walk."

"That's not the point," she said through gritted teeth. "He's going to scare the girls."

"Not if they take after their mother, he won't. Nothing scares that—"

"*Dad!*"

Kieran, who'd been watching their exchange with increasing alarm, began to cry.

"Please, Mom. I'll take care of him, I *promise!*"

Renee closed her eyes again and massaged her temples, trying to stave off a headache. After last night, there just wasn't enough fight in her to win a battle against the two of them. Chances were, the dog's owner would claim it before too long, and in the meantime she'd just have to find a way to keep it in

Wendell's apartment. There was an old baby gate in the attic. If she put it across the top of the stairs, it would keep the dog away from the girls until she could find its owner and send it back where it belonged.

"Fine," she said, giving her father a pointed look. "But let this be on *your* head."

CHAPTER 25

Monday the twenty-third dawned cold and crisp. From the comfort of her warm bed, Renee peered through a crack in the curtains and saw striated clouds strewn across the blue sky like the feathers of some great, wild bird. She yawned and stretched, reluctant to leave the sanctuary of her down comforter. Tomorrow would be Christmas Eve, she thought. Tonight, Jack and his family would arrive, and the house would descend into chaos. She grinned. It was going to be wonderful.

Then she remembered the dog.

The big, hairy, dirty dog that had spent the night downstairs and would still be there when Jack showed up if they couldn't find its owner before then. Her sister-in-law was a clean freak, and a strange dog was just the sort of thing that Megan would flip out over. Never mind that the poor thing was confined to Wendell's apartment, the stairs blocked off with a baby gate, and that the animal was too weak to stand, Megan would clutch the girls to her chest like a mother hen who senses a fox on the prowl.

Renee sighed, wondering if she should have called to warn

them. But what if she had and they'd decided not to come? The fact was, she needed the tumult and crazy joy of Christmas as much or more than her kids did that year. No, she told herself, it was worth taking a chance. Besides, there was one good thing about the dog. It had kept her from obsessing about Travis Diehl.

Fifteen months on her own might not have been easy, but it had taught her one thing: She could live without a man. When Greg left her, Renee had thought she'd never survive—not just financially, or because she'd become a single parent overnight, but because the prospect of being alone every day and every night with no one to share her joys and sorrows with had felt unimaginably grim. But she had survived, and although it still hurt, she'd survive this, too.

There was no rush getting to work that day; Dottie had sent her a text telling her that her first appointment had canceled. It wasn't great news, of course, but the amount Renee earned for the extra color job she'd done on Saturday night more than made up for it. All things considered, she was happy to exchange the lost pay for some extra shut-eye.

Wendell was sitting at the kitchen table, drinking a cup of coffee and working the daily crossword in the *Bolingbroke Herald*. When Renee walked in, he looked up sharply.

"Didn't your alarm go off?"

"My first appointment canceled," she said, stifling a yawn. "I'm fine."

He scowled. "You've had clients hounding you all week for an appointment. Why didn't they call someone on your waiting list?"

"It's okay, Dad. I didn't mind the extra sleep."

She poured herself a bowl of cereal.

"Where are the kids?"

"Dylan's at a team meeting, and McKenna's still asleep. Kieran says he's almost done cleaning his room."

"That was fast."

Wendell smirked.

"I told him he couldn't play with the dog until it was done."

"Good thinking."

Too bad the other two couldn't be similarly motivated, Renee thought. There was still a lot to do to get the house ready for guests. If she hadn't needed the money, she'd probably have taken the whole day off instead of just knocking off early, but between presents and food, Christmas had a way of busting the budget.

"I take it things have cooled between you and Mr. Diehl."

Renee struggled to swallow the last bite of cereal, wishing her father hadn't asked. She'd almost convinced herself it didn't matter, but the sudden tightness in her throat had betrayed her true feelings. She poured herself a cup of coffee.

"Let's just say he's not the man I thought he was."

"Sorry."

"I should be home no later than three thirty. If you can get Miss Mac to move her things into my room and change the sheets on her bed, that'd be great. I'm not worried about Dyl's room. If it isn't clean, we'll just shut the door."

Wendell grunted.

"Jack's email said they should be here by four. I thought I'd pick up some Chick-fil-A for supper."

"Fine."

Her father stared determinedly at the newspaper as she tried to catch his eye.

"I'd appreciate it if you'd try to be pleasant while they're here."

"I *am* pleasant, dammit."

"Well," she said, hiding a smile. "That's good to know."

She finished her coffee and put the cup and bowl in the dishwasher. He'd be all right, Renee thought. When push came to shove, her father would rein himself in—for the grandkids' sake, if nothing else. If he and Jack could just manage to stay away from any contentious subjects, she was sure they'd all have an enjoyable Christmas.

Wendell was still staring at the crossword puzzle, shaking his head.

"What's wrong?" she said.

"I can't get this one."

Renee sidled up and peered over his shoulder.

"What is it?"

"Six letters, starts with an *E*. The clue is: 'Closer to base?'"

She thought about it for a moment.

"How about 'eviler'?"

"Eviler, like more evil?"

"Yeah."

He penciled it in.

"Well, that's just stupid."

The blue sky Renee had seen from her bedroom window was almost gone by the time she left for work. The feathery clouds had coalesced into an unbroken mass of white so thick it left a halo around the sun. As she walked out to her car, she inhaled deeply and wondered if they might be in for a white Christmas.

It was going to be a long day. In addition to five hours at the salon, she still had to clean the house and get everything ready for her guests' arrival. Wendell would take care of the downstairs and pick up the last-minute grocery items on her list, but the kids needed to do their part, too. She was pleased that Kieran had already cleaned his room, but then he'd been excited about staying downstairs in his grandfather's apartment even before the dog. McKenna, however, would no doubt be dragging her feet until the very last second. She hoped that Wendell would be able to light a fire under her before Renee got back from work.

There were patches of ice on the road that morning, making the drive to work treacherous and slow; she was still only halfway to the salon when her cell phone rang. It was Hank Fielding, the principal at Kieran's school.

"Have you got a minute?"

"I'm on the way to work," she said, "but sure. What's up?"

"We've got a problem here concerning our new program. I'd like to ask you a few questions, if you don't mind."

"Is this about Kieran?"

"No, it's about a rumor that's going around. Someone's been telling the parents that medicating their children is the ultimate aim of the program. So far, two families have withdrawn their kids, and I just spent twenty minutes on the phone trying to convince a third to stay on. I'm wondering if you know anything about that?"

Renee pursed her lips, wondering if this had anything to do with Marissa's comments.

"Boy, I wish I could help you, but no one's said anything to me about their kid's being in the program. Did you ask them where they got that information?"

"I did," he said. "They told me it was you."

"*Me?*" She almost laughed. "You're kidding, right?"

"No, ma'am. Both of the families who dropped out told me that *you* were the one who'd passed along the information. I have to tell you, Mrs. Richardson, I'm disappointed."

Renee felt her lips tighten.

"You call and accuse me of spreading lies—without proof—and *you're* disappointed? What kind of b.s. is *that?*"

"I'm sorry," he said, his tone more conciliatory. "I'm only repeating what I was told. Under the circumstances, I thought it best to go to the source."

"What source?" she said. "I don't even *know* the other parents, and if I did, I sure as hell wouldn't be spreading rumors around. Either they're lying or someone's been lying to them, and it sure as hell wasn't me."

Renee's hands were shaking so badly she had to pull to the side of the road and stop the car. She closed her eyes, trying to calm the pounding in her chest. Whatever this was, she told herself, it wasn't worth getting herself killed over.

Principal Fielding cleared his throat.

"Perhaps I need to look into this matter a bit further."

She held her tongue.

You're darned right you do.

"In the meantime, if any of the other parents contact you, I'd appreciate a call."

The salon was busy, its parking lot jammed with the cars of clients desperate to have their hair done in time for the holidays. Renee drove into the empty lot next door, turned off the engine, and set her forehead against the steering wheel. The principal's call had left her badly shaken.

It was devastating to think that anyone would accuse her of spreading lies, but she was especially hurt that Hank Fielding had believed them. She knew when she moved to Bolingbroke that the people there could be suspicious of newcomers, but everyone on staff at the school had been gracious and accepting of her family. The thought that there was someone out there trying to turn them against her made her feel vulnerable.

It has to be a mistake. Sooner or later, things will get sorted out.

But what if they didn't get sorted? She'd bet everything she had on the move to this town; starting over somewhere else wasn't an option.

Then another possibility occurred to her. What if *she* wasn't the target at all? What if it was Kieran that someone was trying to hurt? Mrs. Dalton had told her there'd been some bullying on the playground. Could this be a way to pressure the kids at school who were "different" to leave? The thought was chilling.

Renee took a deep breath and tried to calm the frightened voices in her head. Letting her imagination run wild wouldn't do any good. Whatever was going on, she had to forget about it—for now, at least. She had a job to do. Once she walked into the salon, she'd be busy, and this problem would move into the background. There'd be plenty of time later to fix things, she thought. Right now, there was work to do.

Dottie was at the front desk, looking harried. When she stepped through the door, Renee gave her a quick wave and headed into the back room to hang up her coat. She was just tying on an apron when Dottie stepped in and gave her a bleak look.

"Mary Ruth canceled her appointment."

Renee felt a frisson of fear. Mary Ruth Mayhew and her family had their pictures taken every year on Christmas Eve, and she'd been touched when Dottie told her that Miz Mayhew had made her appointment six weeks in advance so that Renee could fix her hair when the time came. The woman wasn't terribly old, but she wasn't young, either, and she'd had some health problems recently.

"What happened? Is she okay?"

"I don't know. When I came in this morning, there was a message on the answering machine saying she couldn't make it. I tried to call her back, but there was no answer."

"I hope she's all right."

As disappointing as the cancellation was, Renee was far more concerned about Mary Ruth.

"That's not all," Dottie said. "You had two more clients call and cancel within the last half an hour."

Renee was staggered. Absent an epidemic of some sort, this sort of thing just didn't happen—especially not at this time of year. Nevertheless, it made no sense to try and figure out what was going on. Unless she wanted to end up in the poor house, she needed to get her schedule filled. Thank goodness, that wouldn't be a problem.

"Well, it's not great," she said, "but things happen. I'll start calling my wait list and see if I can fill the holes in my schedule."

"I already did," Dottie said. "They all said they were too busy to come in."

"*All* of them?"

"Every last one. Your only other appointment today is at two, and when I called, she said she couldn't make it any earlier. I'm sorry. I did the best I could."

"Of course you did," Renee said. "I'm not blaming you. I'm just . . . surprised. I'd have thought that *someone* would want to come in. I don't know what to do now. I mean, should I stay here or go home?"

"Oh. No, you should definitely stay," Dottie said. "I wasn't able to get any of your wait list ladies in here, but one of your semi-regulars called about ten minutes ago, asking if you had any openings, and I put her in."

Hallelujah.

"Well, that's something. Who was it?"

"Maggie McRay."

Renee's hopes dimmed.

"Oh."

Maggie McRay was a sweet gal and a hard worker, but as a client, she was as frustrating as a recalcitrant child. In spite of numerous entreaties from Renee, she refused to even consider any suggestions about style and color, preferring to let her fine, greying hair hang down, hiding her lovely Irish complexion and sparkling green eyes. No doubt, she'd want nothing but a trim, too, the price of which would do little to make up for the income Renee had lost due to the cancellations.

Nevertheless, she thought, it was better than nothing.

"When's she coming in?"

"I saw her truck pull into the lot next door as I was walking back here."

Renee took a deep breath.

"Then at least I won't have a lot of time to wait," she said.

"Who knows? Maybe we'll get another walk-in later."

"Sure," Dottie said, looking doubtful. "You never know."

Maggie was already sitting in the chair when Renee walked out to her station. Hands gripping the arm rests, her feet planted and her back stiff, she looked about as relaxed as a death row inmate in the electric chair. Renee grabbed a drape from her drawer and shook it out.

"Hey, Miz McRay," she said. "Time for another trim?"

Maggie shook her head.

"No, ma'am."

She turned and gave Renee a resolute stare.

"I want you to make me a sexy senior citizen."

Renee was shocked. Was this the same woman who'd scoffed at the notion of *conditioning* her hair? Who'd refused to let Renee even blow it dry? The one who ended every ap-

pointment by taking out a rubber band and raking her damp
hair back into a ponytail? It didn't seem possible, but seeing
was believing and it was certainly good news as far as she was
concerned. Nevertheless, as Renee set the drape around Maggie's shoulders, she couldn't help wondering what had prompted
this change of heart.

"Hold on tight," she said. "I'll get some color samples, and
you can tell me what you'd like."

Sissy was sitting in the break room, looking bleak. As Renee
walked in to grab an apron and the samples of dyed hair, she
turned away.

Maybe I'm not the only one with cancellations.

"You okay, Sissy?"

The girl shook her head.

"Something on your mind?"

Sissy shrugged, a gesture Renee found especially irritating,
having seen McKenna do it so often.

"Look, if you have something to tell me, just spit it out,"
she said. "I've got Maggie McRay in the chair, and I don't
want her to run off before I get back out there."

"I warned you," Sissy said.

Renee frowned. What was she talking about?

"Warned me about what?"

"About what would happen if you didn't leave Travis
alone."

It took a moment for Renee to put two and two together.

"Are you talking about the cancellations?"

Sissy nodded.

Renee felt her face flush, remembering the cryptic message the young woman had given her on Saturday. At the time,
she'd brushed it off as harmless gossip. Sissy could be credulous
to the point of delusion, given the proper motivation, and

she'd had no interest in feeding her fantasy. Now, however, her comment about Savannah's being jealously protective of her former flame was making a strange sort of sense.

"You mean to tell me," she said, feeling her anger grow, "that Savannah Hays had my clients *cancel* because I wouldn't stop seeing her old *boyfriend?* That's nuts."

The young woman turned, and Renee saw angry tears in her eyes.

"It serves you right," she said. "You never should have made me steal that hair."

CHAPTER 26

"Max! Here boy!"

Travis shivered as another car drove by, creating eddies of bitter wind in its wake. He'd been walking the area around his house for over an hour, talking to neighbors and putting up *Missing Dog* signs, but he still had no idea what had happened to his brother's dog. He'd called the emergency animal clinic and left messages at every vet's office in town—most of which were closed for the holidays—but no one had seen or heard of a lost dog matching Max's description. It wasn't possible for a dog that size to simply vanish, he thought. Max had either been stolen or was dead.

He'd just started back up his driveway, trying to rekindle the faint hope that Max had returned on his own, when his phone buzzed. Travis's heart leaped—finally, some news!—but then he reached into his pocket and saw the caller ID.

"Hey, Hank," he said, trying not to sound disappointed.

"Hey. Got a minute?"

Travis walked to the end of the driveway and peered over the fence. Max wasn't in the backyard.

"Sure," he said. "What's on your mind?"

Hank hesitated.

"Something wrong?"

"No." Travis slipped off his boots and went inside. "I mean, yes, but it's got nothing to do with you. Hugh's dog is missing."

"Have you called the pound?"

"I've called *everybody*," he said. "At this point, he'll either show up or he won't."

He took off his coat and tossed it on a chair.

"So, what's up?"

"It's about the program," Hank said. "Under the circumstances, I wish it was better news."

"Is this about the problem you mentioned at the Jaycees?"

"It is. Those two families I mentioned have dropped out and another is threatening to."

"Why? The program hasn't even started yet."

"Someone told them that the point of the program is to get their kids on meds."

"But that's not true."

"You know it and I know it, but that doesn't mean they don't believe it."

Travis ran a hand through his hair. Of all the problems he'd accounted for, having someone spread false information about the program hadn't even been on his radar. It made him wonder about the source of the rumor. Was this just wild speculation on someone's part, or was there a personal motive involved?

"What if I called and explained that medicating their kids was never the point?"

"I've already told them that."

"But if I—"

"Listen to me. The names of the kids and their families are confidential—something you yourself insisted on when we started the program. The only person besides me who knows their names is my secretary, Debbie, and the only reason she knows is because I asked her to type up the list of families last week."

"Okay, I get that, but—"

"If you breech that confidentiality by contacting those parents, it'll put the whole program in jeopardy."

Travis began pacing the floor. After all the work he'd done—setting up the Diehl Foundation, jumping through hoops for the IRS, consulting with experts to develop the program—it was infuriating to think that the whole thing might be upended by the loose talk of one ignorant person.

"I understand," he said. "I get it; I do. I just want to know who told them."

"I already know who told them. That is, I know who they said it was."

"Then tell 'em to stop!"

"I did."

"And?"

"She said she didn't."

Travis took a deep breath.

"Who is it?"

Hank's laugh was rueful.

"You really think I'm going to tell you?"

"Why not? Don't you think I have a right to know?"

There was a long pause before Hank finally said:

"You and I have known each other a long time—I know you, Travis. You're a hell of a nice guy, but I know how much this program means to you. How do I know you won't try and contact the person yourself?"

"That's not fair."

"Fair or not, I can't take the chance. This program may be

your baby, but I've got a lot at stake here, too. Now, I've already contacted the person, and they claim they had nothing to do with it. If they're telling the truth, then getting in their face about it could bring the whole thing down around our ears."

"And if they're lying?"

"If they're lying—if they really did start this rumor—then I promise you, I will find out. And when I do, I *will* do something about it."

Travis chewed his lip. Hank was right: This program was his baby. More than that, it was a living memorial to the parents who'd raised both him and his brother in difficult circumstances—of course he wanted to set the record straight. The fact was, unless and until the source of the rumor recanted, there would always be a lingering doubt in the other parents' minds.

"You still there?" Hank said.

"Yeah, I'm here."

Travis rubbed a hand down his face. He was tempted to keep arguing, hoping to persuade Hank to change his mind, but it was getting late, and he was still worried about Max. If he was going to get any more searching done before the sun set, he'd have to do it now.

"I'm not happy about it, but I guess I'll just have to trust you."

"Thank you," Hank said. "I'll give you a call if anything changes."

Renee was in a state as she drove home that afternoon. She'd spent six hours at the salon and served exactly two clients—one of whom hadn't even tipped her!—and except for the time when she'd been working, she was thinking about Travis Diehl. The exact thing she'd been hoping that work would distract her from!

At least she and Sissy had finally straightened things out. After blurting out the comment about "stealing" hair from the salon, the poor girl had broken down and confessed that telling Renee to leave Travis Diehl alone had been Savannah Hays's idea. Apparently, Savannah had hoodwinked her into delivering the message by convincing the girl that taking hair from the salon was against the law. Poor Sissy was terrified, sure she'd be punished for "stealing," and it had taken several minutes of reassurance and an intervention from Winona to convince her that she wasn't about to lose her job over the "theft." Winona might have been disgusted, but she was helpless to do anything about it. Like Renee, she owed too much of her success to Savannah's referrals to confront the woman. Unless the situation escalated, she said, the three of them would just have to move on.

Which was fine with Renee. As far as she was concerned, if Savannah wanted Travis that badly, she could have him. There was no way she was going to ruin her reputation and her family's financial welfare for a man she barely knew.

Nevertheless, by the time she got home, Renee was feeling unexpectedly teary. Savannah had been a good customer and the referrals she'd sent Renee had been both flattering and appreciated. She'd even thought of her as a friend. But the woman had thought nothing of setting Renee's clients—some of whom were almost like family—against her. It made her feel vulnerable and scared. Why would Savannah try and hurt her like that? As she hung her coat on the hook by the front door, she felt hot tears sting her eyes.

She couldn't think about it. Not with Jack and his family on the way. There was still too much to do to get the house ready for company, Renee thought. If she let herself get sad and mopey, it would put a damper on everyone's Christmas.

She'd almost gotten herself calmed down when Wendell walked upstairs and stuck his head around the corner.

"Hey there. How was work?"

Renee opened her mouth to speak and choked on the words, then shook her head. Tears filled her eyes as her father approached, his arms open.

"What's wrong, sweetie?"

"Oh, Dad," she sobbed.

Renee leaned her head against his chest and felt a flood of tears course down her cheeks as he patted her back. The relief she felt was overwhelming—it felt good to be patted and told that everything was all right—but it was relief tinged with guilt. Not only were things *not* all right, but once again Wendell was having to support and comfort her. Even worse, there was a small, selfish part of her that wished it was Travis Diehl whose shoulder she was crying on, not her father's.

The wish made Renee feel ashamed. After all her father had done for her, she had no right to be anything but grateful. Who was Travis Diehl to her, anyway? Just some guy who'd asked her out a couple of times. For all she knew, he'd only done it because he knew that Kieran was in the program at school, and he was trying to win her over. Besides, the man belonged to someone else; Savannah Hays had made that perfectly clear. There was no sense torturing herself over something that could never be.

She straightened up and wiped her eyes.

"Sorry, Dad. Just a tough day," she said, forcing a smile. "How were things here?"

"Fine," he said. "Nothing to report, really. McKenna moved her things into your bedroom, and Dyl promised to keep his door closed."

Renee was pleasantly surprised.

"Mac moved *all* her things into my room?"

"Well, she didn't move the *bed*."

"You know what I mean. How'd you do it?"

"I didn't," he said. "The dog did."

Renee glanced toward the stairs where the family's old baby gate was still firmly affixed.

"You're kidding."

Wendell shook his head.

"Strange but true. I told her the dog was off limits until she moved her things." He gave her a knowing look. "Took her about ten minutes."

Renee knew that look. It meant that her father was making a point without actually saying anything—generally because he knew she'd disagree with him if he did. She gave him a look of her own.

"And . . . ?"

"Hmm? Oh, nothing," he said breezily. "I just thought it was interesting."

She felt herself relent. After the day she'd had, she was in no mood to try and extract a confession from anyone. Whatever was on her father's mind, he'd tell her soon enough. The truth was, she was just relieved not to have to fight with McKenna to get her to move her things. If the dog had had a hand—a paw?—in that, then she was glad.

The dog.

Renee bit her lip. In spite of herself, she was curious to see how it was doing. The poor thing had looked so pitiful the day before that she'd let Kieran cover it with one of her old afghans and sleep downstairs next to it. As anxious as she was over breaking the news to Jack and Megan, she'd never considered turning it away.

"So," she said. "How is it?"

"Doing better." Wendell nodded toward the stairs. "You want to come down and see for yourself?"

"Oh, sure. Why not?"

The dog was lying on the floor, stretched out on the afghan, apparently asleep. Kieran was sitting by its head, staring at it adoringly. When Renee came downstairs, he put a finger to his lips. She nodded.

What was that old saying? Let sleeping dogs lie?

She looked at Wendell, and the two of them walked back upstairs.

"Has he been able to stand up yet?" she said when they got to the landing.

"A little," Wendell said. "Kieran got him cleaned up, but I think it wore him out."

"Well, he's certainly looking better than he did last night."

She looked down at her clothes which were covered, as usual, with bits of hair.

"Actually, I think I might just get cleaned up myself. Have you heard anything from Jack?"

Her father nodded.

"He called about an hour ago and said they'd be here by five."

"Okay. So, what still needs to be done to the house?"

"Nothing. I got the upstairs vacuumed, and Kieran made the beds in his room."

Wendell glanced back toward the stairs.

"To tell you the truth, I think the dog's been good for him. He wasn't as fidgety at lunch this afternoon, and he cleared his plate without arguing."

Renee scoffed. "He's brownnosing."

"That doesn't mean it isn't a good thing. They say dogs

can sense things about people. Maybe Rex can tell that Kieran needs a little help."

"*Rex?*"

He shrugged. "That's what Kieran calls him."

Renee closed her eyes. This was what the look had been about: Wendell was angling to keep the dog. He'd seen—or thought he'd seen—some improvement in Kieran's behavior, and now he was going to use that to try to convince her that the dog should stay.

"Don't, Dad, *please.* The dog isn't ours. He has an owner somewhere who's going to show up any minute and take him away. Let's not make that harder for Kieran by pretending he can just give the dog a new name and it'll be his."

"I didn't say it had to be *that* dog," he hissed. "But maybe *a* dog. A pet might just be what the boy needs."

"Okay, all right," she said, feeling suddenly weary. "I'm sorry I jumped to conclusions. Maybe you're right; maybe a dog would be good for Kieran. I just don't want him pinning his hopes on keeping *that* dog. Because *that* dog is not ours and is never going to be. Agreed?"

"Agreed."

"Thank you," she said. "Now, if you don't mind, I'm going to go get cleaned up for dinner."

She turned and walked down to her room, where a pile of clothes had been heaped on the bed. Renee sighed, shaking her head. Technically, of course, McKenna's things had been moved into her room. This just wasn't the way she'd pictured it.

Guess I should have been more specific.

She stripped off her clothes and put them in the hamper, pleased that the workday was over and that the house was ready for company. If having a dog in the house meant that things got done without the usual arguments, then maybe getting one wouldn't be such a bad thing, she thought.

Then Renee stepped into her bathroom and gasped. The place was a wreck! There were two—no, three!—towels on the floor, each of them filthy. And the tub! A ring as thick as her arm encircled it, caked with bits of dirt and grey hair.

Grey hair?

Renee slapped her forehead, suspended between laughter and tears. No wonder the dog looked better, she thought. Her sweet, thoughtful, youngest child had given it a bath in *her* bathroom!

Maybe getting a dog wasn't such a good idea after all.

CHAPTER 27

"Jack! Megan! Girls! Come in!"

Renee stood on the front stoop, waving her arms excitedly as her brother and his family got out of their SUV. Jack looked harried—no doubt, the traffic had been bad—and Megan was a bit tentative, but Grace and Lilly ran for her like greyhounds out of the gate. In seconds, the three of them were caught up in a group hug.

"Oh my gosh, look how much you've grown!" she said.

Grace craned her neck to take advantage of every inch.

"Mom says I'll be as tall as Grandmama pretty soon."

"I'm sure you will," Renee said, too thoughtful to mention that Megan's mother was less than five feet tall.

Lilly pushed her older sister away.

"I'm getting big, too!"

"I can see that. Listen, why don't you two go inside while I help your parents with their things. Grandpa and your cousins are in the family room."

As the girls hurried into the house, Renee went to tell Jack and Megan about the dog. She didn't think her brother would have a problem with it, but if Megan had an objection, she'd rather deal with it out there than risk tainting the mood inside. It had taken a lot of persuading to get Megan to come; Renee didn't want the visit to be ruined before she even walked through the door.

"Thanks for coming," she said, giving her brother a squeeze. "It's great to see you guys."

She collected a tepid hug from her sister-in-law as Jack popped open the hatchback.

"How was the trip?"

"Not bad," he said, glancing at his wife. "Megan got a little carsick, though."

"Oh," Renee said. "Sorry."

Megan gave her a pained look and started for the house. "I need to lie down."

"No problem. Your room's all ready."

She gulped.

"There's just one thing, though, before you head in. We've got a dog staying with us . . . at the moment."

Megan's head whipped around.

"You got a *dog,* and you didn't tell us?"

"Uh, no," Renee said, glancing back at her brother. "He's not ours. We're just waiting for his owner to come and get him."

Jack frowned. "When will that be?"

"As soon as we get hold of him . . . or her. In the meantime, Dad's keeping it down in his apartment. That won't be a problem, will it?"

Jack and Megan exchanged a glance.

"No," he said. "Of course not. I mean, as long as it's not running around or anything. Right, honey?"

Megan nodded, tight-lipped.

"Of course," she muttered. "Not as if I can do anything about it."

As her sister-in-law marched off into the house, Renee turned to her brother.

"Good old Megan. Just as sweet and easygoing as ever."

"Don't start," he said. "It's been a bad week."

"Anything serious?"

He shook his head and set an overnight case on the ground.

"I'll tell you about it later."

She peered at the things in the back of the car. They'd brought an awful lot of stuff for only two days.

"What can I help you with?"

Jack handed her a bag full of groceries.

"Here," he said. "You can put these in our room."

Renee looked at the things in the bag, feeling a twinge of annoyance. She'd already bought most of what was in there, none of which her own kids would eat once they were gone. *Why did I even bother?*

"So," he said, "what kind of dog is it?"

"Hmm?" She looked up. "Oh, big, hairy, grey. It got caught in a snare, and Kieran rescued it."

"Really? Good for him."

He hauled out a suitcase and set it down with a thud.

"How's KK doing these days?"

Renee smiled. Her brother was the only one who ever called her son "KK." It had been Jack's pet name for Kieran ever since he was a baby. This was why she'd wanted him to come, she thought: all those quirky, endearing things that made them a family. It was worth putting up with Megan's attitude and Wendell's guff just to have that connection again, even for a little while.

"He's doing really well," she said. "They've started a program at school for kids with learning disabilities, and I'm cautiously optimistic."

"Wonderful," he said. "I hope it helps."

Jack threw a wary glance at the front door.

"How's Dad?"

"Same as ever."

He smirked. "That bad, huh?"

Renee laughed and threw her arms around him.

"God, it's good to see you."

"You, too, sis." He mussed her hair. "Come on, let's get inside before we freeze to death."

Renee's smile began to fade as soon as she walked through the door. The house looked like it had been divided into opposing camps with each side sticking to its own territory. Megan and the girls were in the living room, talking quietly and throwing the occasional pointed glance toward the family room, while the other four conducted themselves with exaggerated indifference. The snacks that Renee had prepared were set out on the kitchen counter, but so far there'd been no takers.

She put the bag of groceries in Jack and Megan's room and walked back just as Jack was bringing in the last of the luggage. Wendell wandered in, and the two men shared a stiff embrace. So far, she thought, so good.

"We've got nibbles in the kitchen if anybody's hungry," Renee said.

"I am!" Lilly said, jumping up from the couch.

Megan reached out and grabbed her arm.

"Lilly, honey, I'm not sure you should eat any of those things." She turned. "Jack, where'd you put her food?"

"I put it in your room," Renee said.

Megan's eyes remained on Jack.

"Can you please go and get it so our daughter can eat?"

"Of course. I was just heading that way." He picked up the luggage and headed down the hall.

Renee saw Wendell open his mouth and gave him a warning look.

"Did you take a look at the snacks I set out?" she said as Jack returned with the bag of groceries. "I picked up several things at the store especially for your girls."

"This is a new diet," Jack said quietly as he handed the bag to his wife. "Megan read about it online."

"Ah, here we go," Megan said, reaching into the bag. "You'll love this, Lil."

Lilly crossed her arms and gave her mother a stubborn stare.

"I don't want it!"

Megan's smile was tight.

"We already talked about this, remember?" she said. "You agreed you'd try the new food that Mommy bought for you."

The girl's scowl hardened, and her small foot stamped the ground.

"I *did* try it. It felt yucky in my mouth!"

"No, it didn't. Besides, it doesn't matter what it *feels* like. Just try it."

"Noooooo!" Lilly wailed. "*I hate it!*"

Renee froze, unsure what to do. Jack, too, seemed perplexed. Wendell turned away with a smirk, while at the table, Dylan, McKenna, and Kieran ate their own snacks in amused silence. Grace shrank back as if trying to become invisible while her younger sister continued to scream.

Jack looked at his wife.

"Maybe we could make an exception while we're here," he said. "You know. Start the diet up again after Christmas."

"I thought we agreed," she muttered through clenched teeth.

"Yes, but given the circumstances . . ."

"Fine," she said, dropping the bag on the floor. "Do what you want, then. I'm going to go lie down."

With Megan gone, the tension in the room evaporated. Jack portioned out snacks for the girls while Lilly went off to wash her face and calm down in the bathroom. Renee looked around, still hoping to break the ice.

"I'm really glad you guys could come," she said. "It's finally starting to feel like Christmas."

"We saw the tree outside," Jack said. "It's a beauty."

"Thanks. Dad and the kids brought it home last week," she said. "I was hoping you two might put it up tonight."

"Of course."

"It smells nice," Grace said.

Wendell looked at her.

"That's because it's a *real* tree, not a fake one," he said. "Your cousins picked it out and I chopped it down."

The girl's lip trembled.

"You mean you *killed* it?"

"What do you mean, I killed it? It's not alive, it's a god-damn *tree*."

"*Dad?*" Renee said, giving him an admonitory look.

She turned toward Grace.

"The trees at the farm are grown to be cut down for Christmas," she said. "It really doesn't hurt them."

The girl ducked her head and resumed eating. There followed another protracted silence.

"So, Dylan," Jack said. "I hear you're getting an athletic scholarship to Clemson."

Dylan nodded shyly.

"Looks that way."

"Well, it's a good school. They'll be lucky to have you."

When no one else picked up the thread of the conversation, Jack returned to his snack. Lilly set a half-eaten carrot stick down.

"I'm all finished. Can I go see the dog now?"

Renee narrowed her eyes at Dylan, McKenna, and Kieran, who shook their heads in an exaggerated show of innocence.

Jack looked at Lilly.

"What dog, sweetie?"

"The one downstairs."

He glanced up. Renee shrugged.

"When were you down there?" he said.

"When I went to the bathroom," the girl said. "It's a boy dog and it's on the couch. I petted it and it licked my hand. It has an owwie on its neck. Did Grandpa try to cut it off, too?"

Wendell's jaw dropped.

"What?"

"No," Jack said, suppressing a smile. "Grandpa wouldn't do that. Your cousin Kieran rescued the dog from a trap. It must have hurt its neck when it was caught."

Lilly turned an admiring gaze on the boy sitting across from her.

"You *saved* him? All by *yourself?*"

Kieran stared at his plate and nodded.

Grace, too, seemed to gain an instant respect for her cousin.

"Can we play with him? I have my doctor kit with me. We could set up a hospital for him down in Grandpa's room."

"Hey, wait a minute," Wendell said.

Kieran looked at Renee.

"Can we?" he said. "I mean, if we brought him upstairs."

She shrugged. "It's not up to me."

The girls were tugging on Jack's arms.

"Can we, Daddy? Can we?"

"I don't know," he said, glancing toward the bedroom where his wife had gone to lie down.

"Yeah," Wendell muttered. "Better check with *the boss,* first."

Jack set his mouth in a firm line.

"No need," he said. "I can make my own decision."

He looked at the girls.

"If your Aunt Renee says it's all right, then you two can play with the dog up here. Just be careful."

As the girls ran off to get their doctor kit, Jack turned to Renee and sighed.

"Guess I'd better go and break the bad news to Megan."

"Let me do it," she said, walking into the kitchen.

He gave her a skeptical look.

"Are you sure?"

Renee took two wine glasses out of the cupboard and the bottle of Shiraz that Berenice had given her for Christmas.

"I'm sure."

CHAPTER 28

When the white sedan pulled into Travis's driveway at eleven thirty that morning, his first thought was that it was Hank, come to tell him who was behind the rumor at school. Since their conversation the day before, he'd been splitting his time between looking for Max and fuming over the rumor that was threatening to ruin his program. If the person who'd just driven up to his house wasn't Hank, then it seemed reasonable to assume that they had news about his brother's dog. As the driver stepped out, however, his reaction changed from hope to confusion. What was Savannah Hays doing there?

Travis groaned, suddenly remembering her phone call on Sunday. With Renee not answering his calls and both Hugh and Max out of the house, he'd been missing Emmy and feeling sorry for himself; the thought of spending Christmas Eve alone had been looming like the ghost of Christmas past. When Savannah had called, he'd said yes without really thinking; it seemed more likely than not that she'd forget the whole thing once she got a better offer. But there she was, scampering toward his front door in high heels and a fur coat, with a bottle of champagne in her hands. He could think of no good reason to turn her away.

"Merry Christmas Eve!" she cried, holding the champagne aloft.

Travis stepped back from the open door.

"Merry Christmas Eve," he said. "Come in."

She leaned forward, giving him a kiss that just missed his mouth, and Travis took her coat, surprised to see that she was wearing a formfitting red dress underneath. As he hung the coat in the hall closet, Savannah went into the kitchen.

"I hope you've got some orange juice," she said, setting the bottle on the counter. "A mimosa right now would be *heavenly.*"

He turned the label around: *Moet & Chandon.*

"A bit pricey for mimosas, don't you think?"

"Oh, Trav," she sulked. "It's Christmas. Can't we live a little?"

"Of course," he said. "The flutes are in the—"

"I remember where they *are.*"

She opened the top cupboard next to the sink.

"If you recall, I spent a good bit of time here, helping your mama before she passed."

Travis felt chastened, having forgotten all that Savannah had done for his mother in her last months. Never mind that the two of them were as compatible as oil and water, the fact was that she'd been willing to help when everyone else in town had stayed away.

Savannah set two champagne flutes on the counter and sidled over to the refrigerator.

"Aren't you going to open that?" she said, glancing at the bottle.

"Oh! Of course."

Travis unwrapped the gold foil hugging the bottle's neck

and loosened the wire cage enclosing the cork before flipping down the wire "key" pressed up against the glass. It had been a long time since he'd had an occasion to celebrate with a bottle of champagne, and it surprised him how automatic his movements were. As he reached for a dish towel and draped it over the bottle, Savannah purred appreciatively.

"Such moves," she said. "Why, I'm tempted to think you do this all the time."

He gave her a sly smile, twisting the bottle with his right hand and easing the cork out with his left.

"There are some moves a gentleman never forgets."

The cork popped and Savannah held her flute under the neck as the champagne began to flow. When each flute had been half-filled and topped off with orange juice, she held hers up in triumph.

"To Christmas Eve," she said.

"Christmas Eve!"

She raised the glass and took a sip.

"Do you remember our first Christmas Eve?"

Travis hesitated. Of course he did. It was their senior year of high school, and her parents were at a party they'd taken pains to mention that they wouldn't be returning from for hours. Travis was no virgin, but the luxury of making love in a real bed had been almost indescribable. Until that night, his limited experience had been gained in the steamy confines of his father's Camry—the same type of car, he realized with a jolt, that Savannah had just arrived in. Was there more to this visit, he wondered, than just a desire to ward off the Christmas Eve blues?

"I do," he said. "But it was a long time ago."

"Not so long."

Savannah downed the rest of her mimosa and set her flute aside.

"So," she said. "How have you been?"

"Okay, I guess."

"Just okay?" She looked around. "Did things not go well at the group home?"

"No, no. They called me this morning; he's taken to it like a duck to water."

She reached out and set a gentle hand on his arm.

"Then what is it, dear? I could tell something was on your mind the second I walked in. Is it just the holiday blues?"

Travis took a deep breath and rubbed the back of his neck. The frustrations of the last couple of days had churned up his stomach to the point that even the mimosa was hard to swallow. He felt like his emotions were in a pressure cooker—a stew of suppressed fury simmering just beneath the surface calm. It would be a relief, he thought, to let off a bit of that pressure before it burst out and damaged everyone around him.

"Max is missing," he said.

"Hugh's dog?"

He nodded.

"Well, maybe it's nothing," she said hopefully. "Some dogs do like to roam. How long's he been gone?"

"Two days. Hugh let him out on Sunday morning, and I haven't seen him since."

She frowned.

"I'm not going to ask if you've called around. I know you better than that."

"Thank you."

"But with everyone out of town or on vacation, I suppose it's been hard to get any answers."

He nodded, grateful that, for once, he didn't have to explain his inability to recover the dog.

Savannah gave him a hard look.

"I have a feeling, however, that that's not the only thing that's eating you."

Travis looked away, working his mouth. Should he tell her about Hank's call? About the rumor that was threatening to undo everything he'd been dedicating his time and effort to for the last year? If he did, how would he keep himself from showing the bitterness he felt? It seemed almost irrational to him how helpless and angry the whole situation had made him. How could he possibly explain it in a way that made sense to anyone else?

Savannah was still watching him, her soft brown eyes inviting his confession, and he was suddenly transported to that first Christmas Eve. How he'd given himself up to her and she to him. At the time, he'd thought the two of them were meant to be together for always. Who else knew him so well?

No one.

"Hank Fielding called me yesterday," he said. "Someone's been telling the parents in the program at school that the point is to medicate the children in our program. Hank says he's pretty sure who's behind it, but he won't tell me."

As the story spilled out, Travis felt instantly relieved. Just having someone else to share the situation had made him light-headed. But as much of a relief as it was to him, the news seemed to have an opposite effect on Savannah, who blanched noticeably and looked away.

Travis reached for her.

"I'm sorry," he said. "I didn't mean to upset you. I had no business burdening you with my problems."

"It isn't that," she said, looking troubled. "It's—"

"What?"

She sighed and shook her head.

"I don't know if I should say anything. If Hank didn't tell you who it was, then I shouldn't either."

He gripped her arm.

"You mean you know who did it?"

She nodded.

"Tell me."

Savannah looked away.

"I can't. It wouldn't be fair."

"Fair? Are you kidding me? How 'fair' is it to ruin something I've dreamed about for years?" He tightened his grip on her arm.

"Savannah, if you know who it is, you need to tell me."

She looked at her arm.

"You're hurting me."

Travis opened his hand as quickly as if he'd been burned.

"I'm sorry," he said. "I had no right. I'm just—"

He shook his head.

"Forgive me. I've just been so upset."

She reached out and placed a hand on his.

"I understand," she said. "I'd be angry, too. In fact, I was angry when she told me she'd done it. I just—I guess I just didn't think she was being serious."

Travis took her hands in his. They felt cold to the touch, and he realized that Savannah was shaking.

"Whoever it is," he said. "I promise you, they will not find out who told me. You know that, don't you?"

She hesitated a moment before nodding.

"Then tell me, please. Who was it?"

Savannah looked away and bit her lip, as if trying to make up her mind. It was all that Travis could do not to take her shoulders and try to shake it out of her. When she finally looked up, there were tears in her eyes.

"I'm sorry," she whispered. "It was Renee."

Travis released her hands and staggered back. It couldn't be, he thought. Renee wouldn't do that to him. She knew how much the program meant to him. She'd been there when he received his award.

No, he thought. She'd left early that night. What had Marissa told him?

"She looked over and saw you talking to Hank and then she just ran off."

Hank! Hank must have already known who spread the rumor that night. Seeing him there, with Travis, Renee had to have realized she couldn't keep up the ruse. No wonder she'd bolted, he thought. Lying to people over the phone was a lot easier than lying to someone's face. She must have known that if Hank looked her in the eye, she'd give herself away.

What a fool I've been.

"Why didn't you tell me before?" he said.

Savannah's look was bleak.

"Why?" she shook her head. "You think I don't know what you think of me? Or of her? If I'd come to you and told you that Renee had told me in a moment of weakness that she'd been calling the other parents in the program and telling them lies, would you have believed me?"

Travis hesitated.

"I'm not sure," he said.

"Well, I am. You'd have said I was trying to turn you against her, sabotage your relationship."

He shook his head.

"I'd like to think I would have taken you seriously."

"I'd like to think it, too," she said quietly. "But I just couldn't."

A tear ran down her cheek, heartbreakingly slowly, and Travis felt as if his own heart would break. Not just because he'd hurt Savannah, but because he'd thought he might be falling in love with Renee. He felt shaken to the core. How could he have been so wrong?

The phone rang, breaking the tension in the air and making both of them flinch. Travis caught his breath and excused himself as Savannah hurried off to the bathroom. He took a moment to calm down before picking up.

"Hello?"

"Travis Diehl?"

"Speaking."

"My name is Ted Coburn, and I believe I have some good news for you."

CHAPTER 29

Everyone agreed that it was the most beautiful Christmas Eve ever. In spite of the cold, the sun was dazzling and the light dusting of snow twinkled like stars on the ground. After the tension of the night before, Renee couldn't help feeling it was a good omen.

Jack and Wendell were out on the back porch getting the grill ready to cook hamburgers and brats for lunch while Renee and Megan got everything else ready in the kitchen and the little kids set up their "dog hospital" in the living room. The dog—now referred to as "Rex" in spite of Renee's entreaties—had finally gotten up on its feet and was making the rounds through the house, cadging pats and snuffling hands in hopes of finding illicit treats. Jack had gone to the store with instructions to buy dog food only, but had somehow managed to come back with an entire bag of canine goodies. In spite of Renee's warning not to give the dog too many, the level in the bag continued to diminish, and she suspected that someone of a grandfatherly nature was resupplying the youngsters. As the dog returned to his "hospital bed" on the floor, she hoped the animal didn't actually get sick before its owner showed up.

In accordance with Berenice's instructions to keep her houseguest well-oiled, Renee had broken out another bottle of Shiraz, and so far, it was working like a charm. Not only had Megan raised no more objections about the food being served, but she'd grown almost fond of the dog. Renee considered the money she'd spent on alcohol that week to be a worthwhile investment.

Megan took the bowl of coleslaw to the table and glanced into the living room, shaking her head.

"I must say, I am surprised," she drawled, her accent thicker after three glasses of wine. "The girls have never taken to an animal quite like that one."

Renee hadn't drunk as much as her sister-in-law had, but on an empty stomach, the wine made her feel almost giddy. She nodded.

"He's a good patient."

"A *patient* patient." Megan giggled.

She walked back to the kitchen and grabbed the bottle, noting its diminished contents.

"Mind if I finish this off?"

"Help yourself," Renee said. "There's plenty more."

As Megan poured out the last of the Shiraz, Renee took the opportunity to peek into the living room to see how the kids were doing. Her sister-in-law was right: The little ones were playing nicely together. Even McKenna, whose interest in the dog had tapered off quickly, was still hanging around the periphery, playing a game on her phone. Dylan was in the club chair, reading a novel for his English class while he kept an eye on his cousins, ready to step in if there was a problem. He'd taken on so much since Greg had left them, she thought—more than she'd ever have asked him to and probably more than he should have. Renee thought she should probably feel guiltier about it than she did, but it would be a moot point in a few months when he left for college. Until then, she was just grateful for his help.

Megan plopped herself down on the settee and patted the cushion next to her.

"Come tell me what's new and exciting in your world."

"New and exciting? You must be kidding."

"Really? No romance on the horizon?"

Renee took another sip of Shiraz. It had been a long time since the two of them had shared any personal information, and it felt odd to open up now. Still, they'd been close once, and she wouldn't mind having another woman to talk to about the situation with Travis. Maybe this was Megan's way of offering an olive branch. She glanced out at the two men on the porch; Wendell and Jack would be putting the meat patties on the grill soon. Everything else was ready, she thought. Why not?

"Well," she said, taking a seat. "There was this one guy."

"Ooh, I knew it," her sister-in-law said, leaning closer. "Tell me all about it."

"There really isn't much to tell. We met at the school one night, and he seemed nice—"

Megan leered. "Good looking?"

Renee felt a dimple crease her cheek.

"Very," she said.

"And then?"

"And then . . . he showed up at the salon asking for a haircut."

Megan seemed disappointed.

"Oh. So, he was one of your customers?"

"No."

Renee laughed, remembering how Travis had looked, standing at Winona's front counter while the ladies in the salon ogled him.

"I'd told him I was a hairdresser, so he called all the salons in town to find out where I worked."

"Aww," Megan said. "It's like the prince looking for Cinderella after the ball."

Renee rolled her eyes. Megan must be drunk if she thought this was a fairy tale.

Wait 'til she gets to the part about the evil queen.

"Anyway," she said, "we went for coffee after, and it was really nice, then we went Christmas shopping and he helped me pick out a video game for Kieran."

She swallowed, thinking about how sweet Travis had been that day. It was the first time she'd thought that the two of them might have something special going.

"And . . . ?" Megan prompted. "Don't keep me in suspense."

Renee sighed.

"And then my most important client took him away."

"What?"

"It's true. Turns out, she thinks the guy is her personal property, and she's prepared to chase off every single one of my clients if I don't leave him alone." She shrugged. "Sorry, Meg. Looks like the fairy tale has a sad ending."

Megan narrowed her eyes.

"So, that's *it?* You're just going to let some *bitch* take him away from you without a fight?"

Renee glanced toward the living room, hoping the kids hadn't heard.

"It's no big deal," she said quietly. "It's not like we were serious. Besides, the guy was way out of my league."

Megan pointed a finger in her face.

"You know what your problem is? You need to learn to stand up for yourself."

Renee took a sip of wine. Leave it to Megan to take umbrage at someone else's bad behavior.

"This gal, what's her name?"

"Savannah."

"I thought so. Savannah is a Southern woman and Southern women are steely inside. If you don't want her to push you around, you need to put some steel in your own spine and stand up to her. Go for what you want instead of giving up. It would be good for Wendell, too."

Renee frowned. How had the conversation veered from Travis to her father?

"I'm not following you."

Megan set her empty glass on the coffee table and leaned forward. When she spoke, the alcohol on her breath made Renee's eyes water.

"Letting him run the show around here has him thinking he can run our lives, too. That's why he and Jack don't get along. If you'd learn to stand up for yourself, he could back off and let Jack be in charge of his own family for a change."

Renee paused. Megan's logic might be a bit tortured, but knowing her father, it did sort of make sense. The two of them had certainly gotten along better before Greg had left her. Maybe in some strange way, taking care of her had made Wendell see himself as a father again—not just hers, but Jack's, too. Looking at it that way, she could see that their fights weren't just honest disagreements, but part of a struggle to prove who was boss.

"I'm sorry," Renee said. "I guess I never thought of that. Has Jack tried talking to Dad about it?"

Megan laughed.

"Of course not," she said. "My husband's just as spineless as you are."

Renee was about to tell her sister-in-law what she could do with her opinion when the phone rang. She walked over and answered the phone. It was their neighbor, Ted.

"Merry Christmas Eve!" he said.

"Merry Christmas Eve to you, too, Doctor Coburn. How's Molly these days?"

"Oh, fine, fine. I called to tell you that I've got good news."

"Oh?" she said.

"Yes; I've found the dog's owner."

It took a second before Renee understood. What dog? she thought, then she remembered.

Rex.

She stepped over to the living room and glanced at the kids, happily playing with the dog on the floor, and felt a stab of disappointment.

"That's great," she said, forcing herself to smile.

"I hope you don't mind," the man said, "but the man was anxious to get him back. I told him I thought it would be all right if he just headed over now to pick it up."

"Oh," she said. "No, that's fine. Thank you. We'll keep an eye out for him. What's his name?"

"Travis Diehl."

CHAPTER 30

Renee hung up the phone and looked at her sister-in-law.

"You won't believe this," she said, a smile playing on her lips.

Megan gave her a bleary-eyed look.

"Try me."

"That was our neighbor, the one who fixed up the dog. He found the dog's owner."

"So . . . ?"

"It's that guy I told you about. The one my client thinks is hers."

Megan's eyes widened.

"Well, don't that beat all," she said, grinning. "When's he coming to get the dog?"

"Now, apparently. He should be here in about ten minutes."

"Good," Megan said. "Maybe you'll be able to set him straight."

Renee glanced guiltily into the living room where the young cousins were lavishing attention on their "patient." They were going to be brokenhearted, she thought—especially Kieran. Since rescuing the dog, he and Rex had been practically inseparable.

"It isn't going to be easy telling the kids."

"Oh." Megan's neck swiveled like it was on ball bearings. "Yeah, I hadn't thought about that."

Renee took a deep breath. There was no sense putting it off. Travis was probably as anxious to get his dog back as her family would be sad to see him go. She walked into the living room and sat down on the couch.

"Hey, kids. I've got some good news that's also kind of not-so-good."

Lilly was wrapping a dishtowel "bandage" around the dog's front leg.

"It can't be both," she said.

"Well, no, actually, it can be."

Kieran was staring at her, looking pale.

"Is Rex's owner coming to get him?"

Renee nodded sadly.

"I'm sorry, honey, but he has to go home now."

He nodded.

"I understand."

"Well, I don't!" Lilly said. "I want him to *stay*."

She threw her arms around the dog's neck.

Megan brushed past Renee and tried to pull Lilly off the dog.

"Lilly, honey, be careful, or it'll bite you."

"Nooooo!" Lilly screamed. "*I don't want Rex to leave!*"

The back door opened, and Jack poked his head inside.

"What's going on?"

"The dog's owner is coming to get him," Renee said. "Lilly's taking it pretty hard."

He marched across the room and scooped Lilly off the floor

while Megan tried to loosen the girl's grip around the dog's neck. In spite of its injuries, the animal remained calm, and Renee found herself wondering again where Travis had found such an unflappable animal. No wonder the children were being so good. It was as if they were mimicking the dog's calm and gentle demeanor. It wasn't just any dog that could do that, she thought sadly. Losing Rex—or whatever his name was— was going to be harder to deal with than she thought.

Lilly and the dog had been separated, and the girl was in full temper tantrum mode. Jack picked her up and carried her down the hall, trying his best to avoid his daughter's flailing feet. Megan stood and watched them go, seemingly unable to decide whether or not to get involved.

"Can somebody get me a plate for these burgers?" Wendell bellowed. "They're almost done."

Renee nodded. "I'll get one!"

She'd just turned toward the kitchen when the doorbell rang, erasing all thoughts of a plate and burgers from her mind. As she changed course and headed for the front door, she and her sister-in-law exchanged a look. Megan gave her a double thumbs-up.

"Go fight for him," she whispered.

There was a mirror in the foyer, and Renee checked her reflection as she walked by. She felt a frisson of pleasure at the thought of seeing Travis again. In spite of what she'd told Megan, she realized she hadn't quite given up hope. As the door swung open, however, she felt her hope turn to dismay.

Travis's face was grim, his nostrils flared, his mouth so tight that his lips had vanished. It seemed so unlike him that it gave Renee pause. She'd known he might be unhappy that she hadn't answered his messages, but she didn't think he'd be quite so upset about it. It had, after all, been only three days, and with guests arriving and Christmas to prepare for, she'd thought he would understand. Seeing the obvious displeasure on his face, however, Renee realized that she'd been wrong.

"I came to get my dog," he said.

"I know; Dr. Coburn just called. I'm sorry, I didn't know he was yours; I would have called you myself."

"Would you?"

The tone of his voice put her instantly on the defensive.

"Of course I would have. When my son found him, we had no idea who he belonged to."

"Well, you do now."

He looked over her shoulder and raised his voice.

"Max! Come here, boy!"

The dog came trotting out of the living room, trailed by a teary-eyed Grace and Kieran, whose face had erupted in a storm of tics. Renee took an involuntary breath, embarrassed that a stranger should see her son like that, but also intrigued. It was the first time he'd shown any symptoms since the dog had arrived.

What is so special about this animal?

Somewhere down the hall, Lilly's temper tantrum had ratcheted up a notch. Travis looked at the dog.

"Where's his collar?" he said.

"He didn't have one."

He gave her a skeptical look.

"He did when he left home on Sunday."

Renee felt her lips tighten. It was one thing for him to be upset that she hadn't called, but calling her a liar was a different matter entirely.

"Well, he didn't when my son found him *caught in a snare.*"

She pointed at the dog's neck. "The reason Dr. Coburn knew where to find him was because Kieran and my father took him there for treatment."

As Travis turned toward Kieran, he seemed oblivious to the boy's facial contortions, a small kindness for which Renee felt profoundly grateful. The man might be angry with her, but at least he wasn't going to take it out on her son.

He squatted down until the two of them were eye to eye.

"You found him in a snare?"

The boy's eyes filled.

"I shimmied up the tree and cut the rope."

Travis nodded.

"That was a brave thing to do. I'm sure Max appreciated it."

He took out his wallet.

"I'd like to give you a reward for helping him," he said, pulling out a twenty dollar bill.

Kieran shook his head.

"I-I didn't do it for the money."

No, Renee thought, feeling an ache in her chest. Kieran did it for love. She put a protective arm around her son and glared at Travis.

"Well, you've got your dog back now. I'm sure you need to get going," she said.

Travis glanced up at Megan, who stared at him, pie-eyed.

"Can I talk to you outside for a minute, first?" he said quietly.

Renee hesitated a moment.

"Of course."

She turned Kieran back toward Megan and Grace, grabbed her coat, and followed Travis out to his car, feeling three pairs of eyes bore into her back.

Travis opened the back of his Range Rover and put Max

inside, then shut the door. As he turned back, his look had hardened considerably. If anything, he looked even angrier than he had when Renee first opened the door.

"Before I go, would you mind just telling me why you did it?"

Renee frowned as her mouth opened wordlessly. She shook her head.

"What are you talking about? Why did I do what?"

He looked away, chuckling mirthlessly.

"Well, let's see," he said. "First you stole my dog and then you tried to ruin my reputation."

She stared at him, unable to process what he was saying. Was he drunk or just nuts?

"Okay, first of all, nobody *stole* your dog; my son saved its life. If you don't believe me, feel free to ask Ted Coburn what kind of shape Max was in when Kieran and my father brought him to his house.

"Second, I don't have any idea *how* you think I could possibly ruin your reputation, but that's a pretty serious charge, and you'd better have a damned good reason for leveling it at me."

Travis thrust out his chin.

"Hank Fielding told me that someone was spreading a rumor about the program I'm sponsoring at your son's school."

"And you think *I* did it?"

"Well, didn't you?"

"Of course not!"

"Then why did you run off when you saw me talking to Hank at the banquet?"

Renee shook her head.

"When were you talking to Hank?"

"At the bar, just before you took off."

"Well, I didn't see that, but even if I had, it had nothing to do with why I left."

Now that they were actually talking, Travis's ire seemed to have lessened. For the first time since showing up, in fact, he seemed genuinely interested in what she had to say.

"Then why did you leave?"

Renee licked her lips. Since Saturday night, she'd been asking herself why Marissa had told her about Travis's ties to the pharmaceutical industry. She'd even thought of checking it out herself, but she'd been either too upset or too busy since then to do it. Besides, what reason did Marissa have to lie?

"Marissa Daniels told me you used to work for a drug company. She said that was the reason you were planning to medicate the kids in the program."

Travis's jaw dropped.

"I didn't work for a *drug* company. I told you, my work involved the petroleum industry."

"Yes, but Marissa said that most drugs are made from petroleum."

"So, based on that—and without even asking me if it was true—you told everyone whose kids were in the program that I was going to put their kids on medication?"

Renee felt like she might explode. First Hank and now Travis. Had everyone just decided that she was guilty?

"How could I possibly have done that? I don't even *know* whose kids are in the program!"

"Of course you do."

"No, Travis, I really don't. In case you haven't noticed, I'm a newcomer around here, and on top of that, I've got a full-time job. Oh! And did I mention that trying to find a way into one of the oh-so-unwelcoming cliques in this town is about as easy as slipping the proverbial camel through a needle's eye?

Please tell me how, out of all the people I *don't* know in this town, I just happened to know the names of the families whose children are in the program with my son?"

He put a hand over his mouth and ran it slowly down his face.

"Then why did you tell Savannah Hays that you did?"

Renee was staggered.

Of course. Why didn't I see it before?

Suddenly, all the pieces of the puzzle fell into place. Savannah had gotten Sissy to warn Renee away from Travis, and when that didn't work, she'd had her friend Marissa lie to Renee about medicating the students. Then Savannah spread the rumor about medications—over the phone, no doubt, so no one would know they weren't really talking to Renee—making it look as if Renee was acting on the information Marissa had given her. And finally, just in case Renee hadn't gotten the message, Savannah told a few of her friends to cancel their hair appointments; the implication being that there'd be more trouble to come if she didn't back off.

The whole thing was so bizarre, so unbelievably ridiculous, that Renee began to laugh. Of all the petty, jealous, asinine moves, she thought, this one took the cake.

Travis's face was a mask of confusion.

"What's so funny?"

"Nothing," she gasped, wiping her eyes. "Nothing at all."

Renee paused a second to catch her breath.

"Listen, when you see Savannah again, give her a message for me, will you? Tell her I quit. Tell her she won."

Renee turned and walked back inside where she found that the house had descended into chaos.

In the living room, Kieran and Grace were fighting over possession of a small black belt, and Dylan was defending himself against McKenna's charge that he was acting like "the Dad," while in the kitchen, Megan stood toe-to-toe with her father-in-law, holding a plate with a dozen burger patties so shrunken and black they resembled lumps of coal, and a red-faced Wendell demanded to know why no one had brought him the "goddamned plate" he'd asked for. From somewhere down the hall, the sounds of Lilly's outrage continued.

"Quiet! Everyone, please!"

As the noise abated, Renee marched into the kitchen and took the plate from Megan's hands.

"This is my fault, Dad. I said I'd get you a plate and got distracted by the doorbell. I'm sorry."

She dumped the charred, inedible patties into the trash.

"There are cold cuts in the fridge, Megan, and Dad, you know where the bread is. Why don't you two set them on the table while I get the kids sorted out?"

She headed back out to the living room.

"Dyl! Mac! Cut it out. You're acting like a couple of toddlers."

McKenna burst into tears and ran down the hall; Dylan slumped into the club chair and crossed his arms.

"And you two," Renee said, stepping into the tug-of-war between Kieran and Grace. "Give me that."

She reached down and snatched what she'd thought was a small leather belt from their hands. As soon as she had it in her hand, however, Renee realized what it was: not a belt, but a dog collar the exact size to fit Travis's dog. For a moment, she thought that Kieran might have simply bought it for "Rex" after he and her father brought the dog home. Then she noticed the name tag, and as she turned the collar over, saw blood on the underside in the exact place where Max's neck had been injured, and her heart sank. She looked at Kieran, his face a near-constant series of grimaces and facial tics, and closed her eyes.

"Go to your room."

"I can't."

"You know what I mean. Go downstairs—*now!*"

Kieran turned and ran down to Wendell's apartment, his sobs replacing Lilly's as the family's new soundtrack. Renee felt badly for him; the pain Kieran felt was evident in every twitch of his face. She knew he loved the dog, too, and that Max, for whatever reason, had been good for him, but that didn't change things.

He lied to me.

And that, she thought grimly, meant that she owed Travis Diehl an apology.

CHAPTER 31

Savannah was waiting for Travis with open arms when he returned from Renee's. Another round of champagne was poured, and Max's return was toasted, though in truth the dog seemed less than enthusiastic. As Max shambled off to his dog bed, Travis was troubled. In spite of his injuries, the dog had seemed happier at Renee's than he had at home in quite a while, and he couldn't help wondering if it had to do with her son, Kieran. Max's training as an emotional support dog would have made him gravitate toward someone with the kind of facial tics the boy had, and it had probably been the first time since Hugh got his job that Max had felt needed.

Nevertheless, Travis thought, that was no reason for Renee to lie about what she'd done.

"Come and sit down," Savannah said as she led him into the living room. "I want to hear all the dirty details."

Travis collapsed on the couch and shook his head.

"There's not much to tell. Renee says her son found Max in a snare. He and her dad took him to their neighbor who's a retired vet, and when he mentioned the visit to our vet, they put two and two together."

Savannah pursed her lips.

"You don't believe that, do you? I mean, snares are for catching things like rabbits. It couldn't hold a dog that size."

"That's what I thought, too," he said. "But . . . I don't know. Maybe . . ."

He handed her his empty champagne flute, his thoughts in disarray. As unlikely as it seemed, both Renee and Dr. Coburn seemed convinced that Max's injuries were consistent with the story Kieran had told them. And if Max hadn't been caught in a snare, he thought, why would the boy lie about it?

"Can I get you another?" Savannah said.

Travis hesitated. The truth was, he didn't feel much like celebrating at the moment.

"Maybe something stronger."

"I know just the thing," she said, heading for the wet bar.

A smile played on his lips as Travis watched her walk away. He hadn't noticed the bow on her dress before; she looked like a Christmas present waiting to be opened. When Savannah had shown up that morning, he'd regretted asking her over. Now, he was grateful to have her there. Dealing with Renee's betrayal was hard enough; having to do it alone would have been impossible.

"I asked her about the rumor at school," he said.

Savannah walked back and handed him a neat pour of Jack Daniels.

"Have some of this," she said. "It looks like you could use it."

Travis took a sip and exhaled sharply. As the whiskey burned a path down his throat, the fumes traveled upward, making his eyes water.

"Is this the Single Barrel 100 Proof?" he gasped, staring at the glass. "I don't usually drink it this early in the day."

"Well," she said, flouncing down beside him. "I knew you were upset, and I didn't want you to be in a bad mood. We have a lot of things to talk about."

The thought of having to revisit his trip to Renee's prompted Travis to take another sip. This time, the burn was almost comforting.

"You first," he said. "I don't really feel like talking about it just yet."

Savannah's cheeks dimpled.

"All right."

She set her glass down on the coffee table and slipped her arm through his. Travis could feel every curve of her body pressing into his side.

"I've been thinking a lot lately," she said.

He took another sip from his glass.

"What about?"

"About how things change, about how I've changed." She sighed. "After your mama passed, it gave me a new perspective on things. I realized that time was running out."

Travis drew back and saw tears in her eyes.

"Running out?"

Savannah's laugh sounded like a hiccup.

"To have a baby, silly." She blushed. "I'd rather not have one on my own, of course, but if I have to, then I'd at least like it to be yours."

Travis was overwhelmed, unsure if it was Savannah's news or the whiskey that was making him light-headed. He set his drink down on the table and took her hands in his.

"Are you sure?"

She bit her lip and nodded.

"Are you happy?"

"I am," he said. "Of course I am."

With Hugh moving out and Precision Industries on a firm footing, Travis thought, the timing couldn't be better for him to marry and start a family. This should be the best thing that had ever happened to him, and yet . . . And yet there was something about what she'd said that didn't ring true. Savannah had never liked the idea of having children, even as a girl, and her own home—though modest—was a showcase filled with Persian rugs and antique furniture. Would she really be able to reconcile her love of fine furnishings with a life that included kids and a dog?

Travis took a deep breath and ran a hand through his hair, remembering the homey chaos at Renee's.

"What about Max?"

Savannah seemed perplexed.

"Won't Hugh be taking him when he moves out?"

Travis shook his head.

"He can't—not if he chooses the group home he's visiting this week. There's not enough room there for a dog Max's size; plus, they already have a therapy dog."

"Then I'm afraid we'd have to find him another home," she said. "I'm sorry, too, because Max seems like a good dog, but I just couldn't have an animal that size around my baby. You understand that, don't you?"

"Of course."

He turned away and Savannah took his hand.

"It'd be okay, though, we could find him a nice home somewhere else." Her face brightened. "We could give him to one of the kids in your program. Maybe Renee's son would like him."

Travis shook his head. He wasn't ready to forgive and forget that easily.

"All right," she said. "I understand. But what about one of the other families? The Bartons would love to have a dog. Or the Patels. I heard they lost a dog a few months ago."

"How do you know their kids are in the program?"

Savannah paused.

"I don't know. I suppose you told me."

"No," he said. "I didn't."

"Of course you did. You must have."

"Savannah, I don't know who the families in the program are. Hank Fielding told me that he and Debbie Crowder were the only ones who did."

"Well, *someone* told me," she said. "Does it matter?"

Travis pulled back, trying to remember what Debbie had said to him at the banquet. Something about Savannah coming by her office the week before—the day Hank said she was typing up the list of names. What had Renee said to him before he'd left?

"Give Savannah a message for me. Tell her I quit. Tell her she won."

He withdrew his hand from Savannah's and stood up, overwhelmed by a growing sense of horror and disbelief.

"It was you, wasn't it? You called those parents and told them you were Renee."

Savannah took a sharp breath, looking for all the world like she was ready to defend herself, then let it out slowly and gave him a frank stare.

"What if I did?" she said. "You know that Renee is wrong for you; she was just wasting your time."

Travis turned away, his eyes searching for something solid, something familiar that he could hold onto to ward off the sense of unreality that had engulfed him. What Savannah had done—what she was still doing—wasn't just odd, it was barely even sane. Without knowing it, he'd become the prize in a competition she'd invented between herself and Renee Richardson. He'd thought they were old friends, but Savannah didn't even see him as human.

"Get out," he said.

Savannah walked over and put her arms around him, pressing herself against his back.

"Oh, come on, baby," she said. "Now we can get married like we should have years ago. Don't you see? We were meant to be together."

He reached down and pried her fingers from around his waist.

"I told you to get out."

It took another ten minutes before Travis could get Savannah out of the house. By the time he did, there were broken champagne flutes on the floor, an overturned Jack Daniels bottle emptying its contents on the bar, and a scratch on Travis's face that had barely missed his left eye. As her car peeled out of the driveway, he leaned his forehead against the front door feeling shaken and miserable. As bad as the whole episode had been, he thought, at least it was over. There'd be no more sly winks, no "accidental" meetings, no offers of dinner at her place. What had been said and done in the last few minutes could never be undone. Any future they might have had together was gone.

Max was cowering under the breakfast table, the place he'd run to as soon as Savannah started screaming. Travis went in and tried to coax him out with a treat, but the poor guy wouldn't budge.

"I'm sorry you had to see that."

He looked toward the front door.

"I'm sorry for a lot of things right now."

Travis reached up, gingerly patting the sticky trail of blood above his left eye, and winced. First things first, he thought, as he walked into the bathroom and took out the first aid kit. When that was done, he grabbed a mop, dustpan, and broom from the hall closet and walked back out to the living room to see what he could do about the mess. As he stood in the doorway, Travis shook his head. The place looked—and smelled—like the scene of a bar fight.

Twenty minutes later, the glass had been picked up, the furniture righted, and most of the alcohol blotted from the floor and bar top. As Travis took the bagged-up glass and paper towels out to the garage, he saw his phone lying on the floor behind the bar where it had been kicked during the scuffle. He reached down and picked it up. He should give Renee a call, he thought. He owed her an apology.

But there was something else, too, that he wanted to talk to her about. If Hugh decided to move into the group home, he'd be leaving his dog behind, and if Travis had learned anything over the last few weeks it was that Max was miserable being left at the house alone. He'd been trained to help people, and if no one there needed his help, he'd keep running away until he found someone who did. Unless Travis wanted to confine Max to a kennel for the rest of his life, he'd have to find someone who needed him. He hoped Renee would agree that Kieran should be that person.

The sound of a car coming up the driveway caught his attention and Travis felt his heart begin to race. If this was Savannah coming back for another round, he thought, he was going to call 911 and let someone else sort her out. Instead, when he peered out the front window, he saw a white SUV pull up to the house, the blue light bar on its roof flashing.

"It's the sheriff," Travis said, puzzled.

For a moment, he thought Savannah might have reported their fight to the authorities. Then a black Toyota Tundra pulled in behind the police cruiser and Travis scowled.

"What the hell is Trey Daniels doing here?"

He went to the front door and waited for the men outside to ring the bell. He needed a minute to collect his thoughts and had no intention of standing there like a welcoming committee, even if it was the mayor and a sheriff's deputy he was waiting on. As he stood there, listening to the footsteps coming up the walk, he felt a gust of hot breath and wiry whiskers on his hand. A curious Max had shuffled over to see what was going on.

"It's okay," Travis whispered, patting the dog's head. "If she says I started it, I'll be happy to set them straight."

At last, the doorbell chimes rang, and he reached for the doorknob, prepared to defend himself against whatever complaint Savannah Hays had leveled against him. Instead, Travis was surprised to find a boy of about twelve standing on his doorstep, his beefy build and heavy-lidded glower a scaled-down version of the man standing behind him.

"That's him!" the boy said, pointing an accusing finger at Max. "That's the dog!"

"What?" Travis looked at the sheriff's deputy. "What's he talking about?"

The man licked his lips, glancing briefly at Trey Daniels before answering.

"Cody here says your dog attacked him while he was near the woods yesterday."

"Are you sure it was my dog?"

"Of course it was," Trey said. "How many ugly mutts like yours are in this town?"

Travis kept his temper in check; blustering was just second nature to Trey Daniels. Besides, the man was obviously worried about his son. In his shoes, he might have done the same thing. Nevertheless, he thought, returning his attention to Cody, the boy seemed to be unharmed. Whatever had prompted this accusation, it could hardly have been called an attack. He glanced over at Max, who seemed cowed by the boy's appearance.

"I'm sorry if Max frightened you," he said. "But he's really very gentle."

"Gentle, my ass!" Trey thundered. "Look at the size of him! If Cody hadn't gotten away, your dog might have killed him."

Travis looked at the boy on his doorstep, his brow beetled, his chin thrust forward defiantly, and wondered at his demeanor. Why, if Max had attacked him, did he seem indifferent when the dog was standing only a few feet away?

"That must have been scary," he said. "I'm curious, though. How *did* you get away?"

Cody glanced up at his dad.

"I ran real fast."

Travis looked at the sheriff, hoping that he, too, could see the hole in the story's logic. He might not know the whole truth of the matter, but he did know that running from an aggressive dog would only have made the situation worse.

"You mean he didn't chase you?"

Cody hesitated.

"He might have. I don't remember."

Trey put a hand on the boy's shoulder.

"Are you calling my son a liar?"

"Not at all," Travis said. "I'm just trying to find out what happened."

"I told you what happened. Your dog went after my boy for no good reason. That makes him a danger to the community and I want him locked up."

Travis was about to tell Trey to butt out when the sheriff's deputy cleared his throat.

"Was the dog here at home yesterday?"

Travis hesitated, then shook his head.

"Max had been missing since Sunday. I only got him back a few hours ago."

The man nodded.

"Then I'm afraid I'm going to have to take him in for observation," he said.

"What? *Why?*"

"We can't have dangerous animals running loose," the man said. "And it's obvious that you can't keep him contained."

"Wait a minute," Travis said. "When you got here, Cody said the dog attacked him. Now, Trey says the boy ran away. How can Max be considered dangerous if he didn't hurt anyone?"

"It doesn't change the fact that the dog acted in a threatening manner, which makes him a *potentially* dangerous animal, and since you can't seem to keep him on your property, I have no choice but to take him to the pound until this problem can be sorted out."

Travis hesitated a moment longer before nodding silently. He didn't believe for a second that Max had attacked Trey's boy, but neither could he swear that the dog had been in his yard at the time. The sheriff's deputy was right. Unless and until he could find out where Max had been, there was nothing to do but put him where he couldn't escape.

"He doesn't have a collar," he said weakly.

"Doesn't matter," the deputy said. "I have one with me."

He drew a collar from his pocket, stepped forward, and fastened it around Max's neck. As the sheriff's deputy led Max back to his cruiser, the gravity of the situation hit Travis full force. If he couldn't find out where the dog had been, how would he be able to prove that he hadn't done what Cody had accused him of? Max was such a gentle animal that it didn't seem possible he'd actually attack someone. Unless, of course, the boy had done something to provoke him.

Trey Daniels watched as a forlorn-looking Max jumped into the cruiser, and the sheriff's deputy slammed the hatchback shut.

"If I had my way," he muttered, "that dog would be put down *today*."

As the two of them drove off, Travis went back inside, bereft. His parents were dead, Hugh was gone, and now Max had been taken away. He couldn't remember when he'd felt so alone.

He looked down, surprised to find that the phone was still in his hand, and dialed Renee's number. With luck, he would find a friendly voice on the other end.

CHAPTER 32

Back at Renee's, things had finally settled down. Lilly's tantrum had cooled, and Grace had decided that Kieran's temporary banishment was punishment enough for not letting her have Max's collar. Dylan and McKenna were holed up behind closed bedroom doors; a new bottle of wine was keeping Megan pleasantly soused; and Jack and Renee were busy trimming the tree. Wendell, however, was still fuming.

He went into the kitchen and opened the refrigerator. It might be only two thirty, he thought, but lasagna took a long time to prepare, and he needed something to do with his hands while he decided what to do about Diehl.

Who in the hell did that character think he was? Not only had the man snatched his dog away without acknowledging that they'd fed, boarded, and doctored it for almost three days, he hadn't even thanked them for rescuing it from a *goddamned snare!* And if that wasn't bad enough, he'd said something to Renee that had left her in tears, violating the promise Wendell had made after his no-good son-in-law had abandoned her: No one made his little girl cry and got away with it.

As he set his Dutch oven on the stove, Wendell imagined what he would say to Travis Diehl, if he ever got the chance. The man was a worthless SOB who didn't deserve the love of a beautiful, caring, hardworking woman like Renee, and if he ever showed his face there again, he'd . . . Well, what would he do?

From the looks of him, Diehl could probably handle himself, and it had been a long time since Wendell had been in a fistfight. No matter, he thought, if Diehl showed up he'd call the cops and tell them that the man had threatened him. Imagine, threatening an old man in his own home! Why, if Wendell owned a gun, he could probably shoot the SOB himself and get away with it. He smiled and started chopping an onion.

Yep, that'd teach him.

He hadn't noticed that Renee's phone was on the kitchen counter until it started to ring, but when Wendell glanced over and saw who the caller was, it seemed like nothing short of divine intervention. He put the knife down and snatched it up.

"Hello?"

Given the circumstances, Wendell thought he sounded surprisingly calm.

"Oh, hello," the man said. "This is Travis Diehl. May I please speak with Renee?"

Wendell took a step back and peered into the living room. Megan was humming a Christmas carol, and Renee was helping Jack put the star on top of the tree. No one seemed to have heard the phone.

"I'm sorry. Renee is busy at the moment."

There was a pause, then Diehl said:

"Would you mind asking her to call me when she's free?"

"Yes, I do mind."

"I'm sorry, what?"

"I said yes, I do mind. In fact, I suggest you stay away from my daughter from now on, if you know what's good for you."

There was another protracted pause while Wendell quietly seethed, hoping Diehl would try and defend himself so he could deliver the coup de grâce.

"I suppose I'm not very popular over there at the moment," he said. "And I can't say I blame you."

Wendell added the chopped onion to the meat in the pot and stirred it in. If this guy thought he was going to earn any Brownie points for that comment, he was nuts.

"Mmm-hmm. Well, now that you've got your dog back, maybe you can just crawl back under whatever rock you slithered out from this morning and leave us the hell alone."

"I know it probably doesn't matter to you, but I was wrong and I'm sorry."

The onions were making Wendell's eyes water, which irritated him almost as much as the man's apology. After all, it wasn't just Renee who was suffering.

"My grandson loved that dog, you know. He cried his eyes out after you left."

"I know how he feels. It's pretty lonely around here without him."

Wendell frowned.

"You mean you let him run away *again?*"

"No. Apparently, Max attacked the mayor's son yesterday, and the sheriff's deputy took him to the pound. I was going to tell Renee when she called me back."

Wendell could almost feel his blood pressure rising. No wonder this horse's ass hadn't thanked them for taking care of his dog—he hadn't even bothered to ask how long they'd been tending to him! No, all Diehl had wanted was to come over and accuse his daughter of something she'd had nothing to do with.

"Well that just proves what kind of a goddamned idiot you are, Diehl. That dog was here yesterday, weak as a kitten. Something you would have known if you hadn't come charging in like some goddamned avenging angel. Why don't you do us both a favor, pal? Don't call this number again."

Deputy Judd Freeman didn't usually allow complainants to accompany him when he took a suspect into custody. No matter if the crime was horrific or the accused caught dead to rights, the law was the law and every man—or dog—deserved a fair hearing before sentence was pronounced. In the present case, however, Judd didn't feel he'd had much choice. First, because Sheriff Waters was visiting out-of-town relatives and had left instructions that he was not to be disturbed for anything less than the direst emergency, and second because the complainant was Bolingbroke's mayor. That didn't mean, however, that Deputy Freeman was happy about it.

As he pulled his cruiser into the animal shelter's parking lot, he glanced in his rearview mirror hoping that Mayor Daniels would drive on by and keep driving 'til he got home. Instead, the black Tundra with the steel grille guard and matching headache rack pulled in beside him and discharged its occupants. Judd could understand why Trey was anxious to see the dog that had threatened his son locked up, but having the two of them along while he collected the animal had complicated what should have been a simple transaction. The sooner he got the dog inside, the better it would be for everyone.

Judd stepped out of the cruiser and headed up the walkway to the front entrance. Betty Lange, the lady who ran the shelter, had told him she'd come over and prepare a kennel for Travis's dog, but to please buzz her on the intercom when he got there as she didn't want to leave the front door unlocked in case there were rapists in the area. Judd thought her concerns were unfounded, but didn't say so as it would be just his luck if something did happen. The last thing he wanted to do was call the boss on Christmas Eve.

The voice that blared from the intercom was tinny and shrill, but unmistakably Betty's and it promised she'd be out in a minute. Judd thanked her and went back to the cruiser to fetch his prisoner. As he lifted the hatchback, the dog crouched against the cage looking frightened, and not at all like an animal that would threaten anyone. It had gotten into the cruiser without any resistance, too, and hadn't made a peep as they drove to the shelter. If the mayor and his son hadn't been breathing down his neck, Judd would have been tempted to just take it back to Travis's with a warning.

He lowered the tailgate and grabbed the dog's collar.

"Come on, boy. Time to go."

"Careful," Trey Daniels said. "That's a vicious animal."

The deputy nodded.

"Don't worry, Trey. I do this sort of thing all the time."

"Then hurry it up. It's cold out here."

Judd bit back a retort and continued urging the dog toward the open hatchback. The animal had started to resist, digging its paws into the carpeting as its legs stiffened, and it occurred to him that even a gentle dog might be a problem if panicked.

"I'm going to need for you both to step back," he said calmly. "If the dog gets spooked, things could get dicey. I don't want anyone to get hurt."

Trey Daniels ushered his boy back to the truck and lifted him into the driver's seat as Judd tried to coax the dog forward.

"Now what's the problem?

It was at that point that Deputy Freeman lost patience with both the mayor *and* the dog and decided that, rather than try and get the animal to cooperate, it would be faster and easier to just manhandle it out of the cruiser, turn it over to Betty Lange, and go back to ticketing speeders and locking up drunks.

Unfortunately, he was wrong.

As he jerked the dog's collar, the animal tipped its chin down, turned its head, and jerked free. Judd put his arms out, trying to keep the dog contained, but it was too late. Max leaped out and made a dash for freedom.

"Look out!" he yelled. "It's on the loose."

"Not for long," Trey said, reaching into the Tundra's cab. "Get down, Deputy. I'll take care of this."

Judd Freeman stared in horror as Trey Daniels drew a hunting rifle from his truck.

"What in the heck are you doing?"

Daniels lifted the rifle to his shoulder, prepared to bring down the fleeing animal.

"I said get down!"

The deputy hit the ground just as the first shot rang out. The dog was running hard, scrabbling over the patches of frozen ground as a bullet flew by. Judd heard the second shot—

a loud crack that left his ears ringing—and saw the dog stumble and fall.

"You got him, Dad!" the boy cheered.

But as Trey lowered the rifle, the dog scrambled to its feet and ran on. Whether or not the second bullet had found its mark was anyone's guess.

CHAPTER 33

Christmas Eve was turning out to be everything Renee had hoped for. The tree was trimmed, the presents wrapped, and in spite of her confrontation with Travis and the kids' subsequent meltdowns, there'd been no sniping, no recriminations, and—best of all—no arguing between Jack and Wendell. As the family held hands and said grace over her father's lasagna, she was grateful to have her family together again. She didn't think the evening could get any better.

And then it did.

"I'd like to propose a toast," Wendell said, raising his glass. "To my son, Jack."

Renee's brother looked abashed, no doubt expecting their father's toast to mutate into one of his backhanded compliments.

"I know I haven't been a very good father—"

Renee shook her head.

"Dad, don't say that."

"No, goddammit, it's true."

He looked at Jack.

"I might not have been a good father, but I know one when I see one." He swallowed, his eyes shining. "And I just want to say that I'm proud of you, son, for being a better father than I was."

He addressed the table as Renee's brother smiled modestly.

"To Jack!"

"To Jack."

Lilly crossed her arms.

"His name isn't Jack, it's *Daddy!*"

"You're right," Renee said. "To your daddy."

"To my daddy!" Lilly crowed.

Jack gave Wendell a gracious nod, and the two men clinked glasses.

"And to mine," he said.

At that, the others' glasses clinked, libations were sipped, and the salad and bread basket began making the rounds.

"Look!" Grace squealed. "It's snowing!"

And it was.

"To a white Christmas," Jack said, raising his wine glass for another toast.

But before the others could raise their glasses, the atmosphere of goodwill was interrupted by the sound of a ringing telephone.

"Sounds like mine," Renee said as the ringing stopped. "It can go to voice mail."

Megan frowned thoughtfully.

"Who was on the phone before?"

"When?"

"You know. I heard that same ring coming from the kitchen when you and Jack were doing the tree."

Renee turned toward Wendell.

"Did my phone ring when we were trimming the tree?"

Her father took a bite of lasagna and chewed thoughtfully. "It might have."

She narrowed her eyes.

"Why didn't you tell me? It might have been important."

He shrugged and took another bite, an unmistakably guilty reaction that set alarms off in Renee's head.

"Dad," she muttered. "Who was it?"

Wendell picked up his wine glass and took a sip.

"No one important."

She took the napkin out of her lap and set it on the table.

"Excuse me," Renee said. "I'll be right back."

Travis paced the floor in his living room, feeling frustrated and helpless. When Judd Freeman called and told him that Max had escaped, he'd gotten in his car and driven to the shelter. He wanted to look for Max and also to tell the deputy that he had a witness who'd told him that Max was at Renee's house yesterday. When he pulled into the shelter parking lot, though, he was surprised to find Judd in a heated argument with Trey Daniels.

That's when he found out what had happened.

It had taken all the self-control that Travis could muster to keep him from slugging the man who'd fired at his brother's dog—a dog he now knew was innocent of the charge against him. Only the thought of being locked up himself had kept him in check. A quick glance at Trey's truck showed Cody watching the argument wide-eyed, and Travis found himself wondering what the real story was behind the tale he'd told. Had the boy actually been threatened by a dog that looked like Max, or was the entire story a fabrication? And if it was a lie, why had he told it?

In the end, of course, it didn't matter. Once the standoff between Judd and Trey had cooled down, Travis informed them both of Max's innocence and assured them that once the dog was recovered he'd be filing any and all charges that he could. After that, he spent some time trying to follow Max's tracks, but the other men had already left their footprints on the trail. He decided the best thing to do was to leave and wait for Max to find his way home.

That was ninety minutes ago and Max still wasn't there. He still had one hope, however, and that was that when Max had run off, he hadn't been heading home, but back to Renee's. More specifically, back to her son, Kieran.

The second Travis had seen Max with Renee's boy, he knew why the dog had sought Kieran out. By temperament as well as training, Max's whole purpose in life was to comfort people with emotional disabilities. With Hugh out of the house and no one else who needed his help, the poor dog had been deprived of his reason for being. That was why he'd been leaving the property during the day, Travis thought. Max was looking for someone who needed what he could provide.

And I took him away.

He looked at the phone, wondering if he should try and call Renee again. Even after the disastrous phone call with her father that afternoon, he'd still hoped she might call him back; but when she didn't answer his last call, he'd decided not to leave a message. If Max did show up at her house, she'd let him know. In the meantime, there was no sense in making a pest of himself.

The phone rang and Travis snatched it up without even noticing who it was from. The sound of Renee's voice was so welcome it brought a lump to his throat.

"I'm sorry to bother you," she said.

"No, no bother. Thanks for calling me back. Did your father give you my message?"

"No," she said. "In fact, until now I had no idea you'd called before. What's up?"

Travis was surprised. Renee's father must be angrier with him than he'd thought if he hadn't even told her about Max.

"Since he didn't tell you, the first thing I should do is tell you I'm sorry. You were right about Savannah, and I was wrong. After I got home, I found out that she was the one who'd started that rumor. I feel badly for having blamed you."

"Well, it doesn't surprise me. The more I think about it, the crazier Savannah seems."

"You're right; what she did was crazy. I'm just sorry it impacted our relationship."

"Oh, well. *Que sera, sera,* I guess."

Travis nodded.

"So, if your dad didn't tell you I'd called, I don't suppose he told you about Max, either."

"Told me what about Max?"

"A sheriff's deputy came by today and said he'd attacked Mayor Daniels's son, Cody, yesterday."

"But Max was with us."

"I know. Your dad told me, but I didn't know it at the time."

"So, what happened?"

"They were taking him to the animal shelter when he got away."

"Oh, dear. Has he shown up yet?"

"No," he said. "And that's not all. As Max was running off, Trey took out his hunting rifle and fired a couple of shots at him."

"*What?*"

"No one knows if Max was hit or not, but he went down for a moment after the second shot, and I haven't been able to find him."

"Oh, God. Poor Max."

"I know," Travis said, his voice growing thick again. "I don't know what I'm going to tell Hugh when he gets home tomorrow. Max is his dog."

He heard Renee's heavy sigh on the other end of the line.

"What am I going to tell the kids?" she said. "Kieran will be devastated."

"Maybe you should hold off on telling them—for now, at least. If Max comes home or I hear anything, I'll let you know. In the meantime, if he shows up there—"

"We'll give you a call. No problem."

"Thanks," Travis said. "I appreciate it."

Renee felt as if a heavy weight was sitting on her chest as she returned to the table. Even the swirl of snowflakes outside the windows couldn't lift her spirits. She was relieved that Travis knew what Savannah had done, but it would take more than an apology to fix things between them. And she couldn't really blame her father for not telling her he'd called before, either. If she'd seen who was on the phone that afternoon, she might not even have answered it. No, Renee thought, the way she felt had nothing to do with Travis or Savannah or even her father's misplaced loyalty. It had everything to do with Kieran.

When Wendell had told her a dog might be good for her son, Renee had poo-poohed the idea. She'd thought her father was just trying to justify letting Kieran keep the dog he'd rescued. It wasn't until he was gone that she realized how much of a difference Max's presence had made in her son's behavior. There was something about that particular dog that was special, some sympathetic understanding of what someone with Kieran's particular challenges needed. It made her curious about something Travis had told her.

Max was his brother's dog.

Wendell shot her a wary look as Renee returned to her seat. Jack, too, seemed apprehensive. But Megan and the children appeared to be oblivious, and for the time being, at least, Renee was fine with that. She gave her father a tender pat on the arm and gave Jack a wink that had been their special signal since childhood. It meant: I'll tell you about it later.

When dinner was done and the children had made a final inspection of the presents, it was time for baths and pajamas and Wendell's special reading of "A Visit from St. Nicholas" by the fire. As the book was closed, Jack made a show of checking the time.

"Oh, dear," he said. "I hope the kids haven't stayed up too late. Santa Claus can't come if there are any children still awake in the house."

Grace and Lilly sprang to their feet along with a somewhat less sure Kieran, who glanced apprehensively toward his siblings.

"Oh, my goodness, you're right!" McKenna said, smiling sweetly at her older brother. "Come on, Dyl. We'd better get going."

There was a brief moment of tension, but McKenna's sarcasm had gone right over the youngest cousins' heads. The three of them squealed happily and ran to their beds, followed by Renee and a somewhat woozy Megan. Two rounds of kisses, last minute glasses of water, and a dire warning from Jack that he'd heard "reindeer hooves" on the roof and sleep— or a good imitation of it—had been achieved. Renee trudged back up the steps to the living room to give the others the news about Max.

"I can't believe they'd shoot a dog just for running away," Jack said quietly. "Seems kind of excessive, especially since there was no evidence other than the kid's say-so."

"I know," Renee said, hugging her coffee mug. "I'd heard that Trey Daniels was an enthusiastic hunter, but I never thought he'd fire at a dog."

"Diehl didn't say the dog had been shot," Wendell said. "Just shot at."

"You're right," Jack said. "Still, even shooting *at* the dog seems harsh to me."

"Guy sounds like he's got a *problem*," Megan said, tapping the side of her nose. "If you know what I mean."

"Yeah, well, either way," Renee said. "We can't tell the kids until we know more—especially Kieran. For now, I think it's best if we just keep it to ourselves."

There were nods all around.

Dylan had been sitting quietly in the club chair during their discussion, having declined his sister's suggestion that he go to bed. He looked at his mother.

"I could drive around looking for him, if you think it would help."

Renee shook her head.

"That's sweet, Dyl, but the snow's coming down pretty hard, and there's no guarantee that Max would come even if you called him. If he doesn't show up in the morning, we can drive around and take a look, but if he hasn't gone home by now, he's probably found shelter somewhere. I'm sure he'll be okay."

Dylan nodded and stood up.

"I think I'll go to bed then."

"Okay, sweetie. See you in the morning."

As Dylan walked off, Megan stood unsteadily and looked around.

"Me, too," she said.

The other three watched as she tottered off down the hall.

"I'll say this for your wife," Wendell said. "The woman can sure hold her liquor."

"That she can," Jack said. "It's just one of her many fine qualities."

He grinned at Renee, and the two of them burst out laughing.

"I'm going to bed," their father said. "You two are getting silly."

"G'night, Dad."

"Good night, *children,*" he said. "See you bright and early."

As Wendell disappeared downstairs, Renee groaned.

"Ugh, he's right. The kids will be up at the crack of dawn."

"Yup."

"Time to stuff some stockings, Santa," she said.

"Yup."

"Want another cup of coffee?"

Jack looked at his mug.

"Yup."

"Is that all you can say?"

"Nope."

She grabbed a pillow and hit him over the head with it.

"Man, I have really missed you."

CHAPTER 34

Kieran lay in the dark, listening to his grandfather's snores, and watched the glowing numbers on the clock change. When his mother told him that Max would be all right, he'd believed her. She'd always told him the truth, even when it wasn't good— like when she and his dad got divorced. But when he overheard her telling the grown-ups what had happened at the shelter that afternoon, he realized that what his mother had said before wasn't true. And if it wasn't true, Kieran realized, that could only mean one thing: Max was in trouble.

As the numbers on the clock changed from ten thirty-five to ten thirty-six, Kieran squeezed his eyes shut and wished that Mr. Diehl would call and tell them that Max had come home. The more time that went by, the more sure he was that something really bad had happened. What if Max was caught in another snare, he thought, or had lost his way in the storm? What if Max got buried in the snow and froze to death before morning? Then Kieran's eyes flew open as the worst thing imaginable came to mind. What if Cody's dad had killed him?

Kieran sat up and looked around at the darkened room. He had to do something. He couldn't just let Max die out there alone. But he was just a kid. He couldn't drive a car like Dylan or his mom, and if he asked one of them to take him out so he could look for Max, they'd just tell him not to worry, that things would be better in the morning. Except that they wouldn't be better in the morning, he thought, unless someone went out there and found Max—now. Which meant that the only way to save Max was to do it himself.

The thought of going out in the dark and cold made Kieran shiver. The house was warm and Grandpa's couch was comfortable. Plus, in a few more hours, the sun would come up and it would be easier to see where he was going. But what if he waited and Max died before the sun came up?

The boy shook his head, appalled at his own faintheartedness, and remembered what Mr. Baden-Powell had said about the Boy Scout motto: *"Be prepared so that you know the right thing to do at the right moment and are willing to do it."* Well, Kieran thought, this was the right moment to save Max, and it looked as if he was the only one willing to do it.

For a while, his mother and Uncle Jack had been talking quietly and moving around in the living room, but their voices were fainter now, and Kieran suspected they were in the kitchen. He would have liked to wait until they went to bed, but his mom always stayed up later than the rest of the family, and he wanted to get going before he chickened out. It wouldn't be easy getting dressed and ready without getting caught, but he did have one bit of good luck: He didn't have to go out the front door in order to leave the house. Grandpa's apartment had its own door.

Kieran threw back his covers and silently pulled on his

clothes. With the snow still falling outside, he'd have to dress warmly; he didn't want to be forced to return too quickly. He put two shirts on over his pajama top and a sweater over that, then two pairs of socks and his jeans. His heavy jacket had already been moved downstairs to make room for their guests' things, but his snow boots were still upstairs in his closet. Once he'd gotten those, he'd slip out Grandpa's door and head straight for the woods.

When his mother told everyone that the dog would find shelter if it couldn't get home that night, Kieran had immediately thought of the fort. With the branches overhead to keep out the wet and snow and walls to protect it from the wind, it would be a perfect shelter. If he hadn't known about Cody's dad shooting at Max, the thought that he'd be waiting in the fort might have been enough to convince Kieran to stay inside and wait for morning. But if Max had been shot, staying dry wouldn't keep him from bleeding to death, and it would still be too cold for a wounded animal. He had to see for himself whether or not Max had made it to the fort. If he didn't, Kieran knew he'd never be able to sleep.

Kieran put on his jacket and felt in the right-hand pocket for the piece of Max's fur that he'd found that first day in the woods. When Cody had destroyed his hair collection, he'd managed to salvage it, along with a few of the more precious bags inside, and he thought of it now as a good luck charm. Which was good, the boy thought. He had a feeling he was going to need that luck.

He started toward the stairs and bumped his shin against the coffee table, rattling the things sitting on its top. In the bed across the room, Grandpa grunted and smacked his lips.

"What's going on?"

"I have to go pee," Kieran whispered.

"Hmph. Fine."

He heard the bedclothes rustle as Grandpa rolled over. Moments later, he was snoring again. Kieran tiptoed upstairs to get his boots.

At the top of the landing, he paused, listening for the voices in the kitchen. His mother and Uncle Jack were speaking so softly he couldn't make out what they were saying, but Kieran figured it was probably okay. You couldn't see that part of the hallway from the kitchen, so as long as the two of them stayed where they were, he'd be fine.

The door to his room was open a few inches—enough to let his cousins have some light in the unfamiliar room, but not enough for him to slip through. Kieran set his hand against the door and pushed gently.

Grace and Lilly were asleep in his bed, their blond curls weighed down by beads of sweat. He glanced toward the closet, relieved to find the door open and his boots in plain sight. For a moment, he considered taking a hat from his dresser, but the drawers were sticky, and he didn't want to take the chance. The jacket's hood, he decided, would just have to be enough. Kieran crept over to the closet, grabbed his boots, and snuck silently back out the door. He was almost to the first step when he heard a harsh whisper behind him.

"What are you doing?"

He turned, his heart in his throat, and saw Lilly peering at him sleepily.

"Shh!" he said, glancing toward the kitchen. "I'm not doing anything."

"Yes you are," she said, pointing toward the boots in his hand. "You're going to look for Max."

Kieran deflated, realizing that there was no way he was going to be able to fib his way out of this. His only chance was to tell the truth and hope his cousin wouldn't give him away.

"I have to," he said. "I think I know where he is."

Her eyes widened.

"Really? Where?"

He pursed his lips, wondering if he could trust her. He'd already been in trouble for going into the woods by himself during the daytime. If Lilly squealed, he'd be in more trouble than if his mother had thought he was just checking for the dog in their yard.

"Just a place I know," he said casually.

Lilly's expression hardened.

"If you don't tell me, I'll cry. And then my mommy will wake up and she'll know what you were doing."

In the silence of the hallway, Lilly's voice had gotten noticeably louder. Kieran shushed her again.

"Okay, I'll tell you," he whispered. "But you can't tell anybody. Promise?"

Lilly solemnly crossed her heart.

"Promise."

He licked his lips.

"There's a fort in the woods where we like to play. I think he might be there."

"Can I go, too?"

"No, but if you don't tell, I'll let you play there with us tomorrow. Deal?"

"Deal," Lilly said, and toddled back to bed.

Kieran took a deep breath and crept back downstairs, put on his boots, and slipped silently out the apartment door, making sure to close it tightly behind him. In the glare of the porch lights, the front yard looked like a just-shaken snow globe and the ground was covered in a layer of pure white powder. Kieran pulled up his hood and put on his gloves. Then he walked to the end of the driveway, turning left toward the woods, and hunched his shoulders against a wind that was quickly covering up his tracks.

CHAPTER 35

Renee and her brother sat at the kitchen table sipping mugs of spiced apple cider and reminiscing about Christmases past. With the kids in bed and the stockings filled, she knew they should try and get some sleep, but neither of them seemed willing to call it a night. Although everyone had gotten along better that day, their visit had had a rocky start, and there was still Christmas morning to get through. With the fallout from their last holiday together still fresh in her mind, Renee wondered if Jack was thinking the same thing that she was: They might not get a chance to do this again.

"Seems like you and Megan have been hitting it off," Jack said.

Renee laughed.

"She only loves me for my wine."

He shrugged. "Whatever works."

She took another sip of cider and set her mug on the table.

"Which reminds me," she said. "What's with the special diet? Is Lilly allergic?"

Jack sighed.

"No. It's something Megan read about on the Internet."

He gave her a sideways glance.

"Lilly's pediatrician thinks she might have ADD."

"Doesn't surprise me," Renee said. "The kid's a fireball."

"Yeah, well, it's got Megan in a lather to do something about it," Jack said. "And it's driving me nuts."

Renee stared at the cider in her mug, wondering if this explained Megan's treatment of Kieran the day before. Perhaps she was blaming Jack's family for Lilly's "bad genes."

"So, are you going to have her tested?"

"Eventually, I suppose. The doctor says right now we're better off just making sure she gets enough exercise and plenty of rest."

"But Megan doesn't think that's enough."

"Megan never thinks *anything* is enough," he said. "The second they got home from the doctor's, she was on the computer searching for alternative treatments. The woman is obsessed."

"So, maybe it isn't entirely *our* family's fault."

Jack laughed.

"By all means, feel free to tell her that."

"No thanks. There's not enough wine in the world to save me from that."

Jack studied the table top.

"I suppose Greg blamed you for KK's problems, too."

"Yup. According to him, it was either our family's bad genetics or my lousy parenting. Pretty much my fault, either way."

Her brother sighed.

"You miss him?"

"Who, Greg?" Renee shook her head. "The kids do, though. I feel bad about it, but there's nothing I can do."

"I'm sorry your latest prospect didn't work out."

Renee sat back and gave him a frank stare.

"Did Megan tell you that?"

Jack grinned and shook his head.

"Dad and I don't fight all the time."

Thinking about the fights Jack and their father had had since her divorce reminded Renee of her sister-in-law's theory. She decided to run it by her brother to see what he thought.

"Megan thinks the reason Dad's so hard on you is because Greg is out of the picture."

Jack swallowed a mouthful of cider and shook his head.

"Dad's always been hard on me. It's got nothing to do with Greg."

"True," she said, "but I still think she may be onto something. You know, him being here, taking care of us, maybe Dad still feels like the alpha male."

"I think you're both reading too much into it. What Dad really needs," he said, "is a hobby."

Renee giggled. "Or a girlfriend."

He snorted. "Yeah, right."

"Don't laugh," she said. "There's gotta be some old lady somewhere who'll take him."

Jack tapped his chin thoughtfully.

"Let's see, how would that personal ad read? 'Older, infinitely patient single woman willing to play nursemaid to cantankerous old codger. Must be financially independent.' "

"Well, when you put it like that . . ."

Renee's eye roll provoked a fit of giggles from her brother.

"Oh, lord," Jack said, checking his watch. "It's almost eleven thirty. If we don't turn in before midnight, the kids'll wake up and demand to open their presents."

"You really think they'd do that?"

"You think they wouldn't?"

She shook her head.

"You're right. We'd better turn in."

Renee set their mugs in the sink as Jack headed down the hall to join his wife. Talking to her brother had helped her put some things into perspective. She could see her own concerns about Kieran's diagnosis mirrored in Megan's anxiety about Lilly, and Jack's dismissal of his wife's theory about Wendell had helped her feel less guilty about relying on their father for help. As she turned off the lights and headed down for a final bed check, she congratulated herself for inviting them.

McKenna was sprawled on Renee's bed, leaving only about a quarter of the mattress free, and Dylan's door was closed—a none-too-subtle message that he was not to be disturbed. At the top of the stairs, she paused and listened to her father's deep, rhythmic snores, wondering how Kieran was able to sleep with all that noise. She glanced back toward the family room. If he was still awake, she could transfer his sheets and blankets up there and let him sleep where it was quieter. Better that than having him lie awake all night listening to his grandfather sawing logs.

Renee crept downstairs, feeling the temperature drop as she entered the former basement. Even with the extra insulation, Wendell's apartment was always colder than the rest of the house. He claimed he preferred it that way, but the older he got, the more the chill down there seemed to bother him and it worried her. It was a rare day when she found him without an afghan in his lap.

The light from the hallway didn't penetrate very far into the room, and it wasn't until Renee was within a few feet of the couch that she noticed anything was wrong. Her first thought was that Kieran had burrowed under the covers, but as her eyes adjusted to the lower light, she saw that they'd been thrown back, the pillow lying askew on the armrest.

He must be in the bathroom, she thought, then quickly realized that it, too, was empty.

A growing sense of panic engulfed her as she searched the room. Had he gotten into bed with her father? She turned on the light as Wendell roused.

"Dad, is Kieran in there with you?"

"No, why?"

She looked around.

"I can't find him," she said.

"Did you look upstairs?"

Renee chuckled nervously. He must have snuck upstairs to check on the stockings and fallen asleep on the floor. It wouldn't be the first time he'd been anxious to get a jump on Christmas morning.

"I'll go check up there. Sorry to disturb you."

She turned off the light and headed back upstairs, scolding herself for being such a ninny. But Kieran wasn't in the living room. Nor was he in the family room or the little girls' room. As Renee knocked on Dylan's door, her heart was pounding. If her son wasn't in the house, he must be outside. But if he was outside, what was he doing?

Everyone was awake and every room in the house had been searched by the time Renee finally called the police. Her hand shook as she pressed 911 and waited for the dispatcher to answer. It wasn't until she heard the woman's voice on the line that she finally broke down.

"I need help," she sobbed. "My son is missing."

CHAPTER 36

The sheriff's deputies had set up a command post in Renee's family room. Half a dozen volunteers drank coffee and stared at the grid map on the breakfast table while Deputy Freeman gave them their assignments, and a police band radio on the kitchen counter emitted an indecipherable patois of hisses and ominous mumbling. In spite of the furnace running full blast, the front door had been opened and closed so many times that the temperature in the house had become noticeably chilly.

The adults of the family were all up and dressed, as was a grim-faced Dylan, who stood on the sidelines gripping the keys to his car like a lifeline. McKenna and Grace were huddled under a blanket on the couch, half-asleep, with Lilly, who watched the proceedings in mute dismay. In the fifty-three minutes since Renee had called the police, another two inches of snow had fallen, and so far, the only footprints anyone had found were those left by people who were looking for Kieran. As the minutes ticked by, Renee was finding it harder and harder to be patient. Why weren't they doing anything?

As if he'd been reading her mind, Judd Freeman walked over

and quietly explained that they were waiting for the tracker dog and its handler to arrive from Columbia. Not only was it Christmas Eve, but a snowstorm like the one they were experiencing was a once-in-a-hundred-year event, and people weren't prepared to be driving in it. In the meantime, though, the neighbors had been alerted, and he and his volunteers were about to begin a grid-by-grid search of the area.

"Unless you have some idea of where your son might have gone," he told her. "I'm afraid that's the best I can do."

Renee pressed her lips together and nodded, determined not to cry. She'd been almost hysterical by the time Freeman and his team had arrived, and as a result, Jack and her father had had to give the initial report to the deputies. No doubt, they all understood, but afterward she'd felt ashamed and promised herself that she would not do it again. She didn't want anyone thinking she was too weak and delicate to be told the truth. Whatever had happened to her son, she wanted to hear it first and without any sugarcoating.

The volunteers were given their assignments and the six of them left, along with Dylan, Jack, and Deputy Freeman. Wendell had argued that he should be allowed to go as well, but Renee reminded him that two adults were needed at the house—one to monitor the phone and one to watch the kids—and if Kieran were found, she wanted to be able to go and see him right away. In a concession to her father's vanity, however, she had *not* mentioned that the last thing anyone needed was for him to slip and take a tumble in the snow.

With the searchers gone, the house felt cavernous, the girls on the couch so far away that Renee felt she'd have to yell for them to hear her. On impulse, she began walking around the room, picking up discarded coffee cups and putting them in the trash while she racked her brains for anything Kieran might have said or done to indicate where he was going. There was no doubt in anyone's minds, of course, why he'd run off. He was looking for Max.

Renee blamed herself. She should have told him the truth instead of pretending that the dog had simply run off when the deputy tried to take him to the shelter. Thinking back on the powwow she and the other adults had had after he went to bed, she realized that their voices must have drifted down to Wendell's apartment where Kieran, lying on the couch, could hear them. She closed her eyes and felt a shudder pass through her, imagining her baby caught out in the blizzard, searching for a dog that might not even be alive. If only Max had run back home, none of this would have happened.

She looked at Megan.

"I'm going to call Travis."

"What for? He said he'd call if the dog came home."

"I know," Renee said as she called his number. "But maybe he thought it was too late to call."

"Hello?"

Travis's voice sounded husky, and Renee immediately regretted having ignored her sister-in-law's advice. Still, she thought, the man was awake now. Hanging up without saying anything would be worse than asking him a foolish question.

"Hey," she said. "Sorry to bother you, but I wondered if Max had come home yet."

"No," Travis said. "I haven't seen him. Have you?"

Renee swallowed hard, trying to keep her voice under control.

"No," she said. "But Kieran—"

Her voice broke.

"Kieran what? Renee, what's wrong?"

Renee shook her head.

"He ran away. We think—we think he's out looking for Max."

"I'm coming over."

"No, it's okay," she said. "The sheriff and a bunch of volunteers are out looking for him. You don't have to."

"I know I don't have to. I want to. Give me a minute to throw on some clothes, and I'll be right there."

She nodded, feeling both relieved and grateful in spite of the fact that it probably wouldn't help. Unless and until they figured out where Kieran had gone, the best they could do would be to let the volunteers keep searching and wait for the sniffer dog to arrive.

There was a knock at the front door and someone stepped into the foyer.

"Hello!" a sweet voice called. "Anybody home?"

Renee looked up and saw Maggie McRay, a large box in her arms, walk into the kitchen.

"I brought food for your volunteers," she said, opening the top flap. "There's doughnuts and sweet rolls and a couple of thermoses full of coffee, plus sandwiches in case things go on awhile."

She took a tray full of pre-made sandwiches out and opened the refrigerator.

"Mind if I put these in here?"

"No, it's fine," Renee said. "If you can find the room."

Maggie surveyed the contents of the icebox.

"There'll be plenty of room once we take this turkey out of here," she said, giving the bird a yank. "I've got a cooler in the van. You can keep it in there 'til it's time to stick it in the oven."

She slid the sandwiches onto the shelf and shut the door.

"I'll be right back."

Wendell had been migrating closer since Maggie had walked in, and he was standing right behind her as she turned to go.

"Oh! Hey, Wendell," she said as she breezed past.

He watched her go, then turned back, open-mouthed.

"Who was *that?*"

"What do you mean, who was it? That's Maggie McRay."

He glanced back over his shoulder.

"*That* was Maggie?"

"Yes," Renee said. "Why?"

Wendell looked down at the rumpled clothing he'd thrown on in haste and paled visibly.

"I'll be back in a minute."

Wendell and Maggie were having coffee and doughnuts in the kitchen when Travis arrived. Two of the more experienced volunteers had already returned to check the map for another area to search, and Jack and Dylan were filling a thermos with coffee before heading out again. Grace and McKenna had gone back to bed, and Megan was rocking Lilly in her lap, hoping she would do the same. When Renee saw Travis heading up the walkway, she hurried over to open the front door.

He was, she thought, the very definition of a sight for sore eyes. Dressed for the weather in a heavy parka and jeans, the determined look on his face was reinforced by the stubble on his chin and softened by the look of tender concern in his eyes. He looked, in short, like the kind of man you wanted on your side when disaster struck.

Renee stepped back and he came inside, taking a quick look at the command post/kitchen.

"I take it he isn't back yet," he said.

She shook her head, feeling hot tears pressing against her eyes.

Travis took a deep breath.

"All right, what can I do to help?"

Renee shrugged.

"I'm not sure, exactly," she said, looking around. "Everyone's gone out in teams of two, but there's no one here at the moment for you to partner with. Mostly, we're just listening for the phone and waiting for the sniffer dog to show up."

He pulled off his gloves and tucked them into his pocket.

"In that case," he said. "I think we need to talk."

She led him into the living room and took a seat on the couch, wondering what was going on. Travis looked so serious that whatever was on his mind, she feared it must be bad news. Then again, Renee told herself, there wasn't really anything worse than what had already happened, and she was desperate for something to distract her from worrying about Kieran.

Travis still hadn't taken a seat. Renee thought he looked agitated as he loomed over her.

"Why didn't you tell me your son was in my program at school?"

Renee sat back, appalled. This wasn't any of his business.

"What's this got to do with anything?"

"Was it because you didn't trust me?"

"*Trust* you," she said. "Is this a *joke?* My son is outside, lost in a snowstorm, and you want to know if I *trust* you? What is your problem?"

Travis raised his hands in a calming gesture.

"I'm sorry. I know this is terrible timing, but you said there was nothing else to do, and if our relationship is going to have any kind of future, I think it's time we got this out of the way."

Our relationship?

She stared at him, chagrined by an unwelcome tingle of

desire. What kind of person thinks about romance while her kid is missing?

"I'm sorry," she said, "but this is just not the time or place—"

"My brother, Hugh, is autistic. I didn't tell you before now because I thought I might be falling in love with you, and I was afraid I'd lose you if you knew."

He gave her a penetrating look.

"I think maybe that's why you didn't tell me about Kieran, either."

She felt a tear run down her cheek and wiped it away.

"The last guy I went out with told me that Kieran was just trying to get attention. You know, like the poor kid *wants* to get picked on and made fun of in school."

"Guy sounds like an ass."

Renee hiccuped and swiped at another tear.

"He was."

"Then you're lucky you have Kieran, or you might not have realized until it was too late."

Renee nodded and looked down at her hands. She loved her son fiercely, but no one had ever told her that she was *lucky* to have him before now. She smiled and patted the cushion next to her. Travis took a seat.

"So," she said. "Hugh is autistic."

He nodded.

"Among other things, and for now, at least, he lives with me. When we were younger, I promised my parents that he'd always have a home with me. There weren't group homes and halfway houses for the mentally ill back then, and they were terrified he'd end up in an institution."

"That's really sweet," she said. "You were a good son and a good brother."

"I was hoping you'd feel that way. I wish my ex-wife had."

He turned his head and contemplated the Christmas tree for a moment.

"Mother was already ill when Daddy died, and I knew it was only a matter of time. Moving Hugh was out of the question, and I'd already told Emmy when we married that we'd be going back to Bolingbroke one day. When the time came, though, she gave me an ultimatum: I could have her or Hugh, not both."

"And you chose your brother."

"I had to," he said. "My promise to him predated any vows I'd made to her. At the time, I was devastated, but looking back, I think it was for the best. Emmy was never the person I thought she was. I just didn't see it until then."

"Then you're lucky to have Hugh."

Travis ran a hand through his hair and laughed.

"Well, some days it doesn't feel like it."

"And that's why you started the program at the school?"

He nodded.

"My parents worked hard to build a company that would give them enough money to pay for whatever might help my brother make the most of his gifts." Travis grinned. "Hugh might be strange, but he's wicked smart."

"Asperger's?"

"Probably."

She sighed.

"The counselor says that Kieran is very bright, in spite of his OCD. I can't help wondering if there's a connection."

Travis shrugged.

"I have no idea. All I know is, the program Hank Fielding and I have started at the school will give the kids in it a chance to get the kind of help that Hugh has gotten at no cost to them."

"By medicating them?"

His expression hardened.

"I like you, Renee, and you seem like a smart person, but if your son needs medication so that he can have a full and happy life, why would you prevent him from taking it?"

She pursed her lips and thought of all the reasons why the thought of giving her son pills was so objectionable.

"For starters, I don't want him to be labeled. I don't want every teacher and every administrator from now on to look at his permanent record and dismiss him as 'abnormal' before they even give him a chance."

Travis considered that.

"That's a valid point. Our program is considered separate from the regular reporting requirements of the school system. However, it's got nothing to do with whether or not he's on meds."

"That's true."

Renee thought about that for a moment.

"I guess I just don't like the idea of giving him pills to make him behave. He's really a great kid; I don't want him to turn into some sort of zombie."

"Believe me, neither do we. The point isn't to turn the kids into docile little robots, it's to help them learn to manage whatever symptoms they have so that they can learn and retain information in an environment that's safe for everyone. Besides," he added, "no matter what Marissa told you, medication was never going to be the first choice in the program. That was a flat-out lie."

"Yeah," Renee said. "I figured that out when—"

She heard a high-pitched scream coming from the kitchen.

Travis looked around.

"What is that?"

"It sounds like my niece, Lilly," she said, jumping to her feet. "Come on."

Lilly was having a full-blown tantrum when Renee and Travis ran in. Lying on the floor, facedown, she was kicking her feet and screeching as Megan and Wendell tried to calm her down, and Maggie looked on from the safety of the breakfast table.

"Nooooo!" she said, shaking her head. "I can't! He won't let me play if I tell!"

Renee walked over and put her hand on her sister-in-law's shoulder.

"Everything okay?"

Megan shook her head.

"I don't know what happened," she said, looking bewildered. "All I did was ask her if she'd spoken to Kieran last night."

"She's probably just tired of answering questions," Renee said. "When I asked her before, she told me she hadn't."

"I know, but she fell asleep while I was rocking her, and the next thing I knew, she started mumbling about promising not to tell. I thought it might have something to do with Kieran."

Renee felt her temper flare. She wanted to snatch her niece up off the floor and demand that she tell her what she knew, but when she looked at Lilly, lying on the floor, crying and hysterical, it broke her heart. The poor kid had been awake all night, and if she did know something, it must have been eating at her all that time. Perhaps, if they were patient, Lilly's tantrum would run its course, and she'd be able to tell them what was going on.

It didn't take long. The lack of sleep had drained Lilly's usually abundant energy along with her ability to keep the secret to herself. As the adults in the room listened, she repeated what Kieran had told her before he left.

"He said he was going to find Max," she said, wiping her nose on her arm.

"We know that, Lil, but where was he going to find him? Did Kieran say?"

The girl nodded.

"He told me they built a fort in the woods and that Max would be there."

Renee looked at her father.

"Do you know anything about this?"

He shook his head.

"Not about the fort, but I'm guessing he meant the same woods where we rescued the dog."

She nodded and looked at Travis.

"Can you take me there? It's not that far."

"Absolutely."

"Great." She looked at Wendell. "Do you think you could draw me a map of where you found the dog?"

"Hell, no. I'll take you there myself."

"No, Dad," she said. "Travis and I will go and look for him. Megan needs to take care of Lilly, and you need to stay here and tell the volunteers where to go when they get back. I'll take my phone with me so we can stay in touch. Call me if you hear anything."

CHAPTER 37

"Thirty-one, thirty-two, thirty . . ."

Kieran halted unsteadily and looked around. His face and hands were numb, and the frost on his eyelashes was making it difficult to see. He swiped a gloved hand across his face and squinted hard, trying to get his bearings. The snow wasn't as deep in the woods as it had been outside, but what there was had hidden both the trip hazards on the ground and the landmarks he used to find the fort. He shook his head.

What number was I on?

It didn't matter, he told himself. The only thing that mattered was Max. Once he found the fort, he'd find Max. He just had to keep going. Kieran took another step.

"One, two, three . . ."

There was a sapling up ahead on the right, bent over by what could have been snow, but might also be another snare. Kieran shook his head and gave it a wide berth. If he hadn't been so cold, he might have taken a stick and tried to trip it, but he wasn't sure if he could actually pick up a stick with his hands the way they were. He promised himself that as soon as he was warmer, he'd go through the entire woods and trip every snare he found. Until then, he'd just have to . . .

He stopped. What was he doing?

A gust of wind rattled the trees and icy clumps of snow began to fall all around him. Kieran felt the world begin to wobble and realized that he was the one wobbling. He hugged himself and realized he'd begun to shiver. It was nice, he thought. Shivering made him feel warmer. Then he remembered something he'd read about how being too cold made you feel warm and he frowned. He looked down at his feet and willed them to move.

"One, two, three, four . . ."

A crow in the tree up ahead flapped its wing and cawed menacingly at him. Kieran scowled at the bird.

"G-go away!" he said.

It must have a nest nearby, he thought. There was a crow whose nest was near the fort, and whenever he and Max were there, it had cawed at them like this one. The stupid birds were as bad as Cody Daniels, he thought. Why couldn't they just leave him alone?

He paused and looked back at the bowed sapling.

The crow . . . the fort . . . the secret entrance.

Kieran turned quickly and lost his balance, crying out as his knees hit the frozen ground. Unable to stand, he crawled toward the sapling, hoping he was right and feeling absurdly grateful at having been harassed by a crow. When he reached the sapling, he pulled himself upright and his heart leaped. It *was* the secret entrance! He just hadn't recognized it because the other sapling he'd tied it to was broken. He ducked underneath and crawled inside.

"Max, it's me," he said. "It's ok-kay now. I'm h-here."

Kieran looked around, confused. The tree overhead had acted just like he'd thought it would—the ground was dry and almost free of snow—and the wind was noticeably calmer in there, too. Nevertheless, there was no sign of the dog. His knees buckled and he fell, his teeth chattering, his entire body shivering convulsively. He crawled forward and leaned his back against the sheltering tree.

I'll just rest here for a while. I can look for Max again after I take a nap.

Kieran closed his eyes and smiled as someone covered him with a warm gray blanket.

The man with the sniffer dog showed up just as Renee and Travis were pulling out of the driveway. She flagged them down, told the handler where they were heading, and after a brief call to the sheriff's station, the man agreed to follow them there.

"I'll need a piece of your son's clothing," he said. "So the dog will know his scent."

Renee grumbled in frustration as Travis took her back to the house. She ran inside, grabbed one of Kieran's jackets, and jumped back in the car. Minutes later, the vehicles pulled to the side of the road, and she handed it over.

"You sure he's in here?" the man said, as the German shepherd put its nose into Kieran's jacket.

Renee nodded.

"He told my niece he was going to the fort that he built in the woods."

The man gave her a skeptical look.

"In the snow?"

"He's looking for my dog," Travis said. "And it's a long story. Can we just—"

The shepherd lifted its head from Kieran's jacket and sniffed the air. Then it took a step and whined, tugging its handler toward an opening in the trees. The man looked at them and smiled.

"Looks like it's time to go."

Renee and Travis followed behind the man as he and his dog led the way. The animal seemed excited to be out in the woods, sometimes sniffing the air or walking in a circle, sometimes stopping to sniff the ground before whining and moving forward again.

"Why doesn't he just keep his nose to the ground like a bloodhound?" Renee said.

The man shook his head.

"Addie is an air scent *and* a trailing dog. Air scent dogs work well in wild, open areas like this, but if it's windy, like today, they can lose the scent. If that happens, Addie can just pick it up from the ground or the shrubs and keep moving." He grinned. "She's also a girl, so watch yourself."

"Sorry."

"Her name is Addie?" Travis said.

"Short for Adalwolfa Meine Schatzi. My wife thought she should have a German name."

Addie had wandered off the trail again, alternately sniffing the air and the ground.

"What's she doing now?"

The handler frowned.

"I think it's possible your son passed by this way more than once."

Renee looked at Travis, who shrugged and shook his head.

"Why would he do that?" she said.

The man's face was grim.

"Mostly likely, he was confused," he said. "People can get disoriented when they're cold. They start walking in circles."

Addie lifted her head and whined again.

"What's she doing?"

"That's her alert," the man said as she tugged on her leash. "It means she's picked him up again."

Renee hurried forward with Travis at her heels. She knew it was snowing, knew that Kieran would be in danger from the cold, but somehow she'd still been thinking of him as he'd been inside the house: clearheaded enough to find shelter if things got too bad. Now, the sickening realization that he might be stumbling around, disoriented, in the woods hit her like a slap in the face. She found herself praying that Addie would find him soon.

They came to a place in the woods where the ground had been recently disturbed and Addie stopped. She sniffed the ground, whined again, and sat down, glancing back at her handler as if seeking his approval.

"It looks like she's given up," Travis said.

The man slipped Addie a treat.

"No," he said. "She's telling us he's here."

He looked around.

"But I'll be darned if I know where."

Renee grabbed Travis's arm.

"Could she be mistaken?" he said.

The man shook his head.

"No. The boy is definitely here."

"Kieran!" Renee could hear the panic in her voice. "Kieran, where are you?"

Travis took her by the shoulders.

"Tell me again. Where did Kieran tell your niece he was going?"

She took a deep breath and tried to think.

"She said he'd built a fort in the woods and that he and Max used to play there."

He looked at the disturbed ground, saw how it disappeared next to a bowed sapling.

"It's in here!" Travis said.

He yanked the sapling upright and snow went flying. Renee ducked under and saw a small clearing where Kieran sat, his eyes closed and his back against a tree. Lying on top of him, his head resting against the boy's chest, was Max. As she rushed forward, calling his name, Kieran opened his eyes.

"Look, Mom," he said, his voice weak. "I thought someone put a blanket on me, but it was Max."

He sat up straighter and pulled his arms free.

Renee gasped.

"Oh my God! Are you hurt?"

"No, Mom. I'm just cold."

She pointed at his chest.

"Then where did all that blood come from?"

Kieran looked down at the smear of red on his coat and the dog, who lay unmoving across his lap.

"Max!"

CHAPTER 38

Christmas dinner was almost ready by the time Renee and Kieran got home from the hospital. As they stepped into the foyer, the smells of supper cooking brought tears of joy and relief to Renee's eyes, and she felt profoundly grateful for a family she could rely upon in an emergency. She took off her coat and helped Kieran with his, then hung them up and followed him into the living room. Grace and Lilly were in the middle of the floor playing with their new toys under Dylan's watchful eye. When Lilly saw Kieran, she jumped up and came running over.

"We saved your presents!" she cried, trying to drag him toward the neat stack of boxes on the club chair.

Kieran winced and reclaimed his bandaged hand.

"Thanks."

Lilly's lower lip trembled.

"Are you mad that I told your secret?"

He shook his head.

"No," he said. "I'm glad you did."

She looked longingly at the stack of unopened presents.

"If your hands hurt, I can help you open them."

Kieran shrugged.

"I don't know. Maybe."

As Lilly plopped down, waiting for the present opening to start, Renee hoped Travis would get there soon. She was looking forward to meeting his brother, Hugh, and anxious to see how his dog was doing. If it hadn't been for Max, after all, her family might not have anything to celebrate.

When the ambulance arrived to get Kieran, Travis had taken off for the emergency veterinary clinic with Max. As horrifying as the smeared blood on Kieran's jacket had been, none was the result of a bullet wound. Instead, the laceration on the dog's neck had torn open when he pulled free of the deputy's collar, and injured further as Max broke through the frozen branches to get to Kieran. The vet had had to remove one of his back toes, however, but Travis swore that Max didn't seem to notice, though he did seem determined to remove the bandage on his foot. Renee wasn't going to tell anyone about Travis's offer, however, until the three of them arrived. She didn't want to spoil the surprise.

She glanced over at Dylan.

"Do you know whose van is parked out in front?"

He shrugged, pointedly avoiding her gaze.

What was going on? Renee wondered. It wasn't like her firstborn to clam up like this.

"Is something wrong, Dyl?"

He shook his head, coloring slightly.

Was it something to do with the van? she thought, or . . .

Oh, dear God. Have Jack and Wendell had another fight?

She felt her jaw tighten. After everything that had happened, there was no way she was going to play diplomat for those two.

If they'd gotten into another argument, Renee thought, she might just kill them both.

"I'm going to go see if Aunt Megan needs any help."

Renee marched off toward the kitchen, mentally preparing herself for trouble.

Of all the selfish, pigheaded . . . And now, with company coming . . .

She stepped into the kitchen and pulled up short. Megan was putting miniature marshmallows on the sweet potato casserole; McKenna was setting a pan of cookies on the counter to cool; Jack was acting as official broken cookie taste tester; and sitting at the breakfast table, grinning at one another like besotted teenagers, were Wendell and Maggie McRay. Renee smiled.

I guess I don't have to ask whose van is out in front now.

"Hey," Jack said. "Welcome home!"

He walked over and gave her a hug.

"Where's KK?"

"In the living room, opening his presents with help from Lilly."

She lowered her voice.

"What's the deal with Dad and Maggie?"

He snickered.

"As soon as you called and said you were at the hospital, the two of them snuck downstairs. We didn't see them again until breakfast."

Renee nodded, remembering Dylan's awkward silence.

"Maybe we won't have to write that personal ad after all."

"Fingers crossed," Jack said, patting her back.

Renee heard a car drive up outside.

"So," Megan said. "How's Kieran doing?"

"Hmm? Oh, pretty well. He's lost a couple of fingernails,

but the doctor says it isn't frostbite, and his core temperature wasn't much below normal. Thank God Max found him when he did, or he might not have been so lucky."

The sound of their company's arrival was faint, but unmistakable now. Renee could hear men's voices coming up the walkway.

McKenna gave her a worried look.

"How's Max doing? Is he going to be okay?"

The doorbell rang, and she heard a dog bark. Renee smiled.

"Why don't we go ask him?"

Acknowledgments

As always, I'm deeply indebted to the people behind the scenes who helped make this book a reality: my agent, Doug Grad, my editor, Gary Goldstein, his able assistant, Liz May, my publicist, Vida Engstrand, Paula Reedy, my production editor, and many others at Kensington Books who work tirelessly on my behalf and to whom I owe my gratitude.

Many thanks also to my cousin and travel buddy, Nancy Westmoreland, who spent a week squiring me around South Carolina, visiting family, sharing stories, and reacquainting me with the people and places I've missed living here on the left coast. Although Bolingbroke exists only in my mind, I could find it for you on any map.

And finally, of course, love and thanks to my husband, Chris, who enlarges my joys, lightens my burdens, and makes every day a blessing.

BOOMER'S BUCKET LIST

Because dogs can dream, too . . .

Author Sue Pethick presents a warm and fuzzy love story about a passionate pet owner, a smitten newsman, and an unforgettable dog who steals everybody's hearts. . . .

When her cuddly canine companion Boomer is diagnosed with a rare heart condition, Jennifer Westbrook decides to take a leave of absence from her busy PR job—and take Boomer on the greatest road trip of his life.

Charting a course from Chicago to California, Jennifer plans some pet-friendly pit stops for her four-legged friend, including a dog show, a fire hydrant museum, and a factory full of squeaky toys. But when she tries to sneak Boomer into a NASCAR press box—disguised as her seeing-eye dog—Jennifer's cover is blown by a curious, but very cute reporter named Nathan Koslow.

Boomer takes an instant shine to Nathan, unlike the other men in Jennifer's life. When the charming journalist asks to join them on their journey, she can't say no. But when she learns that someone has created a website called "Boomer's Bucket List"—and it's gone totally viral—the trip takes a wildly unexpected turn for Jennifer, Nathan, and the dog who brought them together.

It almost seems as if Boomer's last wish is that his two favorite humans fall madly, deeply, in love. . . .

PET FRIENDLY

**Because dogs deserve a vacation, too . . .
from their humans.**

*In Sue Pethick's witty and heartwarming debut novel, a sweet dog
in need of an owner brings together the perfect candidates. . . .*

Todd Dwyer, a successful app designer, wasn't planning to
adopt a dog, but when his Uncle Bertie dies and leaves his little mutt Archie homeless, Todd can't help welcoming the
pooch home.

Archie could charm the marrow out of a bone, but Todd's
girlfriend, Gwen, is less than impressed with the instant bond
the fluffy white ball of fur makes with her boyfriend. When
things go awry the first night, she insists that Todd give Archie
to his sister, Claire, whose rural home is a day's drive away.

Todd and Archie hit the road, but circumstances compel
them to make a detour to a quaint hotel run by Todd's childhood friend, Emma Carlisle. As it happens, the hotel is hosting
a colorful group of ghost hunters in town for a paranormal
conference, and when Archie starts howling into the air vent,
it isn't long before their road trip turns bumpier than an un-
paved country lane.

But with Archie's unerring canine instincts and loyal heart,
he may help Todd and Emma see the happiness that's waiting
just under their noses. . . .

Connect with Us

Visit us online at
KensingtonBooks.com
to read more from your favorite authors, see books
by series, view reading group guides, and more.

Join us on social media

for sneak peeks, chances to win books and prize packs,
and to share your thoughts with other readers.

facebook.com/kensingtonpublishing
twitter.com/kensingtonbooks

Tell us what you think!

To share your thoughts, submit a review,
or sign up for our eNewsletters, please visit:
KensingtonBooks.com/TellUs.